## SPECIAL MESSAGE TO READERS

This book is published under the auspices of

**THE ULVERSCROFT FOUNDATION**

(registered charity No. 264873 UK)

Established in 1972 to provide funds for research, diagnosis and treatment of eye diseases. Examples of contributions made are: —

A Children's Assessment Unit at Moorfield's Hospital, London.

•

Twin operating theatres at the Western Ophthalmic Hospital, London.

•

A Chair of Ophthalmology at the Royal Australian College of Ophthalmologists.

•

The Ulverscroft Children's Eye Unit at the Great Ormond Street Hospital For Sick Children, London.

You can help further the work of the Foundation by making a donation or leaving a legacy. Every contribution, no matter how small, is received with gratitude. Please write for details to:

**THE ULVERSCROFT FOUNDATION, The Green, Bradgate Road, Anstey, Leicester LE7 7FU, England. Telephone: (0116) 236 4325**

**In Australia write to:**

**THE ULVERSCROFT FOUNDATION, c/o The Royal Australian College of Ophthalmologists, 27, Commonwealth Street, Sydney, N.S.W. 2010.**

# CRAIG AND THE JAGUAR

In Peru, ruthless terrorists plotted to turn an isolated valley into a guerrilla haven, from which they would send bloody revolution sweeping across South America. To blackmail the Peruvian government they kidnapped a group of student volunteer workers, but one was the nephew of the chief of MI6. Sent to investigate, special agent Peter Craig had to pit his own deadly skills against the savage cunning of the rebels in a lonely struggle for the lives of the hostages.

*Books by Kenneth Benton*
*in the Linford Mystery Library:*

A SINGLE MONSTROUS ACT
TIME FOR MURDER

KENNETH BENTON

# CRAIG AND THE JAGUAR

*Complete and Unabridged*

LINFORD
*Leicester*

First published in Great Britain in 1973

First Linford Edition
published 2000



British Library CIP Data

Benton, Kenneth, *1909* –
Craig and the jaguar.—Large print ed.—
Linford mystery library
1. Detective and mystery stories
2. Large type books
I. Title
823.9′14 [F]

ISBN 0–7089–5901–6

Published by
F. A. Thorpe (Publishing)
Anstey, Leicestershire

Set by Words & Graphics Ltd.
Anstey, Leicestershire
Printed and bound in Great Britain by
T. J. International Ltd., Padstow, Cornwall

This book is printed on acid-free paper

# Author's Note

Certain geographical features of the Peruvian high plateau and the *Cordillera Blanca* have been rearranged and given fictitious names for the purposes of the story. I hope that my friends in the Peruvian Armed Services will overlook any unintentional inaccuracies in the descriptions of units and their functions.

K.B.

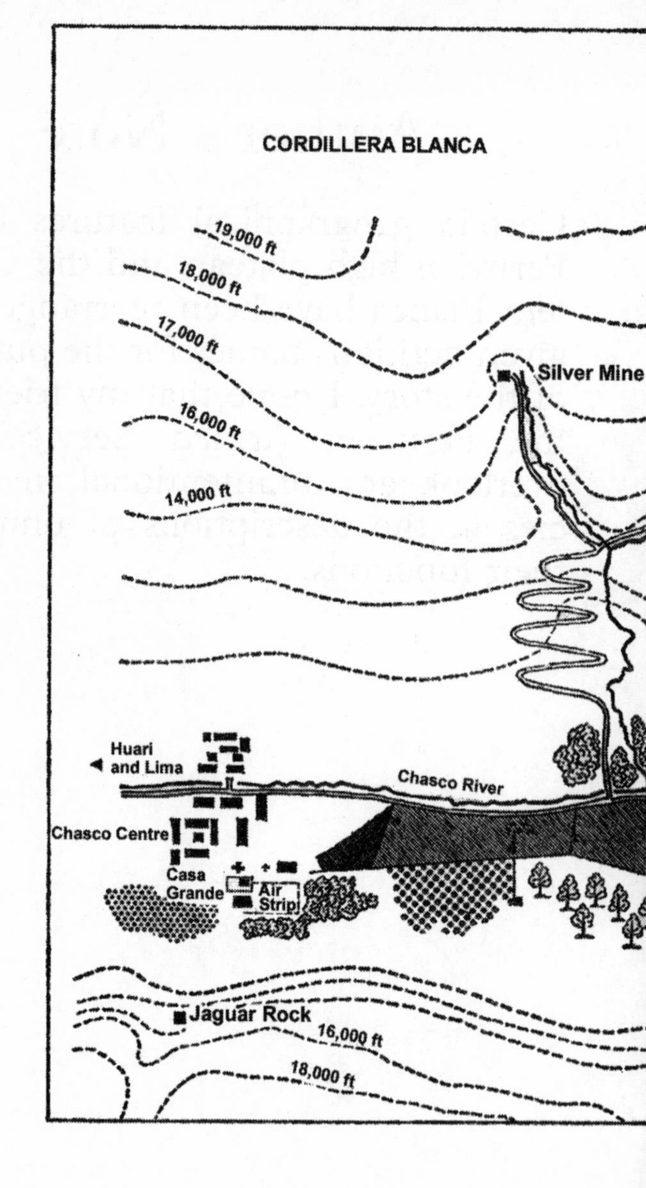

CORDILLERA BLANCA
19,000 ft
18,000 ft
17,000 ft
16,000 ft
14,000 ft
Silver Mine
Huari
and Lima
Chasco River
Chasco Centre
Casa
Grande
Air
Strip
Jaguar Rock
16,000 ft
18,000 ft

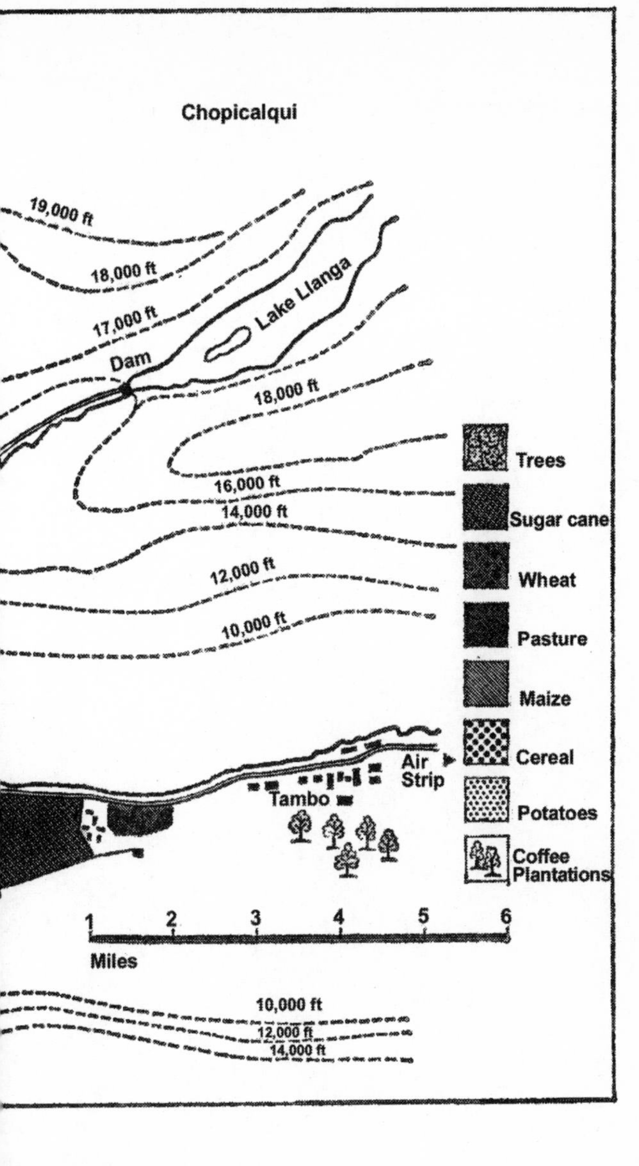
Chopicalqui
19,000 ft
18,000 ft
17,000 ft
Lake Llanga
Dam
18,000 ft
16,000 ft
14,000 ft
12,000 ft
10,000 ft
Trees
Sugar cane
Wheat
Pasture
Maize
Cereal
Potatoes
Coffee
Plantations
Air
Strip
Tambo
1
2
3
4
5
6
Miles
10,000 ft
12,000 ft
14,000 ft

# 1

## Thursday

The man whom Peter Craig found waiting for him in the little pillared hall of the Wanderers' Club was fifty-five, or thereabouts, medium height, grey-haired and worried-looking. A typical civil servant, thought Craig (quite mistakenly). He wondered what this sudden invitation was about.

'Trencham?' he asked tentatively.

'Yes. Glad to meet you, Craig. Dennistoun has told me a lot about you. Let's go down to the bar.' Sir William Dennistoun was the Senior Police Adviser to the Foreign and Commonwealth Officer, and Craig's boss. He had told Craig that a man named Rodney Trencham wanted to meet him over lunch. And that was all he would say.

As they went downstairs to the small bar that overlooks the Carlton Terrace gardens Trencham said, 'I expect you know this Club?'

'Pretty well. Lots of my former colleagues in the Colonial Service are members. I belong to the Oxford and Cambridge, down the street. Bill Dennistoun was a bit secretive about this meeting. Said you'd tell me everything when we met.'

Trencham glanced at him. 'I'm one of the M16 recruiting officers,' he explained simply. Curiouser and curiouser, thought Craig.

The bar was full of members and their guests — overseas civil servants, foreign diplomats of all colours, a sprinkling of publishers, bankers and lawyers and a brace of gaitered bishops. They seemed to have catholic tastes in what they drank, from Guinness through pink gin and vodka Martinis to champagne, which the barman kept accessible on ice under the bar. Trencham found a free table in the window, fetched drinks and sat down by Craig on the window-seat.

'It's good of you,' he began, 'to see me at such short notice. You must be full of preparations for your Peruvian trip.'

'Routine stuff,' said Craig, 'except that I've never been to Peru before. I'm to give the police and security people in Lima some lectures on our ideas of counter-guerrilla techniques. Then they're going to take me upcountry to show me some of their problems — I'm looking forward to that — and then home in about a fortnight.' He sipped his pink gin. 'I don't think the Peruvians have very much to learn from me. They've done a pretty good job. No guerrillas left, so far as I know.' He glanced sideways at Trencham. 'But perhaps you're better informed.'

'No, it isn't that. I'll explain.' He lowered his voice. 'I'm not sure whether you know anything about the way we recruit people into my Service?'

'No idea. I haven't had much to do with your colleagues, as I expect you know. I was a Colonial policeman until a few years ago, and if there was any intelligence needed we either got it ourselves or from the other side of the house — M15.' He smiled. 'So far as I know M16 officers suddenly appear, already trained, and equipped with their little bottles of secret ink and Minox cameras.'

Trencham disapproved of this frivolous approach. He looked at Craig's dark, lined face and the slightly mocking smile. He looked older than his age which was thirty-five, according to the security report. A rugged, taciturn sort of chap, he thought — but Dennistoun had seemed to think the world of him. 'Recruiting and training them is a long process, believe me, and there's a heavy fall-out. Which is why it's so annoying when we find someone who we can see is going to be very good, but not yet — and we have to turn him down. Like Jack Warne.'

'Who's he?'

'Age twenty-two, came down from Magdalen last year with a respectable second in Modern Greats. At the moment he's doing a year as a British volunteer in a settlement in the Andes.'

Craig frowned. 'You mean — that's his cover?'

Trencham almost choked over his gin and tonic. 'Good God, no! That's the first point I want you to get quite straight. If we reject someone — a promising youngster like Warne, for example — well, we reject him. We don't say, 'Go and get some experience of the world and come back in a few years' time.' If he wants to do that, it's up to him, but he gets no encouragement from us. And least of all any sort of intelligence mission. The risk of his doing something silly would be quite unacceptable.' He pointed to Craig's empty glass. 'Same again?'

'No thanks. That was fine. What you're saying is that young Warne *has* done something silly, and entirely off his own bat?'

'Worse. I think he's still doing it, and I want you to stop him.' He rose. 'Let's have lunch.'

Over smoked trout and filets mignon, with good club claret, in the rather splendid Barry dining room on the first floor, Trencham explained.

When he had finished Craig said, 'Let me get this straight. You're afraid that Warne is up to something which he thinks will make you accept him after all as a recruit for the Service. But your only evidence is a letter he wrote to his mother, saying you'd change your mind when you knew what he was doing. It sounds a bit thin, you know. He might simply mean that he was doing adventurous things, taking risks on mountains — '

'That's what he'd do as a matter of course. He was at the base camp on Annapurna when his father was killed. That was four years ago, when he was eighteen.'

A light dawned. 'You mean his father was Randall Warne, the Everest man?'

'Yes. And the boy worshipped him. Still does. But the point is that he's been used to taking that kind of physical risk since childhood. He gets round a cliff face like a goat.'

Craig was puzzled. 'Is all this just the official record?'

Trencham paused for a moment, balancing a piece of Stilton on a biscuit. 'No,' he said. 'I've got a personal stake in young Warne. His mother, Daphne, is my sister. That's why I'm so concerned. I'd have liked to get him into the Service, and in fact encouraged him to apply, but of course I had to get other people to interview him and put him through the hoops. They all agreed that he had a lot of the qualities we want, but — and it's a very important but — he's too enthusiastic and impulsive for an intelligence officer, and has too much sheer unthinking guts. You remember how Richard Hannay described himself — one of the cunning cowards?'

'I do,' said Craig, grinning. 'I've always thought it a masterpiece of false modesty.'

'All right. So it may have been. But we'd rather have cunning cowards than death-or-glory boys.'

'I see. Could you tell me exactly what he wrote to his mother?'

'Said he was on to something that would make Uncle Rodney see how wrong he'd been.'

'Hm. Why is he so keen on getting into the Firm?'

'His father was with us at one time, dropped into Albania during the War, and nearly got his toes frozen off. I told you.

The boy worships his father's memory.'

'All right, Trencham. What d'you want me to do?'

'See Jack, and give him a rocket from me. Find out what he's been up to, and if he shows the slightest sign of not behaving, you can tell the Embassy everything and get them to have him recalled.' He smiled. 'It won't come to that. He's a good lad, even if he is a bit headstrong.'

As they went downstairs for coffee in the morning room a club servant came up to Trencham. 'A Mrs. Warne is on the telephone for you, Colonel. You can take it in the box by the stairs.'

'Thank you, Peters. Excuse me for a moment, Craig. You'll find a coffee tray inside the door. Help yourself and find a seat. I'll join you as soon as I can.'

'I'll get you coffee. Sugar?'

'One lump. Thanks.'

Craig was sitting on a leather settee by the morning-room fire when Trencham joined him. His face was expressionless. He took the cup of coffee and sipped it. 'She's had another letter,' he said between his teeth. 'Says he's taped a lot of Indian songs on the little tape-recorder Daphne gave him before he went out to Peru last year — and one of them is specially for me. The damned young fool! He'll have the Peruvian security on his neck unless he drops this nonsense. He must have penetrated some dissident group, I suppose. That's the only explanation. He knows I'm not interested in songs, Indian or not. When d'you leave?'

'Sunday morning. I get to Lima the same day, because of the time difference. How can I get hold of Warne?'

'I was hoping to keep it out of official channels, because you know what the F.O. are like. Whatever we say, they'll still think the boy was briefed to go snooping for us. But it's too dangerous to wait until he comes home next month, when his year's up. I'll arrange to get Jack summoned back to Lima — the Embassy can pretend it's about a job, or something. You'll have to tell them why you want to see him and use Embassy channels to let me know what happens.

I'm sorry to saddle you with this, Craig.'

'That's O.K. Glad to help. If he's awkward, you agree I can get tough?'

'You certainly may. And I'm very grateful.'

# 2

## Friday Evening

Sunset comes early in the Chasco valley, eight thousand feet above sea level in the Andean highlands, because on the west it is walled in by the Cordillera Blanca, and the twenty-thousand-foot peaks, towering above the valley floor, stop a lot of sunlight.

The Indians who had been sweating under the fierce heat of the sun paused as soon as it sank behind the snowy crests of the range, pulled on their heavy ponchos, woven by the women of the valley from coarse llama wool, and took out their little pouches of coca leaves and gourds of powdered lime. Excessive coca chewing was frowned on by the manager of the Centre, but one wad, chewed slowly during that last chill hour's work before even the light reflected from the eastern mountains failed, made all the difference.

Helmut Springer was standing with one of the *cholo* foremen — a half-breed of Indian and Spanish blood — helping to supervise the laying of an electric cable from the new generator to one of the outlying farmhouses. The little excavator, which the manager had had flown in from the coast to speed up the cable-laying, had done its work well, and the heavy-duty wire now lay at the bottom of a narrow trench eighteen inches deep, reaching across a quarter of a mile of ploughed land. The Indians had grumbled when they saw the machine chugging its way through their precious maize, but now they could see that it not only cut the trench neatly but turned back the soil after the line was laid. Tomorrow the women could replant the maize. They were chattering with excitement.

Helmut turned to the foreman and spoke in Spanish. 'We'll have to dynamite the next bit, Luis, through that outcrop of rocks. Who can do that?'

The *cholo* shrugged his shoulders. 'The manager will borrow one of the men from

Don Jorge's silver mine,' he said. 'I'll tell him.' He looked across the maize fields, on which the second crop was sprouting vigorously. 'Someone's coming from the Centre.'

A man was riding towards them on one of the farm horses, bare-back, with an envelope in his hand. He was stocky and deep-chested, with the flat, copper-coloured face and slanting eyes of the pure Andean Indian. He stopped and spoke to the foreman in Quechua, then handed the note to Helmut, who recognized the handwriting and thrust the envelope into his pocket. 'See you later, Luis,' he said casually, and went off towards the generator shed. Inside, he opened the note and read, 'Come to my hut after the singsong. Miguel.' There was a squiggle under the name, and that meant 'urgent'. Helmut wondered what had happened.

It was part of his job to wait until the lights were switched on in the valley, and the second generator had to be cut in to meet the load. When he started to walk back towards the Centre he could see the last light leaving the tops of the eastern range, and experience the sudden advent of the dark. He was a Bavarian, and mountains had always played a big part in his life. There was a promise of frost in the thin air, and his footfalls rang out on the metalled road. Helmut looked forward to supper with a keen appetite.

What was it, he asked himself again, that Miguel was so anxious to see him about? Could it be that after all the preparations and briefing sessions the Group was to see some action at last? His step quickened.

There were some thirty volunteers, of half a dozen nationalities, working on the Chasco development project, side by side with the Peruvian agronomists and organizers, and it was the Australian who had instituted the weekly singsongs, as he called them. The manager, Major Castillo, had agreed that the mess-hut could be used after supper. Several of the volunteers had guitars or accordions, and they learned each other's songs and roared out the choruses, sitting round the big iron stove, men and girls with their arms round each other's shoulders. Several of the Peruvian staff usually joined them, and *cholos* and their children — fascinated by music, however outlandish — would crowd into the doorways, watching impassively. As a rule, Helmut stayed and sang with the rest, because it was the thing to do, but he often left early to read a few pages of Che Guevara or Chairman Mao before he fell asleep. Tonight, there would be something more exciting to do, he thought.

He came from the dark road into the glow of the lighted buildings, first the warehouses and silos, the agricultural machinery sheds and the fuel stations, then the administrative buildings and the manager's house, and went over the compound to the row of adobe huts in which he had his room. He changed his field boots for loafers, washed hastily, pulled on a heavy sweater over his plaid shirt and ran over the cobbles to the mess-hut.

Inside, the rich smells of cooking mingled with the tang of charcoal smoke and the aromatic scent of the eucalyptus logs sizzling in the open iron stove in the middle of the long room. Along one wall ran a broad tiled ledge with inset braziers. A pig-tailed Indian girl, a brightly patterned scarf crossing over her bodice above layers of woollen petticoats, was ladling out bowls of soup from cauldrons set over the charcoal fires. Helmut quickly went to the range with his bowl and saw that the next course was simmering gently in great pans. Papas a la Huancaina! His mouth watered.

The volunteers had adopted this Andean dish as one of their favourites. Made of a special kind of yellow potatoes cooked in a sauce of fresh cheese, oil and hot peppers, with slices of corn cob and hard-boiled eggs, it took the edge off the sharpest appetite, and very pleasurably. The Indian girl was kept busy until the last scrap of *papas* had disappeared.

There were earthenware jugs of red Peruvian wine and great hunks of freshly-made corn bread.

Helmut shouted greetings to his friends and found himself a seat at one of the long tables. The mixture of clattering crockery and voices raised in many languages was deafening, but the volunteers liked it that way. They only fell silent when the meal was over and a young Spaniard picked up his guitar and began to sing 'La Hija de Don Juan Alba'. Helmut looked at the rapt faces of his colleagues, dark from the burning sunlight of the long day and flushed with food and wine, with affectionate contempt. They little knew, he thought, what some of their friends were secretly plotting to do.

Before the sing-song was over he left quietly, unable to restrain his curiosity, and walked across the compound, now lit by a rising moon, to a two-roomed hut that stood by itself in the shadow of some trees. He knocked and went in. Miguel Cuevas, a volunteer from Argentina, was sitting on his bed — a tall, rangy man of twenty-five, with a pale olive face and passionate dark eyes. They greeted Helmut with a long hostile stare.

'What's the matter?' he asked.

'You'll soon see,' replied Miguel, tightly. 'Wait till the others are here.'

They arrived in a body shortly afterwards, a Colombian, two Chileans, a Frenchman and two girls, Italian and Irish. They had all learned Spanish, and Cuevas addressed them in that language.

'*Must* you arrive together?' he began, bitterly. 'How many times have I told you not to be seen as a group? At least Helmut had the sense to come here alone.'

'What's all this — 'at least Helmut'?' asked the German, laughing. 'What are you picking on me for?'

The Argentine crossed the room in two strides and seized the front of Helmut's cloak. 'You're the electrician,' he said between his teeth, 'so you're the first suspect.' An Indian entered the room quietly and stood with his back to the door.

The German's pale face tautened. He shook himself free and took a step backwards. 'You'd better explain, Cuevas. And quickly.'

'Sit down, all of you,' the Argentine commanded. 'On the bed or the floor

— it doesn't matter where as long as I can see your faces.' His voice had authority, and they'd all sworn allegiance to him. They did as they were told.

'I have called the Group together so that everyone can see how we deal with traitors. You all swore that anyone who betrayed us would be tried and if guilty — we should decide what to do with him. Didn't you?'

There was a shocked silence. The eyes of all the young people present were on Cuevas' face. Of course they had sworn that: it had been rather a thrill.

*'Didn't you?'* he repeated, not raising his voice, but with venomous insistence.

*'Pues si.' 'Si, Miguel.' 'Claro que si.'* The room, furnished only with a rough wardrobe, the bed and a couple of cane chairs, had suddenly become sinister. The glare of the single electric light bulb on the whitewashed walls and on the pale faces of the volunteers became intolerable. The big Breton, Francois, shook himself.

'You're the leader, Miguel, we all agree. But please drop all this melodrama. Tell us what's happened.'

The Argentine pulled out of his pocket a length of fine wire and an object that looked like a large plastic coat-button. He faced Helmut. 'Are these yours?' he asked suddenly.

The young German looked at him, tense but quite firm. 'No. They are not.' He leaned forward to look closer. 'What's that — a microphone?'

'So you recognize it?'

'Of course I can guess what it is. But I've never seen it before.'

'And you're prepared to swear that?' challenged Miguel.

'I certainly will. Where did you find it?'

'As if you didn't know! When it was you who put it in this room, to listen to all we say.'

'Why should I do that?' asked the German calmly. 'I don't have to find out what's said here. I attend all the meetings.'

The Argentine looked disconcerted.

'That's right, Miguel,' put in the Irish girl eagerly. 'There wouldn't be any point. And anyway, fixing that thing wouldn't require an electrician. Where was it found?'

Miguel pointed to the top of the wall above his bed, where the electric light cable entered the room under the sloping rafters. 'It was there, out of sight, hidden on top of the wall.'

'And the wires?' asked the Breton.

'They ran down the outside wall, hidden behind the tree.'

'But weren't they attached to something? I mean, there would have to be a radio transmitter somewhere.'

Miguel hesitated. 'The ends of the wire weren't attached to anything. Just loose, as they are now.'

'Did you look in the tree?'

'Of course. There was nothing there.'

Helmut was still standing, and the light caught the beads of sweat on his pale face. 'So you think,' he said slowly, 'that because I'm a radio ham and have a set in my hut — you *think* I must be the one who put that mike in position. *Gott im Himmel!* You've got a nerve. I swear I did not, and I've said why there would be no point. The only transmitter I have here works on the mains and is too big in any case to be carried around the compound without everyone seeing it. Whoever put that thing where you found it has a small battery-powered transmitter that he can carry in his pocket. When he wants to operate it he attaches those wires to the input terminals and sticks the set in the tree. Then he listens in somewhere near, probably in the Centre. It would only be a feeble signal, I should think. But if you still don't believe me,' he added with a stiff smile, 'you can search my room.'

'That has been done,' said the Argentine. 'You must have hidden it somewhere.' But there was no longer any assurance in his voice.

The German turned away, disgusted.

'Listen,' said the Irish girl suddenly. 'It hasn't got to be a transmitter. Even I know that. It could be a tape-recorder, couldn't it, Helmi?' She turned to the German, who smiled, immensely relieved.

'Of course, that's what it is,' he said to Miguel eagerly. 'You can get a tape-recorder that's no bigger than a cigar box. Like the one Jack has.'

Miguel started. 'Jack Warne?'

The girl said, 'You must have seen it, he's always bringing it to the sing-songs.' She stopped with her hand over her mouth. 'Oh Mother of God!'

'Is there anyone else with a recorder?' asked Miguel ominously.

'He's the only one,' said the Breton.

'It *couldn't* be Jack,' cried the Irish girl. 'It must be the fuzz.'

'What is fuss?'

'*La policia*.'

'There have been no policemen spying here for months,' said the Argentine coldly. 'Why are you so sure it wasn't Warne who planted the microphone?' He looked at Janet Horgan challengingly. The Irish girl's usually cheerful, freckled face was worried. 'Because he's your lover?'

Janet was silent.

He insisted. 'Where does your loyalty lie, Juanita? To your compatriot, or to the Cause?'

'He's no compatriot of mine,' she flashed, 'he's English. But he isn't a spy. I admit he knows some of us meet here — but I made him think it was to discuss politics,' she added in a rush.

'You little fool,' said Miguel bitterly. 'You should never have admitted that we met as a group at all.' He turned away from them for a moment, then squared his shoulders and spoke to the German.

'I apologize, Helmut.' He held out his hand. The German ignored it.

Miguel withdrew his hand slowly. He turned to the others. 'It must have been Warne. I'll see to him. Does anyone know where he is now? I suppose he's gone to bed.'

'He's not in the Centre at all,' said Janet.

'What?'

'He's gone climbing in the mountains. He had five days' leave and left this morning. The manager was asking for him, too, because there's been a message for him from the Lima Embassy. I told him Jack would be back on Tuesday.' She suddenly looked apprehensive. 'But Miguel, you won't — ?' He interrupted her.

'Did you say climbing?' he asked sharply. 'Where? Which side of the valley?'

'On Chopicalqui,' she said sullenly.

He started, and leaned forward, his eyes boring into the girl's face. 'Are you sure?' he asked, harshly.

'Yes. He told me yesterday about the view you can get from the high shoulder.'

The Argentine's face was grim. The group looked at him, puzzled. He was silent for a moment, and then stood up, smiling at them.

'Thank you for coming,' he said politely. 'I'm glad we've solved the problem. Of course it must have been an outsider, and that makes it Warne. I agree there wouldn't be any point in a member of the group trying to record our meetings. You all know what goes on here.'

'Do we?' asked the German, coldly. He turned his back and went out.

# 3

## Sunday

Flying south, the Boeing 707 took a long look at serried ranges of mountains on its left, stretching northwards like the closed fingers of a gigantic hand encrusted with windswept granite crags, sprawling greenish-blue glaciers and, towering above, the great peaks of ice and snow.

The plane turned towards the sea, spiralling to lose height. Below was a floor of cloud, and the shadow of the great wings on the sunlit white pillows began to move faster and expand. Patches of mist raced past the windows and then, quite abruptly, there was nothing to see but the thick cloud condensing on the frozen panes. When the mist cleared they were only a few hundred feet above the ground, a narrow band of desert between the Pacific breakers and the barren foothills that rose from the coastal plain to disappear through the overcast. For eight months of the year the cloud ceiling hangs above Lima, shutting out the sun and holding down the spent air that gets cleaned by rain only once every ten years or so. But during these months, if the Limenos want to see the sun all they have to do is drive up the mountain road for twenty minutes and it's there, waiting for them above the low cloud.

As the big plane taxied in to a halt near the airport buildings a man in a light suit came through the barrier and was at the foot of the steps when Craig put his foot on Peruvian soil. 'Mr. Craig?'

'That's me. Kind of you to meet me.' They shook hands.

'My name's Roger Harris, First Secretary. They gave you a dip visa, of course?'

'Yes.' As assistant in the Police Adviser's Department Craig was allowed to use Counsellor rank on his official visits abroad.

'Good. Give me your passport and the *despachante* will see you get through the immigration and customs quickly.' He handed the passport to the dark-skinned young man who had followed him on to the apron. 'The police rang us, incidentally, and said they'd meet you, but I thought it'd be better if I did. They'll be sending a liaison officer to have a talk with you about your lecture programme tomorrow morning.' He led Craig into the airport foyer.

Craig glanced at him. 'You're being very kind. What about a hotel?' Harris was a man of about thirty-five, his fair skin burned red after a Saturday spent 'up the hill'. He had a pleasant smile, and Craig liked the look of him.

'Well, it's up to you. I've provisionally reserved a room at the Bolivar, but my wife and I would be happy if you'd stay with us. The children are all at school in England, and there's plenty of room.' He hesitated. 'As a matter of fact, it might be more convenient. If you stay in town and we send cars for you there's no knowing when they'll turn up, because of the traffic. Stay with us and my driver can take you wherever you have to go. There's another reason, too, but I'll explain later.'

'Well, I'd love to. Thanks very much. But on one condition. We split my subsistence allowance. That's what I always do and the Office approves.'

'O.K., if you insist. There's Arturo, he's got your baggage cleared already.'

A black Humber was waiting in the diplomatic car park, with a chauffeur in attendance. As they drove away towards the centre of the city Harris said, 'I gather you want to have a talk with young Warne. H.E. would like to know what's it all about, but tomorrow will do. The point is, I'm afraid you won't be able to see Warne for a few days. He's gone climbing.'

'How d'you know?'

'We rang the manager of the Centre at Chasco. He said Jack would be returning on Tuesday night and could catch the Airforce plane on Wednesday. He should be here by lunchtime.'

'Jack?' He looked at Harris. 'D'you know him well, then?'

'Oh yes. He's a very nice boy and often comes to the house when he's in Lima. In fact, he stayed with us last week when he had to visit the Agricultural University about some of the 'miracle corn' seeds they're experimenting with at Chasco. He brought down some of his luggage. You see, he's due to finish his year's stint as a volunteer next month. Which is why,' added Harris with a sideways glance at Craig, 'H.E. is so curious to know why you can't wait until he's in London.'

Craig changed the subject.

* * *

The car drew up in a quiet road in the suburb of San Isidro, a couple of miles from the centre of Lima. While the driver was getting the luggage from the boot Harris led the way through a door in a high wall and between flowering jacaranda trees to the door of the house. It was low-built around a glass-walled patio filled with tropical vegetation. The rooms at the rear looked out through sliding windows on to a wide lawn and a swimming pool.

'There's Sylvia,' said Harris. 'Come and meet her.'

In the moist warm air of the garden the fragrance of the daturas mingled with the more delicate scents of the English flowers in the beds.

Sylvia Harris came across the lawn, slipping a pair of secateurs into the pocket of her gardening apron and pulling off her gloves. She was a good-looking woman of thirty, with a pleasantly shaped figure.

'It's very kind of you to put me up,' said Craig.

'We like seeing people from home. Come inside and let's have some pisco sours.' She looked up at him speculatively. 'Or are you a whisky man? You've got a rugged, Scottish look about you.'

'Can you get whisky easily?'

'Lashings of it, at sixty pence a bottle. So you can take your pick.'

'Then whisky, thanks. Could I have a shower first? Eighteen hours in a plane leaves one a bit sticky.'

'There's one next to your room. And have a swim afterwards if you want to. I shall. Right, then. Drinks when you're ready.'

Later, with glasses in their hands, the two men were strolling in the garden before dinner. The short twilight was already over, and concealed lights shone through the water of the swimming pool.

'You should see us all lit up for a party,' said Harris. 'Coloured lights and spots all over the place, like a scene in a pantomime. Some people think it's a bit too stagey, but I like it and so do most of our guests, especially the women. And anyway, it's what people expect here.' He stopped beside a mulberry tree. 'Just look at this mixed-up tree. It fruits three times a year and flowers at the same time. It's this extraordinary climate; the wretched tree doesn't know what it's supposed to be doing.'

'But that's only down here along the coast?'

'Lord, yes. Just wait until you see what it's like on the altiplano. Incidentally' — he pointed to a wooden hut behind the swimming pool — 'that's where Jack Warne sleeps when he stays with us.' He laughed. 'He's a funny lad. Says he mustn't get soft, and won't sleep in a comfortable bed if he can help it. He just slings his hammock inside the hut and opens the doors and windows.'

'What's the hut for?'

'We had it put up for the children to change in. They have bathing parties for their friends when they're out here for the holidays, and Sylvia won't have them traipsing through the house, dripping. It's locked now, because Jack's luggage is there.'

Craig's interest quickened. He walked towards the hut — and stopped short. A thick chain ran through a staple in the door and another driven into the frame, and was closed with a heavy padlock. There was a mark near the frame staple which Craig's policeman's eye could not mistake. 'D'you mind if I have a look?'

'Of course not,' said Harris, puzzled. 'What's wrong?'

'This.' Craig took hold of the chain and pulled. The staple in the door-frame came clean out of the wood. 'I'm afraid someone's had a go. See that mark? They used a jemmy to lever out the staple.

Then pushed it back so that it wouldn't be noticed.'

Roger Harris swore. 'But we never get thieves here. There are guards on all these roads at night. And anyway, there obviously isn't anything worth pinching in a bathing hut.'

'Except Warne's luggage, perhaps.'

'Bloody hell, I forgot that. We ought to have brought it into the house. Let's have a look.'

Craig stopped him as he ran forward. 'Don't touch anything, Roger. Let me.' He pushed the door open with his foot. It was dark inside, and he felt his way to the window, opened it and threw back the shutters. The light from a lamp standard by the pool flooded the interior. There was a gasp from Harris.

Two battered suitcases had been forced open and their contents emptied on to the floor. There was nothing else in the hut except some bathing shorts in an open cupboard.

'Christ!' shouted Harris. 'The bastards! But they don't seem to have taken much, thank God. Look, there's his Rolleiflex.'

'Yes,' said Craig grimly. 'There's his camera, opened, empty and just left lying around. What's that box?' He pointed to a shallow metal case on the floor, also open and empty.

'Poor Jack!' said Harris ruefully. 'He's going to hate me for this. The swine have pinched all his tapes.'

That word, thought Craig, rang a loud bell. 'Tapes?'

'Yes. He'd made quite a stock of little tape cassettes of Indian songs and dances. He used to play them to us. My God, he'll be livid when he finds they've been swiped. I can't forgive myself for not protecting his stuff properly, but — well you see, it's unheard of.' He bent down to put back the clothes in the suitcases, but Craig stopped him.'

'Look, Roger, I'm sorry, but there's more in this than a simple break-in. We've got to leave everything where it is; it's unfair to the police otherwise.'

'Oh Christ, the police!' He looked at Craig. 'Have they really got to be brought into this? After all, it looks as if nothing of real value has been taken.'

Craig considered. 'There's no one else in the garden, is there? I mean, nobody who could have seen us go into the hut.'

'No. The gardener's gone home, and you can't see the bathing hut from the house, because of the trees.'

'Well, I think there might be an advantage in pretending for the moment that this hasn't happened. I'll explain later. Will you leave it to me? I'll see the police tomorrow.'

'Of course. What d'you want to do now?'

Craig closed the shutters, led Harris out of the door and shut it, replacing the staple and padlock. 'I'll have another whisky, if I may.'

* * *

'After all, darling,' said Sylvia Harris, 'Jack did insist that his suitcases would be all right in the hut. It was his idea, not yours.'

Harris shook his head. 'It was my responsibility, all the same. I ought to have moved them into the house.'

'If you had,' said Craig gently, 'they might have broken into the house to find them.'

Sylvia looked at him, horrified. 'But who are 'they'?'

Craig sipped his brandy. They were sitting on the terrace after dinner, and the air was cool and smelt of watered grass and night-scented stock. 'I don't know. In one of his letters to England Warne mentioned that he was doing something exciting — and secret. Do you think he could have got mixed up with some dissident movement here?'

'Not Jack,' cried Sylvia indignantly. 'He's got more sense than that.'

'You can't be sure,' reflected Harris. 'Almost all the young have a left-wing bias these days. But I must say most of the Peruvian students seem to approve of this Government, for a change. It's a long time since we've had any riots in the Universities, and they were more common than not, at one time.' He made a swipe at a passing mosquito, and added, slowly, 'I've just thought of something. Jack *told* me that there was nothing of value in his luggage. I remember him saying that. There was only his Rolly, and that was broken.'

'Perhaps that's why it wasn't taken,' suggested his wife.

'Perhaps,' agreed Craig. But he thought there might be another reason why the camera had been opened, and left lying. He changed the subject. 'This is my first visit to Lima. What's it like, as a post?'

'The climate's a bit dreary,' said Sylvia. 'All through the middle of the year — which is winter, of course — we sweat it out under this overcast and long for the week-ends when we can get up into the sun. We've just rented a villa at Chaclacayo, thirty kilometres up the Rimac valley, and it's great fun. Sun all the year round, because it's two thousand feet up. Many people with chalets have swimming pools, and we get invited out a lot.' She finished her coffee and picked up the silver jug to pour out more. 'The best thing about Lima is my garden, which is heaven.' She looked across the dimly lit beds proudly. 'I think I've got practically every English flower there is, as well as the tropicals.'

Harris pulled at his cigar and looked at her affectionately. 'What gorgeous nonsense you talk, darling,' he said, and turning to Craig, 'What she means is that she's got more varieties than the other diplomatic wives, and that counts a lot in our tight little society.'

'Is it so tight? You must have a good deal to do with the Peruvian Government. What's it like working under a military regime?'

'Very pleasant. They're doing more for this country than any of the governments — quote — democratically elected — quote — in the past. You can really see things happening. Take this Chasco valley, for example, where young Warne is working. It lies far away from the tourist areas, eight thousand feet up on the other side of the Cordillera Blanca, and for the last hundred and fifty years the whole valley belonged to one family — the Santa Cruz Colmenares. They were good *hacenderos*, by and large, but the Indian tenant farmers were serfs of the Casa

Grande. Almost literally. They could never own their land, and their contracts bound them to give so many days service to the landlord every year, help with maintaining roads, water channels and so on, and provide daughters for service in the big house. What's more, they had to sell their produce through the estate office. And buy stores the same way.'

'It's the classic pattern of the latifundia,' remarked Craig. 'Same in Calabria and Sicily.'

'Same in many parts of the world, but much more prone to abuse when an estate is surrounded by mountain ranges the height of Mont Blanc, and until recently only approachable by mule-back. But it wasn't just the plight of the Indians that needed reform: this was something that affected the economy of the country as a whole.'

'Poor Peter!' said Sylvia, laughing. 'You've started something. It's Roger's hobby-horse.'

'I'm interested,' said Craig. He filled his pipe and prepared to listen.

'All right, then. It's a question of food.

Peru used to import twenty-five per cent of her food, although at least ten per cent of the country — and it's twice the size of France, you know — is cultivable. The population is growing by about three per cent a year and the country must find means of feeding itself. Now, let's take a *good* landlord. Many of them had up to a hundred thousand acres of cultivable land, and some estates were bigger than Wales. All right, so he's a benevolent boss. He looks after his people, gives dowries to the girls when they marry, helps his tenants to get farm tools cheap, doesn't leave his land in the hands of *cholo* agents and foremen while he goes swanning off to Paris — that was the worst thing, of course — and doesn't swindle his Indians over prices for their produce.

'But what is he out to do? Live well, of course, and get richer. So he goes for export crops, like cotton, sugar, coca, coffee and so on. He's not concerned with the fact that Peru is importing wheat and maize from the United States. All he wants to do is make a fair profit as easily as possible. When part of his land would cost too much to irrigate and clear for ploughing he just leaves it, or uses it as a game preserve. He doesn't develop it. That's what caused all the invasions of big estates by the peasants in the sixties — at least, that's how they started, but of course once they had worked themselves up the Casa Grande tended to go up in flames.'

'Drink your coffee, dear,' said Sylvia, suppressing a yawn. 'It'll get cold.'

'There was never a really large-scale rising, was there?' asked Craig.

'Never, because the Indians are mad keen about land. Their own land, in their own valley. They're not the least interested in what happens over the mountains. If their families grow too big the younger men don't go and try to farm somewhere else — they wouldn't have a chance, anyway. They get down to the coast and start to learn Spanish and get jobs. There are about half a million of them living up in the hills around Lima, squatters on Government land. They go down into the town to work or beg, and even if they make money they never think of going back to the plateau. That's what the new Government want to stop. Make them want to stay in their valleys.'

'So they dispossessed the landowners?'

'Yes, leaving them only enough to farm and live on. But it's a slow business. The opposition of the great landlords has been extreme in some parts, and the task of converting a vast estate to small but still economic farms and co-operatives, and training and equipping the new owners to develop them as the Government wants — and not necessarily what the Indian farmers themselves want — is formidable, and will take a long time. One of the shining examples is the Chasco valley, where the *hacendero*, Jorge Santa Cruz, has actually cooperated with the Government over the dissolution of his empire. This is what has so seized the imagination of young people, and that's why more than thirty volunteers from different countries have gone there to help.'

'But who does the organizing? There can't be all that many skilled farm managers who're prepared to spend their time hundreds of miles from civilization.'

'But that's the whole point. The Army. They include the only large body of educated men who know the Indians and speak their language. They have to, because that's where half their recruits come from.'

'*Half?*'

'Yes. There are about six million Indians living on the plateau, and the Army has to recruit from them, teach them to speak Spanish as well as Quechua or Aymara, give them primary education and train them in their skills. For years the Staff College and the Centro de Altos Estudos Militares — like our Imperial Defence College — have been teaching officers the basics of economics and food production, and it's these men who are everywhere, setting up agricultural training schools and co-operatives and managing the large estates that can't be split up for economic reasons. I tell you, there'll be a lot of mistakes and botches before they're through, but it's a very remarkable experiment, and I take off my hat to them.' He finished his brandy and grinned at Craig. 'There's a lot more to it, but that's the essence.'

'But surely there must have been attempts by left-wing groups to take over the land-reform?'

'Lots. But mostly from the old-fashioned Socialists and trade unions. The young people have been very pro, on the whole. University classes go and spend their long vacations up in the sierra, trying to help.'

'It's interesting, Roger. I'm glad you told me. I think I'd better go to bed now. Sylvia has been rather pointedly falling asleep for some time.'

'My dear Peter,' she said, sitting up and frankly yawning. 'Don't think it's your company. It's just that I seem to have heard Roger on this subject before.'

# 4

## Monday

The British Embassy occupied two floors in a modern office block on the Plaza Washington. Mr. Frederick Townsend, the Ambassador, received Craig in his room at nine o'clock. A rather intense-looking man in his early fifties, with a thin, clever face, he was fidgeting with his cigarette-lighter as he talked.

'I had a telegram from the Office,' he said, 'asking me to call young Warne back to Lima, so that you could talk to him. What is this about? I gather from Roger that Warne is suspected of getting mixed up in some political activity. Strikes me as odd; I thought the boy had a reasonably sensible head on his shoulders.'

'There is this break-in at Harris's house, sir.'

'He told me about that. But it isn't very positive evidence, surely? The thief might have got scared and run for it, snatching up the only thing he thought might be interesting.'

'In that case, sir, he'd have taken the box, too. But there's a bit more to it than — '

'Ah, I thought you hadn't told Harris everything. Why not?'

'I intended to tell you first. You see, in a letter to his mother Warne wrote that he'd made a tape which would interest his uncle, who is in the Intelligence Service.'

His Excellency's hackles rose. 'D'you mean to tell me he was sent out here, *as a volunteer*, with some damned intelligence brief?'

'No, sir. That's exactly what he was not given. I had a categorical assurance to that effect from his uncle. No. It was something he was doing on his own initiative.'

'You're quite convinced of that, Craig? It could be very important.'

'I am absolutely sure.'

'All right.' Townsend thought for a moment, flicking the lighter on and off. 'So whoever broke into that hut was after the tape. And got it,' he added, crisply.

'If it was there. But Warne told the Harrises there was nothing of importance in the luggage. So perhaps it wasn't.'

'I'm not so sure,' said the Ambassador. 'I'm just thinking — if I had a tape-recording I didn't want anyone to find, I'd give it a phoney label and put it in a box with two dozen others.'

Craig looked at the other man with respect. 'I hadn't thought of that. But I still think it wasn't in the box. Why did they go through everything else? It's as if they couldn't be sure that it was one of the tapes in the container. So we must assume that Warne still has it with him, twenty thousand feet up on a mountain called Chopicalqui, or else hidden somewhere in the Centre. I'm afraid we'll just have to wait until he gets to Lima on Wednesday.'

'Why? I don't want any trouble, Craig. My relations with this Government are excellent, and I mean to keep them so. Can't you go to the Centre before Warne gets back from his climb? I know it's several hundred miles away, but the Air

Attaché might arrange for you to get a lift to the Air Force base at the end of the valley, and you could get a jeep to take you to the settlement.'

'I start my lectures this afternoon, sir, and they go on throughout the week.'

'Cancel them. Postpone them till next week.'

'It'd upset the Peruvians. And anyway, I think we must explain to them without further delay what has happened, and leave them to take action.'

The Ambassador tapped his foot impatiently. 'I don't like waiting.'

'No, sir. But if anything did come out, wouldn't it look better if we'd already told the Peruvians what we suspect?'

'Damn! You're right, of course. What contacts d'you want?'

'I'm seeing the Deputy Director of the *Direccion General de Seguridad* for lunch today, with the police and security liaison officers. If you've no objection I'll tell him the whole story, omitting of course the connection with MI6.'

'All right. Go ahead. I know Urrutia. He's a sound man. Army colonel, seconded to the police. Yes. Tell him the whole thing, but for God's sake make it crystal clear that the boy had no kind of I. brief from us. Ask his advice, and follow it.' His Excellency glanced at his watch. 'We must do our best to make your visit pleasant, Craig — I mean from your point of view. My wife'll be getting in touch with you through the Harrises; we'd like you to come to dinner one day this week. But let's get this damned thing straightened out first.' He thought for a minute pausing on his way to the door. 'Listen, Craig. If you find that Warne has attracted any attention from the Peruvian police — or the security fellows for that matter — you have my authority to say he will take the first plane home as soon as he arrives in Lima. Understood?'

* * *

The Plaza San Martin, in the centre of Lima, is laid out in grand style, with the statue of the Liberator in the middle and several of those clubs dear to the hearts of fashionable Limenos.

The Club Nacional has something of the characteristics of both the Athenaeum and the Royal Automobile Club, and is bigger than either. It was built for the rich and powerful — the rubber and sugar kings, the owners of gold and silver mines, bankers, generals, admirals and politicians. Within its pillared halls and private rooms, in the Turkish bath, the library, the gymnasium, and across the shining tables of the dining room financial empires have been founded and governments undermined. The Club has immense dignity, yet with a touch of that raffish spirit of daring and enterprise which has given Peru, since the days of Pachacuti, the ninth Inca, its kaleidoscopic history.

The police liaison officer led Craig up the wide staircase to the first floor. In an alcove near the windows two men rose from a leather sofa. Colonel Urrutia was a man of medium height, with the broad shoulders of his Basque forebears, a strong-featured pale face and a prominent jaw. He wore a grey lightweight suit and a silk shirt and tie. The man with him was young, dressed in elegant tweeds, with a thin, intelligent face — very Spanish-looking.

'Welcome to Peru, Mr. Craig,' said Urrutia, in excellent English. 'Your first visit, I think?'

'I've been looking forward to meeting you, *mi Coronel*, and seeing your beautiful country.'

'We're delighted to have you with us. You know Inspector Gonzalez already. This is Captain Loyola, of the National Intelligence Service.' Loyola bowed formally, and the two men shook hands. Urrutia settled Craig on the sofa and sat down on his left. A waiter apeared with four glasses of pale liquid, topped with foam. 'You must try one of the Club's pisco sours.'

Craig sipped the sticky mixture of cane-spirit and fresh lime juice through the layer of white egg foam, and said the flavour was excellent. Which it was, if a little too sweet for his liking.

He found a lot to interest him in his hosts. The inspector was a type he recognized easily, a dedicated Special

Branch officer, proud of his English and French and eager to talk about the anti-guerrilla campaign in which he had taken part in 1965. Loyola, a cavalryman, interpolated jealously that it was the Army, under the President, then Chief of Staff, who had crushed the guerrilla movement, but Gonzalez said the police had carried out operations in the towns at the same time, and the two campaigns had complemented each other. They were both politely interested to know what Craig had to say about counter-subversion, but he told them, laughing, that he didn't want them to be bored when they heard his views all over again in his lectures. Colonel Urrutia listened attentively, without saying much. Then he put some pointed questions about operations in Northern Ireland, and Craig did his best to satisfy his curiosity.

By the time they had finished an excellent meal of *ceviche* — raw white fish steeped in fresh lime juice — and charcoal-grilled steaks, and were sitting over coffee and brandy, Craig felt that he could decently bring up the subject which was on his mind.

'I should be grateful, Colonel, for your advice on a problem which is of concern to our Embassy. His Excellency suggested that you might help us.'

'I have great respect for Mr. Townsend,' said Urrutia simply. 'Go ahead.'

Craig explained that Jack Warne, working in the Chasco valley as a volunteer, had written to his mother that he had stumbled on information of intelligence value. Some of it had in fact been recorded on a tape cassette, but he had not said what he intended to do with this. Craig made no mention of Warne's relationship with Trenchman and MI6, but went on to say that the Embassy had been told to summon the young man to Lima so that Craig could find out what it was all about. He added that Warne was apparently away from the Centre at the moment, climbing on the slopes of Chopicalqui.

'Is he accompanied by guides?' put in Urrutia sharply.

'I don't think so. But the boy is an

experienced mountaineer. His father was killed in the Himalayas, and young Warne was with him on the expedition.'

'He'll meet the same fate, unless he's lucky,' remarked Urrutia grimly. 'I know that area well, and the eastern slopes of Chopicalqui are dangerous. But what is it you want, senor? I presume you will interview Mr. Warne when he turns up at the Embassy, and of course inform us if indeed he has any information of interest.'

'Yes, that is His Excellency's idea. But in the meantime something very odd has happened.' He retailed the story of the discovery of the rifled suitcases. The young inspector bristled.

'You did not call us in last night, sir?'

'I should have done so, of course, but that would have let everyone know that the theft had been discovered. I thought you might see some advantage in keeping it quiet for the moment.'

Urrutia nodded. 'Perhaps you are right. But I shall want to send an inspector this afternoon, to make a thorough investigation. I don't think I need ask,' he added, smiling, 'if you disturbed anything?' But the question was there.

'No, Colonel. Nothing was touched. I discovered this morning that Mrs. Harris went to the hut two days ago, to fetch a bathing-dress. At that time the suitcases were closed. Since then no one appears to have gone near the hut — except the thieves.'

'I see. Let's hear, Gonzalez, how you interpret what Mr. Craig has been telling us.'

The young police officer sat up straight. 'It appears likely, *mi Coronel*,' he said in Spanish, 'that Warne has become a member of a group of persons inimical to the State. He was able, using a small pocket-type tape-recorder of the kind Mr. Craig has described, to record the discussion at one of the meetings he attended, and planned to take the recording with him to England. Or he may have intended to hand it over to his Embassy for passing to us. But I don't think so.'

'Why?' asked Urrutia, smiling.

'Because he is a very young man and

would no doubt wish to get maximum credit for his discovery in his own country.' Jumping to the right conclusion, thought Craig, although the logic was questionable.

'You think he must be a member of this so-called group?' asked Urrutia, still with his cat-and-mouse smile.

'Yes, of course — er, no, sir. I see what you mean. He could have planted the microphone in the place of meeting. It is easy to buy cheap microphones in Lima.' He thought for a moment. 'But connecting it with the tape-recorder would not be easy.'

'Right,' said the Colonel. 'But of course, there's no reason why it should have been a group of dissidents. He could have held a conversation with a single person, and switched on his apparatus in advance. Still, I agree that the group is more likely. Young people fall naturally to talking politics in groups.'

'I have a suggestion, Colonel,' said Craig. 'By all means send your officers to investigate the scene of the theft, but could they come after dark, in civilian clothes, as if they were paying a social call?'

'They could. But why should they?'

'I am putting myself in the place of the person who planned the raid, Colonel. Either he found what he wanted, or he didn't. If he did not, he is thinking at this moment that Warne will have it with him, or concealed somewhere at the Centre, perhaps. So he will try to rob him again. But if it becomes known that the hut has been broken into he will expect Warne to be informed — by the Embassy, that is — and take precautions accordingly. So there is an advantage for us in keeping the break-in secret, for the time being.'

'Because the person behind the theft will expect Warne to make no special effort to conceal the tape, and thus be easier to rob?'

'Yes. I'm assuming, of course, that you can alert your local police officers at the Centre to give Warne discreet protection from the moment he returns from his climbing expedition until he is safely on the plane to Lima. And thus catch the person responsible.'

The three Peruvians smiled ruefully. 'It is quite impossible,' said Urrutia, 'to give what you call discreet protection to one of the volunteers at the Chasco Centre. We have no resident police there, and to bring in one of the officers from our base at Tambo, down the valley, would cause comment at once.' He sought for the right expression, and produced it triumphantly. 'He would stick out a mile.'

Craig laughed. 'You see I've been speaking without local knowledge, which is a policeman's worst sin. I suggest, then, that you arrest Warne as soon as he gets back to the settlement.'

'On suspicion?' said the Colonel, raising his eyebrows.

'Protective custody. After all, if they can't get the mysterious tape they can always have a go at Warne himself. What's on the tape is also locked up in his head.'

'We should lose our chance of trapping the criminal,' objected Loyola. 'And after all, the tape may have nothing to do with the Centre. It may have been recorded while Warne was in Lima, and the people who planned the theft may be here.'

'I realize that,' said Craig, 'and must leave it to you to decide whether what I've suggested is the right course. One thing I can assure you is that the Ambassador will raise no objection. He told me to say that if there is any evidence that Warne has been misbehaving himself — politically — he will be sent back to England at once.'

'There is just one point, Mr. Craig.'

*'A sus ordenes, mi Coronel.'*

'I was going to ask if it didn't occur to you or Mr. Harris that it might have been the police who broke into the swimming hut.' He was half-smiling as he spoke, but his eyes were fixed on Craig's face.

'It certainly occurred to me — not, I think, to Harris. It was my first thought. I knew the young man had been mixing himself up in something he shouldn't have touched and it would have been quite natural if you had shown interest in his luggage. But of course it was quite impossible.'

'Why?'

'Because if you had had Warne under suspicion you'd have known that he would be leaving Peru in a few weeks' time. That would have been the opportunity to search all his effects — at the airport. Not take the risk of alerting him in this way. And no policeman worth his salt would have scattered the contents of the suitcases all over the floor. Everything would have been put back in its place, and very carefully.'

'Well argued,' said Urrutia with his bland smile, 'and the subtle flattery is noted. In fact, we didn't. This is the first time Warne's activities have come to our notice. All right, then. You can tell His Excellency that we will take Warne into protective custody as soon as he returns to the settlement, and see that he is escorted to Lima. I will send the forensic officers to the Harris's house after dark.'

Craig thanked him. Then he said, 'Harris was telling me a good deal about the Chasco re-settlement project. I gather it is your colleagues in the Army who do most of the organization?'

'Yes. The manager at the Centre is a retired major of engineers, Castillo — a very dedicated man. He's lucky in having a local landowner who will co-operate. There are eight thousand hectares of first-class land to be divided up, and it's a very difficult task.'

'Good God, that's twenty thousand acres. And the *hacendero* owned the lot?'

'Under the agrarian laws of our national revolution Don Jorge Santa Cruz lost all his land, except for the large home farm and his house and its grounds. But of course he got compensation,' added Urrutia hastily. 'In — er — Government bonds. He still has his silver mine and was able to sell his wool and corn processing plant to the Centre.'

'All the same, it's a pretty big loss.'

Urrutia was silent for a moment. 'Don Jorge has collaborated correctly, and takes a close interest in the new Centre and the communal factories and markets. That is what I hear. I know him slightly, since he is a member of this club, of course.' He smiled. 'Before you begin to feel too sorry for him, Mr. Craig, I should add that he still has a yacht at Cannes, a villa near San Tropez and I am quite sure a large numbered account in a Swiss bank. The rich men in Peru, before we took over, were very rich indeed.'

All the same, thought Craig, as he went out into the Plaza San Martin to the car which was waiting to take him to the Military Academy for his first lecture, Don Jorge Santa Cruz must have a very mild, or a very forgiving nature. He was to remember that assumption later, with wry amusement.

⋆ ⋆ ⋆

About the same time, on that Monday afternoon, but nearly three hundred miles to the north-east and sixteen thousand feet nearer the sky, Jack Warne reversed his ice-axe, holding it firmly between his gloved hands, and glissaded down the last of the snow slopes between buttresses of gleaming blue ice. At its foot the loose schist began, with scattered scrub, and he found a place with some shade to take a rest.

He took off his rucksack, put on the anorak — for the air was cold after the blazing sun of the high snows — and ate a bar of chocolate. Then he changed his climbing boots for thick rubber-soled shoes and stretched out for a few minutes before descending the last two thousand feet to the lake. Over to his left he could see the towering wall of the glacier falling towards the water that lay hidden by the curve of the mountain.

It had been an exciting climb and he felt, as always, physically soothed. The view at dawn from outside the snowcave where he had spent the night, snug in his sleeping bag, had been glitteringly beautiful as the sun caught the succession of snow-covered peaks — Aguja, Artesonraju, Chacraraju, Huandoy, and nearer at hand the twin crest of Huascaran, twenty-two thousand feet high, and first climbed at the turn of the century by a woman of fifty.

His own father had been killed by a fall in the Himalayas — he could never forget the awful stillness of the frozen body — on a mountain whose challenge was known and respected. But the Andes were incalculable. They would allow a woman to climb their summits and then, without warning, destroy thousands of lives within a few seconds.

Warne shook himself and got to his feet. His body was as tough as whipcord and his face weathered by wind and sun, except where the snow goggles had left pale circles. He took the descent easily, using his axe. Here and there the first trees appeared among the scrub.

Within an hour he had reached the shore of the lake. Llanga, it was called. Fourteen thousand feet above sea-level, and like all the glacier lakes in this part of the range, steadily growing through the gradual recession of the snows.

From where he stood on the shingle beach the narrow lake came twisting from the left between the ribs of the mountain. He could just see the glacier sprawling down from the high snows like melted blue wax.

Far to his right, past a small off-shore island, was the dark mound of earth and rocks which had formed a natural dam to hold back the mass of lake-water from the valley below. Warne shivered.

The sun was sinking behind him over the mountain at his back, and he began to think of supper. There was a collapsible spinning rod in his pack, and Warne tied a spoon on the trace and began to cast from the shore. There were huge rainbow trout in the lake, by all accounts, but if so they paid no attention to his amateur's lure, and he was glad to have hooked a couple of one-pounders after half an hour's fishing. They would do for his supper. He would descend to the valley the following afternoon with more trout, if he could catch them, and they'd have a party. He would have to keep the fish in a wet cloth during the long walk down, or they'd be as high as Huascaran.

# 5

## Tuesday

Ten miles downstream from the Centre the broad green valley of the Chasco river narrowed, and the stream ran between steep banks into the little village of Tambo, whose main importance was the small Army base and the airstrip of beaten earth that served it. Fifty years before, the village had been wiped out by a flood, and most of the houses in which the Indians and *cholos* lived showed signs of having been patched together after the disaster. But the new Army hutments were smartly maintained in their neat rows along the river bank, and the hangars which housed the transport planes were brightly painted. It was still a month before the rainy season would begin but there was always plenty of water in the stream bed, for the Chasco was fed by the *quebradas* that brought down meltwater from the high ranges on both sides.

A Military Police jeep drove out of the camp and up the tarmac road that led to the Centre, and beyond it to the head of the valley. The man beside the driver was Major Bernardo Rodriguez, of the Military Intelligence Service. He was reading the long signal that had come from Lima during the radio operator's night-shift. *Muy curioso*, he decided, and put the paper away to enjoy the morning sunlight on the green fields and whitewashed cottages of the settlement.

This was how it ought to be everywhere, he thought, where the great estates had been confiscated under the new laws. Every family now had its own house and plot of land, and together they formed the co-operatives which worked the main crops that needed development by mechanical means. Each family provided labour and took its share in the profits. The men who held the franchises for milling, lumbering and so on, in areas remote from the Centre were allowed to make a fair profit, and no more. Of course they grumbled, as the Indians always did, but there was no doubt about it, the whole valley was becoming a prosperous and largely self-supporting society, and providing more food for the coastal plain than ever before. And it was the Army men who had planned the whole project.

Rodriguez had a genial contempt for the experts at the universities in Lima and Trujillo. They couldn't understand the Indians as the Army did. He himself could speak tolerable Quechua and had made friends among the *alcaldes* of the villages in the Chasco valley.

Yes, it was a great achievement, and he had to admit that without Don Jorge Santa Cruz it would have been a slow and awkward business. But Santa Cruz had seen the writing on the wall and instead of sabotaging the scheme — as he could have done, at first — he had collaborated, using his influence with the *alcaldes*, allowing his great barns to provide the nucleus for the communal market, and helping to open up watercourses which had been unused since the time of the

Incas. Of course, having spent most of his life on the estate, he knew it like the palm of his hand and spoke Quechua like a native, which all helped.

The jeep passed, on the right, the wide boulder-strewn bed of the stream that joined the Chasco river. It came from the glacier lake Llanga, high up in the mountains, and during the winter rains — and worse, when the thaws came in the spring — it was a raging torrent. Further on, from the same side, a dirt road joined the highway, and Rodriguez could see a heavy truck approaching, bringing down either ore or men from the silver mine, which was situated not far from the lake. If it was ore, the truck would only halt at the Casa Grande for control and a meal for the driver and then go on up the valley to where the road turned west and wound its slow way through the Cordillera, over a high pass and down to the coast, a hundred and fifty miles away.

The jeep passed through two or three hamlets and approached the Centre, still following the course of the Chasco river. On the other bank were the new lines of houses for the men working at the Centre and their families, white-painted and arranged around a market square. The car swung left between the main administrative buildings and stopped outside the door of the manager's office. Rodriguez ran up the steps and went in.

Major Castillo, the manager, was a tanned, eager little man, bald-headed and wearing steel-rimmed half-spectacles. He was working at his desk, and looked up in surprise.

'What brings you here, Rodriguez? There's no trouble as far as I know. I'll get you some coffee.'

Rodriguez took off his cap and mopped his forehead. He sat down. 'Thanks, I could do with it. It's a hot drive. You've got a young volunteer called Warne, a Britisher. D'you know him?'

'Of course I know him. He helps the agronomists. The British Embassy telephoned the other day, saying they wanted him to go to Lima, and I agreed. But I had to tell them he wouldn't be available until tonight.'

'I did hear that he was away, climbing

on Chopicalqui. The thing is, Major, I have to tell you in confidence that the young man may be mixed up in some political activity. That's why they want him in Lima, for questioning.'

Castillo's face darkened. 'You haven't been infiltrating spies into this settlement without my knowledge, have you?'

'Of course not. You know perfectly well we should approach you first. I think it must be something he's done in Lima.'

'I should hope so. Good, here's the coffee.' He waited until the Indian servant had left the room. 'So what d'you want to do?'

'I'd like to search his room, as a start.'

Castillo frowned, then shrugged his shoulders. 'Oh, all right. The volunteers are all at their jobs just now, so there shouldn't be anyone about in their compound. Otherwise it'd get round the Centre like a bush fire.'

Rodriguez hesitated. 'I'm afraid, Major, it's going to do that anyway. You see, I've orders to arrest young Warne as soon as he returns here tonight.'

The manager stared at him. 'It's

serious, then. This is a nuisance. The last thing I want is for the volunteers to think the Army is spying on them. They all work well and I like them, mostly, but they have preconceived ideas about the police, military or otherwise.'

'I'm sorry, but my orders come from Lima.'

'O.K. Let's get it over.'

Castillo led the way out into the brilliant sunshine and across the compound to a smaller area, beyond, where there was a row of adobe huts. He pushed open a door and walked into a short corridor with doors on both sides, one of which he opened. 'This is Warne's. Pretty spartan, isn't it? But they don't seem to mind. The door at the end of the passage gives on to the courtyard, with a wash-house in the middle.'

The room was indeed bare of furniture except for a bed, wardrobe, desk and some wooden chairs. Rodriguez closed the door behind him and went through the room systematically — mattress, pillows, the inside of the desk after removal of the drawer, the top of the wardrobe and underneath the bed. He found nothing. He examined the pockets of the clothing in the wardrobe and the lining of the battered suitcase standing in the corner. Again, nothing.

Then he stared thoughtfully at the floor near the bed, covered with a fine layer of gritty dust that had blown in from the parched earth outside. 'That's odd,' he said and pointed. The mark where he had supported himself on his hand to look under the bed was clear, but so was another mark six inches away. 'When are the rooms swept out?' he asked.

'Once a day,' said Castillo shortly. 'You can't expect more than that. The dust blows in everywhere.'

'I merely wanted to establish when somebody else looked under this bed,' replied Rodriguez drily.

'Oh, I see. Yes, it does look like that. The rooms are swept before the volunteers get back for the evening meal. Whoever did that must have come in here this morning, I should think, when there was already dust on the floor.'

'I wonder why.' Rodriguez brushed

himself down. 'Well, that's my job for the moment. Let's get back to your office. If you can spare me a few minutes I want to hear all you know about Warne.'

Castillo had little to tell. 'He's a nice fellow, doesn't quarrel with the others, but can be boisterous when he's that way inclined. He sings and plays the guitar and has recorded Indian music, I know that. I heard something about him and the Irish nurse, Janet Horgan — Juanita, we call her. They seem to disappear together occasionally, but that happens with many other couples. We've had no pregnancies yet. If they're Catholics,' he added primly, 'they're not very good ones.'

Rodriguez laughed. 'Well, I'll have to wait around until he turns up. Can you arrange to have me informed immediately? I'll get him to pack his baggage — there isn't much, as you saw. He left most of it in Lima — and take him back to the base.'

'Of course. I hope he returns before the volunteers get back from their tasks, so that there won't be any fuss. If he does, I can tell the others that he has to return to Lima in a hurry, and leave it at that.' An Indian brought in a note. Castillo opened it and looked up, smiling. 'That's nice. Don Jorge has heard you're here and asks us both to lunch, just the two of us.' He looked at his watch. 'You've got thirty minutes. That'll give you time for a shower. D'you want a clean shirt?'

'That's a very kind offer. The dust gets into everything.'

* * *

Senor Jorge Santa Cruz Colmenar received his guests in the patio of the Casa Grande. It was partly covered by a sloping roof of red tiles, supported on white-painted columns, which ran round all four sides and gave protection from the vertical rays of the noon-day sun. In the paved court was a fountain in the middle of a lily pond, and the gentle splashing of the water among the ferns provided a restful background to the talk that followed.

Don Jorge was a man of sixty-two,

tall and lean, with a tanned, lined face and dark eyes under drooping lids. He was dressed for riding in the Spanish *campestre* style — a short jacket over a frilled shirt, with shining leather riding boots appearing under the narrow twill trousers.

'*Que tal*, Castillo? Nice to see you. Major Rodriguez, I think?' He held out his long brown hand.

The Major stood to attention and bowed. '*Mucho gusto*, Don Jorge.'

A butler brought a silver tray with a decanter of fino sherry. Santa Cruz said, 'I drink sherry myself at this hour of the day, but if you'd prefer something stronger — ?'

The two men shook their heads and took the tall glasses in their hands. They sat down at a table under the overhanging roof. The *mayordomo*, an old, impassive Indian in green livery, placed bowls of celery and olives, lying in crushed ice, on the table and withdrew.

'I was admiring the way the settlement is growing, Don Jorge,' said Rodriguez. 'In the few months I've been stationed here the difference is impressive.'

Santa Cruz patted the Manager's arm. 'Major Castillo is an organizer of outstanding brilliance,' he said, smiling. 'And he knows he can count on me for any help I may be able to offer.'

'Don Jorge's experience of the valley and his knowledge of these Indians has been of the greatest value to us,' said Castillo, continuing the exchange of compliments. 'The Government owes him a debt of gratitude.'

'The Government,' retorted Santa Cruz drily, 'owes me a good deal, one way or the other, but I don't complain. Many of my old friends with great estates have just left the country in disgust, allowing their lands to be chopped up like diced cheese.' His face darkened. 'And grow rotten,' he added bitterly.

Rodriguez said quietly, 'I have seen many estates, sir, where the landlords had let the tenants be exploited and oppressed, and it's only now that the land is being properly developed for the good of the country.'

'But not here, senor,' cried Santa Cruz

fiercely. 'My father and grandfather — God rest their souls!' — he crossed himself, rather sketchily — 'neither they nor I left the state to our agents to run. We might be away for a few months of the year, for as a family we have other commitments, but don't imagine that we did not know every tenant, and every hectare of the best land in Peru.'

'The Government couldn't make exceptions, Don Jorge,' said Rodriguez. 'Everyone realizes that it is hard that the good landlords — if I may use the expression — have to lead the way while the others do their best to delay the process, but at least the Government tries, under the new laws, to reward those who co-operate.'

'Reward? You said reward them? What you mean, my dear Rodriguez, is that if a landowner behaves himself like a good boy the Government kindly allows him to keep a slightly higher proportion of what is his.' He finished his sherry in a silence that could almost be felt. He smiled ruefully at his guests and shook his head. 'Forgive me, *amigos*. I am not as young as I was, and am not used to change. As you know, I have bowed to the storm. In this valley, at least, the land is being properly developed and the people are happy and contented. And this,' he added gravely, 'means more to me than what happens to my own fortune. Ah, here's Fidel.' He saw the *mayordomo* appearing in the entrance to the dining room and stood up. 'Let's see what we can do with that six-kilo lake trout they brought me this morning. I must make my wife's apologies for her absence. She is at our villa on the Cote d'Azur for the European summer. I shall join her a little later.' Rodriguez noticed a curious glint in the older man's eyes as he paused, and repeated, 'A little later, just before the rains begin.'

* * *

They were sitting again in the patio, drinking coffee and smoking Cuban cigars, when Santa Cruz said, 'I noticed your jeep carries the insignia of the

Military Intelligence Service, Major Rodriguez. I hope we haven't been at fault.' His eyes twinkled amiably.

Castillo glanced at Rodriguez, who said, 'I'm afraid there has been an enquiry into the activities of one of the volunteers employed by the Centre. I have to escort him to the Base and put him on the plane to Lima.'

'D'you mean he's been making trouble here?' asked Santa Cruz, raising his eyebrows. 'If so, I'm very glad you have found out.'

Castillo was going to reply, but Rodriguez cut in smoothly, 'Not here, Don Jorge, as far as I know. It is probably something the young man did in Lima. He spent a few days there recently, and perhaps he got into bad company.'

The eyes under the drooping lids narrowed. 'I'm surprised. They seem sensible young people, from what I've seen of them. They invited me to attend one of what they call their 'sing-songs', and I must say I enjoyed myself.' He laughed. 'They even succeeded in making me dance a *marinera* with one of the

— er — very nubile young women. If only she had taken the trouble to brush her hair and take a bath — but it's too much to ask of the young, these days. My grandchildren are still young, but their parents live in Europe and have already forgotten the manners and discipline they learned in Peru. I can't tell which of their children are girls and which boys; the hair length is the same. I doubt whether they will ever grow up to add elegance to a civilized drawing room.' He added suddenly, 'Who is it?'

'It's no secret, sir. An Englishman named Warne.'

'The mountaineer. I don't think I've had more than a few words with him, but I gather he's a good climber, like his illustrious father.'

The others looked puzzled.

'Oh, yes, didn't you know? His father was Randall Warne, the Everest man. He had the bad luck to die on Annapurna. I wouldn't have thought the boy had much interest in politics.'

'I don't even know if it is a question of politics,' said Rodriguez firmly. 'All I know is that he has to go back to Lima as soon as he returns to the Centre tonight.'

'What's he doing, then?'

'Climbing on the Chopicalqui shoulder.'

'By himself?'

'Yes.'

'I wish I had known, Castillo,' said Santa Cruz, turning to the manager. 'I would have advised against it. He should have been accompanied.'

'He's been on the slopes before,' said Castillo, defensively.

The older man shook his head. 'It's a dangerous mountain. If he slipped off one off the ice cornices — ' he made a gesture with his hands — 'you might never find him again.'

⋆ ⋆ ⋆

The afternoon sun was still some way above the mountains when Warne stopped fishing and looked with satisfaction into the net he had sunk in the shallow water near the shore. Six trout, and one or two of them whoppers. He would ask Janet to cook them when he got back to the Centre. He grinned. You had to feed the girl to get her amorous.

He had been standing in the sun for hours, and the sweat was soaking his shirt. He stripped it off, then his jeans, and looked longingly at the green water. Why not? It was too warm to take those fish home yet, and if he started at five, when the sun left the lake, he could still make it downhill on the road, using the short-cuts he had tried out before, and arrive in time for supper. The island was almost opposite him now, because he had been working down the shore in the direction of the dam. It only looked three hundred yards away, and worth exploring. The water couldn't be as cold as all that, near the surface, after a day of hot sun.

There was a change of underclothing in his pack, so he kept on his woollen vest and trunks to break the chill and entered the water. Within five yards he realized that the water was very cold indeed, and struck out in a fast crawl.

Half-way there, the cold dissipated the outer warmth of his body and he felt as if every limb were creaking with dull pain. But he was ashamed to turn back, and raced through the last hundred yards at his best speed. Hauling himself out he lay shivering on the sandy shore of the island, letting the fierce sun bring back life and warmth. He stripped off his underclothes, wrung them out and spread them on a hot layer of rock to dry. It wouldn't be a blind bit of good, of course, since he'd have to put them on again to swim back. That layer of wool had probably saved his life, he said to himself dramatically.

He walked round the island, which was sixty yards long and ran in a ridge parallel with the long axis of the narrow lake.

He wondered what had caused the island to be formed, and decided that the original glacier had split into two branches, piling up debris between them. He remembered that the lake was supposed to be a hundred feet deep at the lower end, so the scouring action must have been enormous. Idly, he turned and went up the slope towards the centre of the island — and stopped dead.

Out of sight from the shore, hidden in a

little depression among the trees, was a small hut, about eight feet by six, built of stout planks, with a low pitched roof covered with bituminous felt. On the side nearest him there was a door, secured by a stout padlock, and a small window.

Warne tried the padlock without success, and went to the window. The inclining rays of the sun lit up the interior and he could see into the small room, furnished with a table and chairs standing on a thick llama-skin rug. There were shelves and tins of food and in a corner — of all things — a skin-diver's rubber suit, complete with flippers.

Warne looked at them longingly. It was the flippers that would make all the difference — but if he could borrow the suit as well he wouldn't have to face that searching cold on the return swim. Every minute it was getting colder as the shadows lengthened over the water.

The window was far too small, even for his wiry body, and the padlock looked impregnable. He sat down opposite the door on a rock and thought. Presumably the hut was used by someone who liked to catch his trout the hard way — although he had seen no sign of a trident or an underwater gun — and came to spend a few days here from time to time. What would he do with the key? He looked round under stones near the door, but found nothing. Beneath the eaves, by the door? Nothing there either. Finally, he went round the back of the hut and tried again.

He found it. Running his hand along the ledge under the eaves — just the place where he had hidden the mike in Miguel's hut, he thought — he felt something cold, and that was it. The key was not rusty at all; must have been used quite recently.

He went round to the door and thrust the key into the padlock. It opened. He released the hasp and opened the door.

This, he thought, was breaking and entering — or at least, entering. He was still shivering and pulled the table to one side so that he could pick up the llama rug — it smelt to Heaven — and wrap it round his naked body. He ran out of the hut and went to the end of the island, where he could see the dam, but there was no one in sight. Back in the little room, he tried on the aquasuit. It fitted quite well, except for being too short in the leg, and he decided to go the whole hog and borrow both suit and flippers. Dressed in black rubber he picked up the llama skin and was about to spread it on the floor when he noticed, in one of the floorboards, a small narrow panel of wood, flush with the surface.

It looked odd and he fingered it and found that he could push one end down and prise up the other. Underneath was a recessed handle, and he could now see that it was in the middle of a large panel, cut out of the floor-boards but fitting very neatly, with dust in the cracks so that it was scarcely visible. Bending down, he got his fingers round the handle and pulled. The trap-door came loose, and he found himself staring down into a compartment under the floor, filled with wooden boxes. They had rope handles at the ends and were securely bound with steel tape.

He lifted the end of one of the boxes. It was heavy, and there was a skull and cross-bones and some lettering stencilled on the wood. '*Explosivos Peruanos*'.

'Dynamite!' said Warne, aloud. He looked down on the box with loathing. So that was the explanation of the aquasuit. The bastard's idea of sport was to set off a charge, and then use his suit to cover a whole area of dead and dying fish. Well, one thing was certain, his gear was going to get lost!

Warne was leaving the hut when his eye caught something else he had not seen before. Above his head, resting on the roof joists, beneath the low-pitched ceiling, were a number of cast-iron pipes, about four inches in internal diameter and varying in length. He scratched the rubber cowl on his head. What on earth were they for? He gave it up, went out of the door and closed it behind him, re-fastening the padlock and returning the key to its place. If anyone found the diving gear missing they might wonder how he'd got in, but who cared?

The suit leaked a little, as he had expected, and his half-dried underclothes were chilly, but with the flippers threshing behind him he made the shore in rapid time. He stripped off the rubber suit, webbed gloves and flippers and hid them in the bushes, changed his underclothes and pulled on his shirt, jeans and anorak. Then he paddled out to the place where he had tethered the net of fish, brought it back and strapped it to his rucksack. Dry socks, shoes, ice-axe — all complete. As he made his way through the pines along the shore the last sunlight left the lake but still shone like bright gold on the great spur of Chopicalqui on the other side, ravaged by deep crevasses in purple shadow, and on the granite slopes below.

At the end of the lake the bare earth of the morainic ridge stretched from one side of the valley to the other, a natural dam. In its centre a sluice-gate held back the water, which spilled over the top to fall into a deep flume, lined with stone, that ran right through the dam before emptying in a spectacular fall into the gorge below. Among the trees at the near end of the dam was a stone hut with a flat roof. The door opened at his touch. It was quite empty, solidly built with a small window. No glass in it.

He turned to look back at the lake, now covered with gossamer drifts of mist, and felt a curious feeling of repulsion. Thankfully, he turned towards the road. There was something sinister about the lake, and the sooner he could get away from it the better.

There was an area of beaten earth near the hut, large enough for a car to turn round in, and from it the dirt road led down the side of the gorge under the sheer face of a cliff. Warne began to walk downhill, swinging his axe. His spirits were rising. There were two hours or more of steady descent ahead and time to look round, now and again, and watch the evening glow on the mountain crests fade to a delicate violet as the last light withdrew. Supper at the Centre, and Janet. It was really time she decided between him and her precious group of conspirators.

God knew what they were conspiring about. The tape recorder, which he had rigged up to show Janet that the secrecy of her so-called political meetings wouldn't stand up to professional counter-espionage methods — and that voice-operated mike *had* been a truly professional touch — had produced something that still puzzled him. He hadn't told the girl. She always shut up like a clam when he was curious about her meetings in Miguel's hut, and the tape showed why. They weren't just talking world revolution on Maoist or Guevarist lines; they were actually plotting something.

On the tape he had heard Miguel laying down the law about security — and that was a laugh! — but he had gone on to talk about Day One, Day Two and so on. And there was something about 'rounding them up and taking them to the refuge'. What refuge, for God's sake? There wasn't a building in the valley, except the Manager's house, that wasn't open for anyone to go in. And when someone — from the accent it sounded like Helmut — had asked where it was, Miguel had said there was no need for him to know until Day One. The talking in Spanish had stopped there, and the rest — there might have been quite a time gap, because the special gadget he was using with the recorder only switched on the microphone when it heard human voices — the rest of the talk was incomprehensible. It was in Quechua.

Miguel had started, speaking very slowly and hesitantly — it was news to Warne that the Argentine could speak the language at all — and then someone else had taken over, clicking and coughing out the words at high speed, like an Indian. But yet — he hadn't sounded like an Indian. There was something familiar in his voice, but not enough to identify him. Others had joined in, and the whole of this part of the conversation was still unfinished when the cassette had come to an end. He had collected the gadget and the recorder the following day, leaving the mike in case he wanted to use it again. If anyone found it they would think it was the police, which would give them food for thought, and serve them right.

But they *were* plotting something, that was clear, and he had to prevent Janet from being involved. Politically, she was just a natural Irish rebel, and a push-over for anyone with a wild scheme to set the world to rights. He would have to tell her what he had discovered, and hope to shake some sense into her silly head. Get her into his room after supper, and then — later, of course, when she was at the clinging stage — switch on the recorder and let her see what a dangerous game she was playing.

He could at least prove to his uncle that he could carry out a James Bond act and get away with it. He was still congratulating himself when he heard the noise of a car in low gear, ascending the road. The roar of the torrent down below on his left had hidden the sound until now. A jeep approached round a bend in the road.

There were two men in it, an Indian whom he had seen at the Centre, and Miguel. The Argentine stopped the car before it reached Warne and got out. He had a sub-machinegun in his hands. Warne could scarcely believe his eyes. There was no mistaking the thing. He walked forward slowly, gripping his ice-axe. When he was a few paces away he could see, in the failing light, that Miguel's face was sweating and green. Or was it the reflection of the light from the high snow? '*Que tal*, Miguel,' he greeted him quietly. 'What have you got that thing for?'

'For you, Jack, if you don't behave.' Miguel's voice sounded thick and strained. The Indian took the wheel and drove past Warne in the direction of the dam.

'What *are* you talking about?'

'I want a word with you, *amigo*, before your military police friends take you away.' He had his head lowered, and the words came slowly. Warne moved nearer. The man must be off his rocker, but if he could get close enough he might have a go with the axe and get the gun away from the Argentine before he did something silly.

'You're talking nonsense, Miguel. I haven't any police friends.'

'Military police.' The man's face was ghastly, and he was speaking in jerks. 'You spy!' Miguel took a step forward, and suddenly dropped the gun and knelt on the road, vomiting uncontrollably.

Warne reached out quickly with his ice-axe and neatly hooked the machine-gun towards him. He knew what was the matter with the Argentine. *Soroche*. He himself could cope with mountain sickness, and in any case he *walked*, when he climbed mountains. The jeep had probably come up the six thousand feet from the valley fast, and the *soroche* had struck. He picked up the gun, and backed away.

He heard the noise of the jeep, which had turned round at the dam and was descending. Warne pointed the gun at the Indian as he approached. The man stopped and put his hands above his head, staring at the Englishman impassively, his jaws working slowly as he chewed a wad of coca. Behind him, Warne could hear Miguel still retching helplessly.

'Go past me and pick up the senor,' Warne shouted, wondering if the gun was cocked. Born too late for National Service he had been shown these things in the school O.T.C. but had never fired one. Still keeping his eyes on the Indian, who was slowly moving forward to stop the jeep alongside Miguel, he felt for the lever and pulled it back.

There was a sharp 'clonk', and a cartridge leapt out of the breach. So it *had* been ready to fire. The man must have been crazy.

The Indian got down, picked up Miguel, now empty but still writhing in pain, and lifted him into the back seat of the jeep as if he were no weight at all. Then he climbed behind the wheel.

'Stop!' shouted Warne, running towards the car and pointing the gun at it. The Indian turned round and suddenly dived over the back of the front seat towards Miguel's body. His hand came up with an automatic and he fired. The noise of the shot, magnified by reflections from the other wall of the gorge, was deafening, and halted Warne in his tracks, wondering whether he had been hit. Then, as the jeep engine sprang into life, the Indian turned again and fired over his shoulder. Warne heard the loud buzz of the bullet flying past his ear, and his finger closed convulsively on the trigger.

Luckily, it slipped off again as the gun jumped in his unpractised hands, but not before four shots had rung out in a continuous roar, repeated over and over again by the echoes. The jeep was swinging madly round the corner. Warne dropped the gun and put his head in his hands, waiting to hear the machine go over the edge of the gorge. But the engine whined on and on, growing rapidly fainter, until its sound was swallowed by the noise of the stream.

Warne drew a deep breath. *Could* he have missed at that close range? The jeep hadn't been more than ten yards away when he'd fired. He obviously hadn't hit the driver but — oh God! — it must be because Miguel's body was in the way. He hadn't aimed, of course, but the gun was pointing in the general direction of the car when it went off — just as if it had fired itself. But no — he couldn't get out of it like that. The fact remained that he *had* pulled the bloody trigger, and Miguel was almost certainly dead by now. Dead! Murder, or manslaughter, if they made that distinction in Peru. Or self-defence? It didn't matter. The fact was there. He had killed someone. Even James Bond wouldn't have waited until his enemy had spewed his guts up before filling him with lead.

He sat down on the edge of the road, his legs dangling over the drop. What on earth had Miguel been doing with all that armament? And what had he said about the cops — no, the military police, and something about him, Jack, being a spy, and the police coming to get him? For God's sake, he'd done nothing against the Peruvians. If they had found that mike how could they have connected it with him, and even so, why should the Peruvian police object? He was only doing their job for them. There was nothing for it but to wait and see.

The last light had gone, and the thought of the long walk downhill in the dark, before the moon rose, was suddenly uninviting. If they came up the road to look for him they'd have to go up to the dam before they could turn round, so he might as well wait for them there, in the hut. What was more, he was hungry, and could light a fire of pine cones in the hut and grill one of those trout; there was still a tin of butter left in his pack, and some salt and biscuits, and the last few bars of chocolate. His spirits rose, and he began to walk briskly back towards the dam. Let them come for him! At least he'd have a meal first.

* * *

It was an hour later, as the volunteers finished their supper and came out into the dark compound, that Janet Horgan heard her name called: 'Juanita!'

She turned, and saw the young German. 'Hello, Helmut, where did you spring from? I didn't see you at supper.'

He took her arm and led her away towards the sleeping quarters. 'Get your medical kit, Juanita. Quickly. Meet me in Miguel's hut, he's badly hurt.'

'I'll get the doctor.' She was turning away when he pulled her back, sharply.

'No, you won't. This has got to be kept secret. It's Group business. Do as I say.'

She shook herself free. 'I'll have a look at him, but if you're right we bloody well can't keep it secret.'

When she came into the hut she saw Miguel groaning on his bed, face down. His body was covered with a blanket. 'What's the matter with him?' She was a qualified nurse, and had rolled up her sleeves and was opening her box as she spoke.

'He's had a bad attack of *soroche*, but it's worse than that.' The German was pale.

'Poor Miguel! He's had these attacks before. I'll give him an injection and he'll be O.K. by the morning. What else?'

'He's been shot.'

She stared at him. '*What?*'

'He went up the mountain to find your boy-friend Warne, in the jeep, and the Indian who was with him won't say what happened. But his jeans are covered with blood. Look!' He snatched back the blanket.

'Mary and Joseph, what a bloody mess!

He'll have to have the doctor.'

'We can't have him here. He'd tell everybody.'

'Listen, Helmi. If the bullet's inside him and he's losing blood still, he'll need proper surgery and a blood transfusion.' She had her watch out and the other hand on the Argentine's wrist. 'It's weak, but that may be only the *soroche*. Help me to get him on his back.'

'It'll hurt him.'

'Don't be silly, man. How can I unzip his flies as he is?'

Miguel groaned loudly, but they got the jeans off and the blood-soaked trunks. 'Get water. Warm, and clean, for God's sake. No, wait. Give me that bottle of brandy he's got in his wardrobe. Thanks.' She took lint and began to wipe away the blood. Then she burst out laughing.

Helmut shook her. 'What's the matter with you?' he growled.

'It's only a flesh-wound, you silly. Look at it. He's been very lucky.' She opened a sealed packet and produced a pair of rubber gloves, which she pulled on.

'We've all been lucky,' muttered Helmut.

'There'll be no need to get the doctor, then.'

'No, as long as I can get Miguel on his feet by tomorrow. But I'm not so sure about that.'

Helmut stared down at the long groove in Miguel's backside, welling blood, and winced. She probed it gently, and the Argentine uttered a deep groan. Janet put her hand on his head. 'Quietly, Miguelito. It's nothing to worry about. No bullet. I'm going to stop the pain.' She bared his arm and washed it with brandy, then found her hypodermic. 'Keep the lint on the wound until he's gone to sleep. I'm going to give him another injection, to stimulate his heart.'

Helmut did as he was told. Suddenly he laughed. '*Komisch, was?*' he said, and switched to Spanish. 'The great Miguel, our leader, goes out to hunt down a man with a machine-gun in his hands, and comes back with a sore arse, and no prisoner. *Das ist ja herrlich!*'

She looked up sharply. 'He took a *gun*? To *find Jack*? What on earth are you talking about, Helmut?' She was usually a little afraid of the big German, but here by the sick-bed she was secure in her authority. Seeing him hesitate, she said sharply, 'I've got to know what happened, if you want me to keep this away from Doctor Suner. Go on, what d'you know?' She was holding Miguel's wrist and looking at her watch.

'Miguel told me — ', he looked down at the Argentine, who was lying with his head turned on the pillow, his eyes closed. 'Is he — ?'

'It's all right, he's asleep. Hold his arm while I give him this injection. Good. Now tell me.'

'He told me this evening he was going to find Warne and bring him back before he did anything else to damage our plans. I don't know what he meant by that, but he was serious enough and had a gun in his pocket. He said it was urgent.'

'*Urgent?* Why? Couldn't he have waited until Jack came home? And for God's sake, what did he want to tote a gun for? And by the way, what's happened to Jack? Have you seen him? He wasn't back for supper, and he's not one to miss it?'

'Oh, don't ask all these stupid questions. I don't know.'

'Has Jack got anything to do with this?' She gestured at Miguel's rump.

'I tell you, *I don't know*. Ask Miguel when he comes to. How is he going to be? You won't have to give him a transfusion?'

'*Claro que no!* These beef-eating Argentines can lose a quart of blood, and all the better for it. He hasn't lost as much as that, anyway. But I can't make it out. You say Miguel had a gun; Jack obviously hadn't. Then how did Miguel get hurt? It must have been somebody else, I suppose. And Jack had nothing to do with it.' She looked up. 'What happened to the driver?'

'He's as scared as a rabbit. Went off to get drunk, I should think.' He looked at what she was doing with horror. 'What's that for?'

'I've got to stitch him up, silly. Bring the lamp nearer.'

# 6

## Wednesday at Noon

Craig had finished his lecture and was talking to a group of officers in the tree-lined quadrangle of the Military Academy, when Captain Loyola came up to him.

'I've had Colonel Urrutia on the telephone, Mr. Craig. Your Ambassador has persuaded him that your lecture this afternoon should be cancelled.'

'Cancelled?' said Craig sharply. 'What on earth for?'

'His Excellency wants you to go to the Chasco settlement. Young Warne has disappeared.'

'You mean he just didn't turn up at the Centre, after his climb?'

'Yes, sir. But they sent out a search party early this morning, and they returned an hour ago. They'd found no trace of him.'

'What does His Excellency think I can do, I wonder,' said Craig resentfully.

'Apparently he thinks there may be some connection with the break-in at Mr. Harris's house. In any case, he must have been very insistent, since Colonel Urrutia has arranged for you to leave at once. An Army plane is waiting and if you agree I will accompany you to the Centre. There will be a sandwich lunch for us on the way. Mr. Harris has been informed, and will meet us at the military airport with a suitcase of warmer clothes for you.'

His Excellency, thought Craig, could certainly get things and people moving. 'All right,' he said shortly. 'But I'd like to speak to the Ambassador first, if you don't mind.'

'Of course.' Loyola led the way to a telephone in the hall of the building and put through the call.

Townsend cut short Craig's reasoned objections. 'I'm sorry to give you this job, Craig, but I'm afraid I must insist. As I told you, I don't want to risk having any trouble with the Peruvians. It looks to me if the boy has found out that we want him here, and is playing hookey. I've told Urrutia that, and he agrees that it's best for you to see for yourself. When you find young Warne, bring him straight back here. I'll give him a piece of my mind and send him home. Have a good trip.'

Craig knew there was nothing for it but accept. While in Peru he was under the Ambassador's orders.

* * *

The Alouette aircraft was fitted with VIP accommodation, and the picnic lunch was excellent, rosy giant prawns with chili-flavoured mayonnaise, chicken sandwiches and a bottle of iced white wine. They were still flying north above the pale ribbon of the coastal desert, three hundred feet below. On the right, the mountains rose in a sheer wall of desolate grey. Only here and there a thread of water from the heights, frugally distributed by irrigation channels, blotched the arid plain with living green.

'We shall begin the climb in fifteen minutes,' said Loyola. 'I wouldn't advise soda with your whisky, Mr. Craig.'

'I never touch it. Just a trace of water, thanks. It's excellent whisky.' He looked at his companion. 'But why not soda?'

'It expands in the stomach and causes — er — discomfort.'

'The change in altitude? Of course. What's this mountain-sickness you get here? People tell me it's very unpleasant.'

'It is. It's a curious thing and strikes quite suddenly. Even people whose hearts are resilient can get an attack if they behave unwisely.'

'Meaning?'

'You must let your heart get used to the change gradually, and not eat too much.'

Craig laughed. 'A fine time to tell me that, when we've just eaten a splendid lunch and are about to climb — how much?'

'The high pass is at sixteen thousand, so we've got to go a few hundred feet higher than that. If you feel any nausea we have oxygen bottles.' He pointed to a rack above his head, from which two thin rubber tubes hung down, ending in bone nozzles. 'Put the nozzle in your mouth or nose and turn on the tap.'

'I'm used to heights,' said Craig confidently.

The plane was flying over a large area of sugar plantations, watered by a substantial river flowing down from the mountains. 'That's the Paramonga estate,' said Loyola, with pride. 'It used to be American before the revolution. We make pisco as well as sugar, and the leaves of the canes make paper. Ah, this is where we begin the climb.'

The plane turned out to sea and made a long spiral to gain height. It reached the coast again well over cloud level and thrust upwards into the thinner air. The grey mountains began to pass below them, and quite suddenly everything changed. First a grimy glacier penned in between granite walls, then snow slopes and great seracs of brilliant ice and snow appeared, edging the stony ribs of the Andes that still swept upwards towards the unseen peaks.

There was a road far below the plane, a thin chalk line that zig-zagged up the side of a broad valley, dived into a tunnel and re-appeared higher up, clinging to the side of a precipice, and always on and upwards, sometimes buried under drifts of snow. There had been a few towns and villages in the lower valleys, but here the landscape was harsh and desolate, grey and glistening white granite, with snow lying in the crevices. But there were still houses, like crofter's cottages in Scotland, thought Craig, with thatched roofs and smoke curling up from the stone chimneys. An impressive mountain, all ice and snow, appeared on the left.

'Caullaraju,' said Loyola, 'where the Cordillera Blanca begins. You can't see it from here, but the Santa valley is down there, running between the Cordillera Blanca and the Cordillera Negra, which is parallel and nearer the sea. The Santa forms the Callejon de Huaylas lower down, where we had the disasters in 1970. Now we go over the top.'

Craig's heart was beginning to thump and his stomach was queasy. He reached up, reluctantly, and switched on the oxygen, putting the mouth-piece between his lips. Anything was better than being sick in front of the younger man. Loyola, who had waited for Craig to make the first move, followed suit, gratefully. They breathed in the sickly gas and felt relief stealing through their bodies.

The plane passed over a lake, where the road to the Santa valley struck off to the North. The other branch continued eastwards, still climbing, and passed into a tunnel. On both sides of the aircraft, so close that they seemed to hem it in, appeared snow peaks, and the little plane dodged between them, twisting its way through a natural pass in the range. Beyond, the road came out into the sunlight and began to descend, winding down a valley. The plane ceased to follow the road and headed almost due north, along the side of the Cordillera Blanca.

'The road goes to Huari first, and then there's a long detour round the mountains before it can get into the Chasco valley. We are taking a short-cut.' Ten minutes passed before they climbed over the barrier and began to descend into the Chasco valley. The mountains of the Cordillera, on their left, were a stupendous series of twenty-thousand-foot peaks, casting long shadows into the valley. The river formed itself almost as they watched, joining together the white torrents that cascaded from the precipitious walls of granite and snow. On the right-hand side, to the east, there was another range of mountains, lower but also snow-topped, and between the two ranges the valley deepened and grew greener as it stretched into the distance. First scrub and isolated pockets of trees, and then rich green plantations of firs and spruces and eucalyptus, with patterned fields of yellow barley and maize, and the bright glint of flowers in the potato furrows. The steep sides of the valley were terraced to form serried contour lines, each with its tiny crop. The highest terraces must have been a thousand feet above the valley floor.

'The Incas built them,' explained Loyola, 'and many still retain the original irrigation channels, some cut through the solid rock — and all made before any iron came into use.' But who, wondered Craig, but an Andean Indian would toil up from terrace to terrace to tend the topmost strips which couldn't be longer than a cricket pitch or wider than a man's outstretched arms?

Small villages appeared, and isolated farm-houses, white-painted and set in little patches of green. The road changed from dust to tarmac and straightened out, following the broad river towards the Chasco settlement. The Alouette began to lose height.

Craig could see, over the shoulder of the pilot, a small modern village, and opposite it, on the right bank of the stream, beyond the line of eucalyptus and willow trees that bordered the road, the older buildings of what had been the heart of the Santa Cruz estate and had become the Chasco Centre. They were grouped around compounds, and beyond, he glimpsed the low white lines of the Casa Grande, the 'great house' of the landowner, with its small Baroque chapel roofed with lichen-stained tiles. The house was surrounded by smooth lawns and tall shade trees. There was a blue flash from a swimming pool, the silver gleam of a hangar roof, and the plane was coming in to land on the strip of shorn couch grass that formed the runway.

A young man wearing a short-sleeved khaki shirt and slacks came across the grass to meet them as they descended. He had a nervous, sallow face with dark eyes and a hair-line moustache, and looked like someone who was always in a hurry. 'Engineer Francisco Lopez,' he introduced himself, '*a los ordenes de Ustedes*.' They gave their names and shook hands.

Craig stood still for a moment, savouring the intense sunlight and the thin air. There was a scent of grass, and a delicious whiff borne by the breeze from the eucalyptus copse, shimmering in a blue mist under the burning sun, that stood between the hangar and the wall of the Casa Grande. How different, he thought, from the muggy damp atmosphere of Lima and the mechanical smells and sweet reek of oxygen in the plane. He turned to follow Lopez.

'I am Deputy Manager,' explained the young man. 'Major Castillo, the Manager, is expecting you in his office.' He led the way past the hangar, round the high wall of the Casa Grande gardens and between buildings to the main compound. There seemed to be a great deal going on, with typewriters clattering behind open windows. Castillo's office was in the middle of the administrative buildings. A truck bound for the coast, piled high with potatoes held in by nylon netting, was at the door. Inside a dark-complexioned man of about fifty, with grey receding hair and steel-rimmed half-spectacles, was signing the waybill which the truck driver had brought from the checking office. Craig thought of the long, desolate stretch of dusty road in front of the man before he could span those savage mountains and reach the valley sloping down to the Pacific. 'How long will it take him?' he asked.

Lopez shrugged his shoulders. 'The best part of ten hours down to Paramonga, on the coast, and then a quick three-hour trip to Lima on the

Pan-American highway. He'll be there tomorrow noon.'

Major Castillo greeted the two newcomers and turned to Lopez. 'Thank you, Paco. You'd better get over to the machine shop now. They're having trouble with a turret lathe. Come in, senores,' he added, turning to Craig and Loyola.

He led them to some chairs grouped round a table in the corner of his large office and made them sit down while he rang for a servant. Craig said, 'Senor Lopez looks very young for such an important appointment. Is he in fact your chief assistant?'

'He's a lot more than that,' said Castillo. He took off his glasses and squeezed his eyes between finger and thumb. 'I don't know what I'd do without him. Until he arrived a year ago I was rapidly growing a crop of stomach ulcers. There's a lot to do here, and he's a well-trained engineer and a first-class organizer. Surprising, for a man who only finished his course at the Engineering University in Lima two years ago, but it's true. He's a born leader. Father was in the Army, of course,' he added, smiling.

'As you were, Senor Director,' commented Loyola. 'How do you like changing the *vida castrense* for this work?'

Castillo poured out coffee and handed it to the two men before he answered — and then rather solemnly, almost like a man taking an oath, 'It is the most challenging, most worthwhile task I have ever had entrusted to me,' he said. 'I wouldn't change it for a general's pay.'

* * *

It was half an hour later, Loyola had left for Lima in the Alouette. Craig and Castillo were still talking around the table. Lopez had returned and was sitting at his desk, dealing with callers and answering the telephone on behalf of the Manager.

Craig pointed with the stem of his pipe at a place on a contour map of the valley where, four miles downstream from the Centre, a road branched off to the left.

'From the map it's obvious that Warne would have followed this road up the side of the range to here, where it divides, like a Y. Good God, that's fourteen thousand feet already.' He traced the left-hand branch of the Y. 'This one goes up a ravine, a branch of the main gorge, to where it stops at the foot of a mountain wall, and that's where Don Jorge has his silver mine. By the look of the contours, almost on top of each other, it's very steep for the last few kilometres.'

Castillo said drily, 'It has a slope of one in four on the bends, but the trucks are heavily laden only on the way down. It's not a road for a careless driver. The drop into the ravine is about two hundred feet.'

'And the right-hand road?'

'It's not much more than a track leading up even more steeply to this lake, formed by the glacier of Chopicalqui, about the same height as the silver mine on the other side of the shoulder. The track ends at a natural dam at the lower end of the lake and is seldom used, and then only by Don Jorge and his friends for fishing, or when a man goes up to open the sluice-gate when there's a threat of heavy rain or thaw.' He smiled. 'I've been up there once or twice, but it's not my idea of pleasure. The lake's at — what would it be in feet? — about sixteen thousand, eight thousand above the floor of the Chasco valley.'

'I see. And the normal way up the shoulder of Chopicalqui?'

'It's not marked on the map, but it lies between the two branches of the Y, that is between the mine and the lake roads. The climbers go straight up for four thousand feet to the snow line, and then it's real climbing technique to get to the top of the shoulder, let alone the summit.'

'So you assumed that Warne took that route, and that's the way the search-party went?'

Castillo turned. 'Here's Major Rodriguez. He'll tell you.'

Craig rose and shook hands. Rodriguez's face was burned dark red, except where the sun-goggles had protected his eyes. He sat down, rather stiffly. 'I'm not quite as young as I was,' he said, 'but I made it with the guide and one of the volunteers, a young German. He scampered up. By the time I got back to the fork in the road, where we'd left the Land-Rover, I'd had quite enough for one day. I slept like a log after lunch. Sorry. I wanted to be here to greet you.'

'Major Castillo has been filling me in on the background,' said Craig. 'I gather there's no chance of going up to the lake today?'

Castillo smiled. 'It'd be dark by the time you got there. But we'll start again at dawn.'

Rodriguez turned to Craig. 'I know it's frustrating, Mr. Craig, but the obvious route to try was the straight one. I agree with you that he might have come down the longer way, past the lake, but he could have fallen anywhere on those slopes and it'll take time to explore them.'

'But supposing he got down to the lake itself,' suggested Craig.

'Then he'd have had only the road to walk down. We did find some of his tracks when we were half-way up the shoulder, so he must have gone up that way. But the slopes become icy as you go further up and the wind blows the loose snow away. What I'm afraid of is that he slipped somewhere near the top of the shoulder, which is horribly easy to do, and slid down a crevasse. But I'll try from the lake side tomorrow, and perhaps we could take the same group.' He turned to the Manager. 'They were very fit and willing.'

'By all means,' said Castillo. He said to Craig, 'Would you like to go with them?'

'Yes, please. There's just one question,' he added, turning to Castillo. 'Can we ascertain whether any of the other volunteers went up the mountain road yesterday?'

Castillo looked surprised. 'You don't think — but anyway I can find out.' He called to Lopez, who came over to the table, and asked him the same question.

'I gave permission,' said the young man, 'for Miguel Cuevas, the Argentine, to take a half-day off yesterday. He borrowed the volunteers' jeep and took it up the mine road to see the sunset. He came back with a bad attack of *soroche* and has been in bed all day.' He frowned. 'The young fool! He knows he's a weak head for the altitude and he must have driven up too far and too quickly.'

'Did he see any sign of Warne?'

'No. I asked him that, of course. He said it was dark when he felt able to drive down, so he wouldn't have seen him anyway unless he was actually walking down the road. And no climber would do that. He'd take the short-cuts.'

Castillo was showing signs of restiveness and looking at his watch. 'I must ask you to excuse me, gentlemen. Paco Lopez and I have a great deal to do. My wife is expecting you both for dinner. In the meantime you might like to take a look round the Centre.'

Craig and Rodriguez went out into the sunshine, still hot although the sun was approaching the rim of the western mountains. They walked out of the compound, crossed the road, and stood on the bridge, looking down at the swift green water flowing in the middle of its wide, rocky bed. Women were beating clothes with wooden paddles and spreading them on the hot stones to dry.

'You know the background to this enquiry, Major?'

'Yes. I was fully briefed by Lima. I told

Castillo yesterday.'

'So that's why he didn't ask me what I was here for. I expect you searched Warne's room?'

'Nothing there. But somebody else had been looking before me.' He explained about the mark in the dust.

'That's interesting,' said Craig thoughtfully. 'It goes to show that what Warne discovered was here, not in Lima. Would you mind if I had a look at his room, too?'

'Of course not,' said Rodriguez smiling. 'But I'll be surprised if you find anything I missed. It's this way.'

They returned to the compound and entered the square of buildings used by the volunteers. No one seemed to be around. It took Craig less than five minutes to check that Rodriguez had spoken with justice. There was a small tape-recorder in the drawer of the desk, but Rodriguez showed him that it was empty, and there were no tapes with it. Craig sat down on the bed and considered.

'I'm trying to put myself in Warne's place,' he explained. 'He's made this mysterious tape and wants to hide it. For all we know it was among those he took with him to Lima, which were stolen. But if so, why should someone search his room? I think it's either with him now, up in those mountains, or it's hidden somewhere here. Not, we agree, in this room. Where else would he be able to hide it without being observed?'

A smile spread over Rodriguez's face. '*El retrete*, where even the King is alone. The volunteers, I'm told, are always in and out of each other's rooms, but there he'd be safe.' The Peruvian led the way into the passage that divided Warne's room from the next in line and out through a door at the rear. 'I thought of this yesterday,' he admitted, 'but at that time I expected Warne back, and didn't want to draw attention to myself; besides, there were too many people about. I could only search the one I used myself.'

In the big patio was a large wash-house, divided into sections for men and women, and containing shower cubicles and lavatories. There was no one around, for the volunteers had not returned from their work. 'I imagine we can confide our attentions to the men's side,' said Rodriguez, grinning. 'Taped behind the cistern or under the flat part of the pedestal — any other ideas?'

'Inside the cistern.'

'Inside — you mean in a waterproof wrapping?'

'It's worth trying, isn't it?'

Three minutes later they met, exchanging rueful smiles. Craig was drying his hands at a towel-dispenser when he exclaimed, and pointed to a tank high up on the wall above the urinals. He gave the Major a knee to stand on and a moment later Rodriguez gave a cry of triumph and jumped down, a small wet package of cellophane in his hand.

He looked down at it, puzzled. 'I can see how he could have thrown it in, but fishing it out, without help, would be another matter.'

'He's a climber, don't forget. He could probably hang by one hand from the support and reach into the tank with the other. But it was a good hiding-place.' He put the packet into his pocket. 'Let's get back to his room.'

As soon as they had closed the door of Warne's room behind them he pulled out the parcel and began to unwrap it carefully. Rodriguez stared, bewildered, at a small metal case, not much bigger than a match box. On the surface was printed, in clear white lettering, 'VIVA VOCE.' At each end of the box was a pair of terminals.

*'Jesus Maria, que es eso?'*

'I think I know,' said Craig thoughtfully. 'I saw something like this in Rome, not long ago, and the name clinches it. I think this one's Japanese, but the Germans sell a gadget called an Akustikon, or something similar, which does the same thing.'

'But what *does* it do, man?' asked Rodriguez impatiently.

'It's a device you connect between a microphone and a transmitter — or a tape-recorder. When the microphone doesn't hear human voices the device cuts off the recorder. As soon as it hears human voice-frequencies, it starts it up. Otherwise, you'd waste most of the tape for nothing.'

# 7

## Wednesday Afternoon

'It's a pity none of the volunteers are about,' said Craig.

'There's the nurse, who's supposed to have had some sort of liaison with Warne. She's looking after the Argentine, Cuevas.'

'Liaison? That's interesting. Who told you that?'

'Castillo. She's an Irish girl called Janet Horgan, and he said she and Warne tend to disappear together. I didn't have a chance to question her yesterday. It was nearly midnight when Castillo and I decided something must have happened to Warne and made arrangements for the search-party, and she was already in bed. Let's try Cuevas' room.'

'O.K. What do you know about him, incidentally?'

'He's older than the other volunteers,

about twenty-five, and was allotted a hut that's bigger than the rest. It's over there, among the trees. He doesn't mix much with the others, according to Castillo, but he's a useful member of the team. He took a degree in Buenos Aires in animal husbandry and Don Jorge told me he's borrowed him to advise about his precious herd of Herefords on the home farm. Cuevas' father is a big ranch owner near Cordoba, and the young man evidently knows a lot about cattle.' They were walking across to the solitary hut as he spoke.

The door opened and a girl stepped out, blinking in the fierce sunshine. She called back through the door, '*Pues bien. Ahora tienes que dormir.*' Then she closed it, and turning round saw the two men.

'Oh my God!' she said. 'The fuzz.' The intonation was Irish.

Craig looked at her in amusement. The spotless nurse's uniform set off her inviting figure and the mass of auburn hair coiled below the cap. A Nightingale badge was pinned above a firm breast.

'You're a Thomas's girl, I see.'

'Nothing escapes you!' she said scornfully.

'My name's Peter Craig, and this is Major Rodriguez of Military Security. We'd like a word with your patient, Miss Horgan.' The thought had come to Craig on the spur of the moment.

'He's asleep,' she said quickly. 'I'm afraid you can't see him now.'

'He wasn't asleep a moment ago,' said Craig, 'when you spoke to him.' The two men moved forward.

The girl barred the way. 'Listen. Senor Cuevas has a bad attack of *soroche*. It would only make his head worse to talk to you. I'm sorry, but he's my patient and I don't want him disturbed.'

'I'll ask the doctor, then,' said Rodriguez, turning.

'No. I really don't think there's any need to worry Doctor Suner; he's got quite enough on his plate already.'

'Has he seen the patient?' asked Rodriguez, his interest caught by the girl's defensive attitude.

'No, he hasn't. I can deal with it quite well. Come back later, please.'

'Senorita,' said Rodriguez firmly,

'you're being unreasonable. We only want to speak to Senor Cuevas for a moment, I assure you.'

She looked at him defiantly, then changed her mind. 'All right, if you insist. Five minutes only, please.' She entered the hut and they heard her speaking inside, and a voice protesting. Then she re-appeared and motioned to them to come in.

The shutters in the bedroom were half-open, but shaded by the trees outside. The Argentine was lying on his side, his face turned towards the door. The look in his dark eyes were unwelcoming.

Rodriguez and Craig introduced themselves and sat down in chairs by the bed. Miguel made no response. The girl stood hovering, and Craig could feel that she was tense and anxious. He left Rodriguez to ask the questions.

'We're sorry to disturb you, senor.'

The man on the bed spoke in a sullen voice, 'Who's the Englishman? And I don't mean just his name?'

'He's a senior police officer from England, on a visit to our own police services.'

The dark eyes widened, then closed again as if in pain. 'There's nothing I can tell you,' he muttered.

'You can see — ' began the girl. Rodriguez interrupted her. 'Please be silent, Miss Horgan. I only want to ask Senor Cuevas a few questions he can answer very easily.' He turned to Miguel. 'You drove down the valley yesterday afternoon, senor. Why?'

'I've said all this before to Engineer Lopez. I decided to go up the mine road to see the sunset. Then' — he shuddered, and closed his eyes again — 'this thing came over me.'

'I see. How far did you get?'

'Up the place where the lake road branches off. That's where it happened. I was very sick.'

'Did you see any sign of Mr. Warne?'

'No.'

'You're quite sure of that? You heard nothing either?'

'No.'

'Well, there you are. That's all we wanted to know.' Rodriguez' eyes flickered around the room, and Craig saw his nose lifted for a moment, sniffing. Craig smiled; he had noticed the same smell.

'You drove down in the dark, I suppose?'

'Yes.'

'But all the same, if Warne had been walking down the road, you'd have seen him?'

'Of course. *If* he was taking the road. But he might have used the short-cuts.'

'A dangerous thing to do in the dark,' remarked Craig mildly. 'But you didn't see him?'

'No. *Caray!* Must you go on repeating yourselves?'

'It's taking you a long time to get over a simple dose of *soroche*, isn't it?' asked Rodriguez sharply.

Janet was up in arms at once. 'I told you, it was a very bad attack. It strained his heart, which is quite a common side effect. All he needs now is rest, and not a lot of questions. And your time's up.'

'We'll go,' said Rodriguez. He rose and moved quickly towards the bed with his hand outstretched — and saw the Argentine's eyes flicker. But the Major merely reached for the young man's hand and shook it. 'Thank you, Senor Cuevas. I wish you a quick recovery.'

The girl led them out into the sunshine. She was going to turn back, but Craig said, 'Let him sleep, Miss Horgan, as you prescribed. I'd say he's had a *very* unusual kind of *soroche*, wouldn't you?' Behind her back he caught Rodriguez' quick nod of agreement.

She was at once on the defensive. 'I told you it was a bad attack, and so it is. But nothing more.' She stood still. 'If all you want to ask about is Jack Warne, ask me.'

Craig took her arm, quite gently, and led her towards Warne's hut. 'Let's do it comfortably, then. You see, there appears to be only you and Senor Cuevas left in the Centre — of the volunteers, that is. Let's go to Jack Warne's room.'

Janet shook her arm free and walked ahead, well aware that she was giving the men something to look at. But in fact their eyes were on each other, in a swift exchange of signals.

Rodriguez pointed to the lithe figure of

the girl and raised his forefinger to touch the corner of his eye. He jerked his thumb over his shoulder at the hut they had just left, and made the same Latin gesture, that says, *'Cuidado!'* and means just plain 'watch it, chum'.

Craig nodded, and then made a curious gesture of his own. He held his hands in front of him and raised and lowered them alternately. Rodriguez grinned, and gave the thumbs-up sign. The whole exchange took only a few seconds, while Janet thought they were admiring her legs, as they should. She rolled her hips a little, to keep them interested. Men were all the same, she thought: a girl could always keep them guessing, and she had to take their tiny minds off the subject of Miguel.

'When did you see Warne last, Miss Horgan?' Rodriguez' voice, sharply raised, came from just behind her shoulder. She whipped round.

'A few days ago. I can't remember when exactly. Is there any news of him?'

He was silent, but opened the door of Warne's hut and let her go ahead. Craig hurried to draw up a chair and made her sit down. 'I suppose you knew him rather well,' he said, with a smile. 'Being the only two British volunteers in the Centre.' He perched on the bed, while Rodriguez took a chair slightly behind the girl.

'I don't think it's any of your business,' she replied tartly. 'And anyway, I'm Irish, not British.'

'Oh dear!' said Craig ruefully. 'I *have* got off on the wrong foot, haven't I? We're only trying to find your friend Jack for you.'

'He's not my friend any more.'

'Why's that?'

'Find out for yourself.'

'I don't like people,' said Rodriguez harshly, 'who are unhelpful with the police.'

'And I don't like policemen. We call them 'fuzz'.'

'Can't you find another name for us?' asked Craig. 'What's wrong with 'bluebottles'?'

'It happens to be as dead as Oliver Cromwell,' she said scornfully, 'And anyway, it has a sort of fatherly sound, like friends of the people, and all that jazz. 'Fuzz' is just contemptible. But I can call you pigs, if you like.'

'You forget, senorita,' broke in Rodriguez angrily, 'that you're in Peru, and if you say such things in Spanish you'll be in trouble. Answer our questions. I suppose some people would call you good-looking. Did Warne think so?'

She flushed. 'You've got no right — '

'Are you and he lovers?'

She looked at Rodriguez defiantly. 'Yes. If I don't tell you one of my dear friends will. At least, we were, for a time.' Rodriguez snorted.

'Poor girl,' said Craig solicitously. 'You must be very worried about this. I'm afraid we have no news at all. We shall be going up to the lake to look for him tomorrow.'

She started. 'Can I go with you?'

'Why not?' said Craig. 'But I thought you weren't interested in him.'

'I'm a nurse,' she explained impatiently. 'He may be hurt. There must be something wrong or he'd be back by now. I wanted to go with the search party, but I couldn't — ' She broke off.

'Because of Miguel Cuevas?' Craig's voice had suddenly become menacing. 'Because you didn't want anyone else to look after him? Is that why?'

'He's my patient,' she said sullenly.

'It's not just that, is it?' Craig's voice rose. 'Is it?'

'Please don't shout at her, Craig,' said Rodriguez. He leaned forward and touched the girl's arm. 'He doesn't mean to be unfriendly, Miss Horgan. Nor do I. But you see, we both know there is something more than *soroche* that is wrong with Senor Cuevas. Why don't you tell us?' He patted her arm. 'After all, even the fuzz know that you don't use surgical spirit to cure *soroche*.' He chuckled merrily. 'Unless you made him drink it?'

'Surgical spirit?' she stammered.

'The room was reeking of it. I suppose you'd dressed the wound?' he asked casually.

'It's not a *wound*,' she said loudly. 'He fell and scratched himself. On the mountain,' she added, facing him. 'Just a little scratch, but it can be dangerous, you know.' She widened her grey eyes. That often had an effect.

But not on Craig, apparently. 'How did you know we were police officers?' he asked roughly.

'He came yesterday,' she said, pointing at Rodriguez, 'and everybody knew he was here about Jack.'

'Did they indeed? And what about me?'

She hesitated. 'They telephoned from the Embassy that a policeman was coming

'Who told you that?'

'I can't remember.'

There was a long, unbelieving silence. Rodriguez rose to his feet. 'These things take time,' he said in a kind voice. 'I'm sure you'd like some coffee, Miss Horgan.' He walked out of the room. She looked at Craig, who seemed to have become less menacing. He had pulled out a pipe and was filling it slowly and carefully.

'What does he mean?' she asked, irritably. 'What takes time? I'll tell you something; I have a lot of things to do.'

‘Like running back to Cuevas, I suppose, and telling him what the nasty men said.’ He cupped his hands and puffed out smoke. ‘Sorry. I forgot to ask if you’d like a cigarette. All nurses smoke,’ he added, smiling.

‘This one doesn’t. You’re not doing a blind bit of good with your winning ways. Ask the rest of your boring questions, and let me get on with my work.’

‘Not till Major Rodriguez whistles up that coffee, surely? Besides, he may want to ask you some questions of his own. He’s in charge, of course. I’m just helping. *Did* you quarrel with Jack Warne?’

‘Not exactly. It’s just that we don’t believe in the same things.’

‘Like politics?’

She lifted her head defiantly. ‘Like politics. Jack is very immature, politically speaking.’

Craig drew a bow at a venture. ‘And I suppose — it’s quite natural, after all — he didn’t like you going into a corner, so to speak, with people who thought the same as you.’

'I didn't say that.'

'But it's true, isn't it? He thought you were being secretive, and no man likes his girl to have certain things she can't discuss with him at all.' He paused, looking steadily at her troubled face, and added mildly, 'And you *were* being secretive, weren't you?'

'What would I be secretive about?'

'If you knew something was going on, and he didn't.'

'But he — I don't know what you're talking about.'

Rodriguez had come into the room, followed by an orderly carrying a tray with a pot of coffee and cups. 'You were going to say,' he said sternly, reverting to his earlier role, 'you were going to say, 'But he did.' We know he did. Warne knew something was going on, here at the Centre, which he didn't approve of at all. Will you have sugar?'

'You don't know anything, really,' she was beginning.

'One lump or two?'

'You're just trying to find out. Well, you can try someone else. And I don't want your bloody sugar.' She got to her feet, a little uncertainly.

'Like Miguel Cuevas?' snapped Rodriguez.

'Leave him alone,' she cried angrily. 'He's got enough to worry about. And he won't tell you anything either.'

'He's in it, too, of course,' said Craig, turning to Rodriguez.

'Oh go to hell!' she shouted. 'It's so typical. You come here, a couple of great brutes, and fire these questions at me, one after the other. I'm not going to reply any more.' She turned away, and blew her nose loudly.

'The fuzz, as you call them, can't afford to be chivalrous.'

'You can say that again!'

'Warne may be dead,' shouted Rodriguez.

'How d'you know?' she cried wildly. 'Anything may have happened. You've no reason to think that, have you? I mean that isn't why — '

He shook his head. 'We're just trying to find out what could have happened. And we think the key to that lies here, at the

Centre. In your head, perhaps.'

'What d'you mean?'

'I'll show you,' said Rodriguez, friendly again. He pulled open the drawer of the desk and drew out the little recorder, which he put into her lap. She recoiled. 'Come on, Miss Horgan. You know what he used it for.'

She flushed angrily. 'There you are. As if you didn't know already. He was doing it for you, wasn't he?'

'He used it to record some conversations he shouldn't have heard. Is that it?'

'You know he did. That's what they said he was, a police spy. And they were right, or you wouldn't be here. I wouldn't have credited it if you hadn't told me. I thought he was . . . And all the time he was a crawling, sneaking police spy.' She burst into tears.

Craig took a large white handkerchief from his breast pocket. He put his arm round the girl's shaking shoulders and let the handkerchief fall into her lap. '*We* didn't say that, as a matter of fact. *Who did?* Was it Miguel?'

She nodded, sniffing. Absentmindedly,

she picked up the handkerchief and blew her nose.

'What is wrong with Miguel, Miss Horgan?' asked Rodriguez sharply.

'*Soroche*.'

'What else?'

Craig intervened. 'Don't worry her, Major. You can see she isn't in a fit state to answer questions. She told us he fell and — er — scratched himself. That's all it was.'

'Where was he hurt?' insisted Rodriguez.

'In his bottom,' she muttered, sniffing.

'I see. Just a scratch on his backside. But so deep that you had to dress it again today, nearly twenty-four hours afterwards. But not serious enough to call in Doctor Suner. Did you have to stitch it up?'

She was silent.

'*Why* didn't you want the Doctor to see the wound?' asked Rodriguez suddenly. 'Was it a gunshot wound?'

'No,' she cried, desperately. 'It was just — '

'It was a gunshot wound,' shouted Craig. 'You don't have to answer. The

Doctor had better see it at once.'

'Blast you!' screamed the girl, venomously. 'You don't think I'd let you play these corny tricks on me, acting tough and smooth alternately, if I wasn't worried out of my mind. Fuzz tricks!' She caught her breath in a deep sob. 'It isn't serious. Just a long flesh wound. I've stitched it up and there's no inflammation. But *please* don't tell Doctor.'

'I can see why you're worried,' said Rodriguez soothingly. 'Cuevas told you he'd had a gun-fight with Warne — '

'And that Warne was wounded, too,' cut in Craig. 'And you just kept silent about it, knowing that Jack might be bleeding to death somewhere up in the mountains, without help. And I suppose Cuevas told you where — '

'Of course he didn't,' she burst out, furiously. 'Miguel wouldn't tell me anything, except — ' She stopped.

'Except what?' shouted Craig, seizing her by the arm.

'Oh leave me alone. All he said was that Jack had got hold of a machine-gun. For all Jack knows Miguel may be dead. He riddled the jeep with bullets. That's why he's hidden himself, I suppose.'

* * *

Craig rose and fetched Janet's handbag from the table where she had dropped it. 'Your nose is shiny,' he said kindly. 'Make some running repairs while we leave you for a moment. We'll be outside, so don't run away just yet.'

She made no reply, but opened the bag and took a shocked look at her face in a mirror.

Craig and the Peruvian went outside and halted a few yards away, out of earshot. 'It's up to you, Major, but if you agree I'll take her statement while you make the other arrangements.'

'Good idea. I'll get the doctor to examine the wound, and place my corporal on guard outside Cuevas' door, with instructions to keep him incommunicado. Then I'll look for the jeep. I'll be back soon.'

'Yes. And thanks, amigo.' He put his arm lightly round the Peruvian's shoulders, in the South American *abrazo*. 'We make a good team, don't we? Breaking down a hardened criminal like that!'

Rodriguez smiled. 'I don't suppose either of us is proud of that interrogation, but it worked. It takes time, but the erosion method usually does work. Straight-forward bullying would have made her shut up like an oyster. What are you going to try now?'

'Sweet reason.'

'Father Craig at the confessional?'

'Something like that.'

'Good luck. My driver will be outside the door if you want me.'

When Craig returned to Warne's room the girl was sitting straight up in the chair, legs demurely crossed below the knees, with a look of dogged determination on her pretty face. 'You're going to caution me, or something, I suppose. Well, I want to see my lawyer.'

'You're in Peru, Miss Horgan,' said Craig mildly. He sat down and relit his pipe. 'You may not think so, but I'm on your side. I don't *want* you to be handed over to the Peruvian police for examination.'

'But — but I've done nothing wrong. They can't charge me with anything.'

'I'm afraid they can. Major Rodriguez has gone off muttering about concealing evidence of the use of offensive weapons, failure to report a gunshot wound to higher authority and so on. He hasn't mentioned conspiracy,' added Craig, leaning back in his chair, relaxed, 'but that's what I think I'd go for. It's a cinch.'

'But we haven't *done* anything yet. The twisty bastard! Acting so friendly, and thinking up how he could make a charge stick. And you're just the same. I suppose you're going to start bullying again, any minute now?'

'Not me. It's his job. I'm just keeping you quiet until he's ready to have another go. Be careful what you say about that group of yours, for God's sake. Plotting against the State is a serious crime in this country. As you say, you haven't done anything yet — but planning and plotting is just as bad, you know.'

'But — and anyway, he's got no evidence.'

'Hasn't he?'

'That bloody tape, you mean? I suppose Jack's handed it over to him, and that's why he came here, to ferret out more on the spot. Is that it?'

'You can't expect me to tell you what Major Rodriguez has or hasn't got, in the way of evidence. That's for him to do. I told you, he's in charge. I do suggest to you, very earnestly, that you should think out what you're going to tell him if he faces you with concrete evidence of a plot against the Government of Peru.'

'But if he thinks that, he's got it wrong. It isn't against the Government. He must have told you that. It's a scheme to help those poor devils who're on the run,' she cried — and then stopped, with a hand over her mouth, horrified.

Craig's unruffled face re-assured her. 'Of course. But he won't see it that way. He'll see it as an attempt to help people who are enemies of the State.'

'Oh don't be silly. They aren't even in Peru.'

'But they were coming here, weren't they?' asked Craig, groping in the dark.

'How could a small group of people up here, hundeds of miles from anywhere, give any help otherwise? I suppose you were going to hide them somewhere in the valley until the hunt was over.' He stretched himself, yawned. 'It doesn't sound much of a plot to me, but Rodriguez hasn't told me everything.'

'We were going to do a hell of a lot more than that,' she declared, annoyed that he seemed to be taking no interest.

'So you may have been. But it's all over now, because the Peruvians are wise to your precious plot. So the thing for you to do is to see how best you can get out of the mess you're in. I'll help, if you'll let me.'

'I'm not going to say who the other members of the group are.'

'All right, then. Just tell me what you can.'

'It was all Miguel's idea,' she said in a rush. 'He wanted to help the Tupamaros in Brazil. A whole group of them have gone into hiding, not far from the Peruvian frontier. The Brazilian police captured two of them and tortured them horribly.'

'Who says?'

'Miguel, of course.' She added, with a touch of drama, 'He's a Tupamaro himself.'

'The Tups have done a bit of torturing themselves,' pointed out Craig, drawing on his pipe. 'Not to mention killing off people they don't like.'

'That's just what the capitalist papers say. Miguel knows what he's talking about. I don't like him particularly — he's got very Latin ideas about the status of women — but you have to admit he's dedicated to the Cause.'

'Ah yes, the Cause. Defeating neo-colonialism, is it? Undermining the Latin-American police states, lackeys of Wall Street?'

'Of course not. It's liberating political prisoners all over South America, starting with those poor Tupamaros in Brazil.'

'But they're not in gaol. What you mean is harbouring them, so that they can rest up before having another bash at some miserable bank cashier to get at the lolly they need.'

'They can't work without funds, and

the banks are full of it. It's not like taking money off people who need it.'

'Oh, don't be so childish. You know better than that,' said Craig. 'How are they going to get here?'

'I don't know. They'll just turn up, and we'll get them away to the refuge.'

'I wonder what's happened to Rodriguez. Hang on a moment.' He took out his notebook and scribbled, 'You'll need an M.P. section from Tambo. Give me another ten minutes.' He went to the door and gave the note to the driver of the Land-Rover. When he got back to his chair the girl was looking at him suspiciously.

'What was that in aid of?'

'I've asked him to leave us alone a bit longer. I'd rather he didn't come in with his ideas of forceful interrogation — not just yet, anyway. We've got to get your story hanging together first. How many people are in your cell?'

'It's not a *cell*. We're just a group of eight people who happen to think the same way.'

'I see. But only one of you, Cuevas, has

any contact with these Tupamaro refugees?'

'Well, yes.'

'Do you know where the place is — the refuge, where you're going to put the Tups?'

'No. It's a question of security, you see. Only Miguel knows.'

'So the rest of you have no contact with anyone outside, except through Miguel? You just do what you're told.' She nodded.

'Exactly. It's what we call a cell.' He was making it sound far too pedestrian and unromantic.

'The whole thing depends on the quick way we'll act when the Tups are due to arrive. We shall take them to the refuge, provide food — we've been storing that already — and not only them, but — '

'Hostages?' asked Craig wearily.

'Yes. We'll take some of the volunteers with us. We shall be armed, of course, but they'll go along with the plan as soon as they understand what's at stake. We've already decided more or less which ones to choose.'

Craig took a deep breath. 'How have you done that?'

'We have these sing-songs in the evenings, and other kinds of get-togethers, and people often talk politics. It's easy to tell the sheep from the goats.'

'By sheep, you mean the ones who'll allow themselves to be herded quietly into this place of refuge, as you call it. It sounds a good name for them. But supposing you find there are goats among them? You could have been mistaken. Someone might object.'

'They'll be taken by armed men and held under guard, but treated quite well.'

'Where do these armed men come from?'

'I told you, there'll be guns for all the group, and the Tupamaros will bring more with them.' She frowned. 'At least, I think so.'

Craig couldn't contain himself. 'Christ!' he exclaimed. 'How old are you?'

'Twenty-two. What's that to do with it?'

'It makes a life sentence even longer. What d'you think would happen if one of the goats resisted, and got shot for his pains?'

She hesitated. 'That wouldn't happen. But if it did, well, it'd be his fault, wouldn't it?'

'Not in the eyes of the law. Every last one of you would be tried for it in a Peruvian court, for conspiracy and armed revolt. The least you'd get would be ten years, and it wouldn't be funny.'

'But it can't happen now, can it? You know about the whole thing. That's why you came here. It wasn't only to find Jack, was it?'

'There's the question of that tape, you see.'

'What was on it?' she asked curiously. 'Miguel doesn't know, and it's driving him crazy. He found the microphone in his hut and searched Jack's room and found the tape-recorder, but it was empty. I told him it was probably harmless, because how could Jack know when we'd be talking in Miguel's hut? If he'd followed us we'd have seen him.'

Craig reached into his pocket and put the little black box on the table. 'That's how he did it. With this gadget, the recorder only works when it hears voices.'

She stared at the thing in horror. 'But what a beastly thing for Jack to do! I suppose the police gave it to him. I'd told him we met in Miguel's room to talk politics, and all he said was he'd always known Miguel was a raving red. And then he must have gone off to the police and told them to give him this box, so that he could eavesdrop.' She looked up. 'It doesn't make sense. Jack isn't like that. He's not a police nark.'

'But Miguel thought he was, didn't he? He went out yesterday to find him.' Craig raised his voice. 'And with a gun, I suppose.'

She was silent.

'When did he get back to the Centre? And what did he tell you?'

'About half-past seven, I should think. But Hel — one of the others told me after supper to come to Miguel's room quickly, and I found him with this wound, and a really bad *soroche* hangover. He must have vomited everything he had in his stomach,' she added, reverting for a moment to her official manner.

'And later Miguel told you Warne had shot at him, and riddled the jeep with bullets from a machine-gun. It doesn't sound likely does it?'

'No,' she said in a low voice. 'It doesn't sound like Jack at all.'

'*Unless Miguel fired first*. He did have a gun, didn't he?'

'Yes. Someone told me he had an automatic.'

'Who did?'

'Someone in the group.'

'All these names will have to come out some time, you know.'

'I don't like telling tales. It makes me feel dirty.'

'I'm sorry, but you've been acting far, far more foolishly than you realize, and I hope you're glad the whole thing has blown up in your face.'

'But you don't understand. We expected to be blamed, and run the risk of police persecution. We knew that in the end public opinion would be on our side. And anyway, the whole idea was that part of the bargain over the release of the hostages would be a safe conduct for all members of the group to leave Peru.'

'I thought that would be included. Were you given any training in the use of arms?'

'That was to come later.'

'And were the details of the plan to round up some of the other volunteers fully worked out?'

'No. But my job was clear. I was to take care of sickness and, well, injuries.'

'I see. The doctor to the revolt.'

'Of course not. But minor wounds — like the one Miguel got — '

'How stupid can you get?' said Craig angrily. 'Have you ever seen a man after being hit by a burst from a machine-gun? Can you amputate a limb? What about blood transfusions? Even if you had plasma in your precious refuge, could you check the blood groups?'

'I didn't think it would ever come to that,' she said sullenly.

'You just didn't think. In fact, all your cell ever did — I want to get this quite clear, in your interests — was to promise loyalty to Miguel, and willingness to do anything he chose to ask, at any time. Was that it?'

'I — I suppose so. And absolute secrecy — ' Her voice faltered.

'Exactly. You swore to say nothing at all if questioned. As now, for example.'

'You're a bully, aren't you? I told you it was only because I was worried.'

'You'd be a damn sight more worried if the plan had come off. Listen. I expect any one of the others in your cell would have acted just as you did. Ordinary people *do* break down under quite simple, fair police interrogation. Don't you see, that's why you were never told any details of what you were supposed to do. And that's why, if the balloon went up, the only man you could point to would be Miguel — and by that time he'd have disappeared. You and the rest would be charged with the whole conspiracy, and believe me, you wouldn't have an easy time.'

'You're just guessing.'

'I'm not. There's been a lot more going on than you know. When did Miguel discover the microphone?'

'That was the evening of the day Jack left — Friday.'

'I thought so. On Saturday, *in Lima*, there was a break-in at the house where he'd left his luggage. His suitcases were the only things touched, but they ransacked those thoroughly — and do you know what they took away?'

'No.' This was the real stuff, she thought.

'His tapes. All of them.'

'He'll be wild. But it serves him right, if he really is a copper's nark.'

'*Why* did they take the tapes?'

'How do I know?'

'There may have been more on the tape than just the record of one of your amateur meetings of conspirators. Why d'you think Cuevas took a gun — as you say he did — and went up into the mountains to find Warne. Because he'd seen Rodriguez at the Centre, enquiring for Warne. He jumped to the conclusion that Warne had asked Rodriguez to come because he had something important to tell him. So he tried to get Warne first.'

'But isn't that just what Jack *did* do?

He was in touch with them wasn't he?' Her face darkened. 'I still can't believe it of him.'

'And you're quite right,' said Craig. He was feeling tired of the sheer stupidity of the whole affair, and a little ashamed of himself for leading her on. It was like taking milk from a baby.

'What d'you mean?'

'Jack Warne was never in contact with any police, British or Peruvian. He was just curious, that's all.'

She jumped out of her chair. 'You utter bastard! You made me think you knew all about us. But — say that again. Was Jack a police spy?'

'No, of course he wasn't. And I never said so, did I?'

'Oh thank God!' She had tears in her eyes. 'I've been thinking of that all the time. I couldn't believe it but it seemed so — ' She faced him angrily. 'You just led me on, didn't you? It was just a game to you, wasn't it?'

'I did lead you on, or — put it another way — you just talked. And quite right, too. But believe me, it isn't a game.' He heard footsteps approaching the door and turned with relief as Rodriguez came in.

'I found the jeep,' he said. 'Somebody had plugged the holes with fibre-glass and mastic and painted them over. They'd washed the interior but there was blood between the springs of the back seat.' He spoke to the girl. 'It wasn't exactly riddled, you know. Just two holes. All the same, it's very lucky only one hit Cuevas.'

'Miss Horgan's been very helpful,' said Craig. He gave the gist of what she had told him in a few sentences. The girl sat listening with a black scowl on her face.

Rodriguez whistled. 'So that's it. The doctor's seeing Cuevas now, and afterwards he'll be kept in his room until I've time to interrogate him. If the story about the Tupamaros is true we may have to fly in more troops from the coast. It's quite correct that there is a group of Tupamaros on the run in the Mato Grosso, and we know they're well supplied with funds. They robbed a bank in Cuiaba last week and commandeered a Dakota from the airport. One of them, at least, is a pilot. He took them off without the slightest hitch and flew away to the north-west below radar level. They must have landed on some jungle airstrip and it's quite possible they've got other friends this side of the border, and are planning to make their way here — or even land on the strip. But how?' He frowned. 'It sounds a very odd plan. Do they think that because we have a Government that's opened diplomatic relations with Cuba they'll be received with open arms.' He grinned cheerfully. 'That would be a very big mistake. Now I shall want all the names of the members of this fancy group from Miss Horgan.'

'She's refused to give them.'

'Oh has she? Well, *hija*, you'd better start now. We have to know who they are. Then we can send them to Lima tomorrow, with you, too, and you can all contact your Embassies and get the lawyers working for you. That's sense, isn't it?'

'I won't do it.'

Craig saw a troop-carrier swinging into the compound.

'Your Section's arrived.'

'Good, I'll deal with them. Now, Miss Horgan, let's see if there's paper and pencil here.' He rummaged in Warne's desk and produced a pad and a Biro. 'Start writing down in Spanish what you've told Mr. Craig. I'll send a guard to stay with you. If you don't want to put down the names of your friends you'll be very unwise. That's all I'll say.' He went out.

'I'm not going to,' she said stubbornly. 'He can beat me up, but I won't.'

'All right then,' said Craig calmly. 'Don't. We'll find out soon enough, I think.'

'You're not going to torture Miguel?'

'No. I'd be surprised if the names of the cell-members don't emerge by what I might call a natural process. Now get on with your job. You've told me the main facts as you know them. Now write them down.'

# 8

## Wednesday Evening

Eight men and a sergeant of the Military Police at Tambo were in the compound when Craig was relieved by a corporal as guard for Janet Horgan. He found Rodriguez giving instructions to the sergeant, surrounded by a crowd of volunteers, who had returned from their work and were curious to know what was happening.

It was the first time he had come in contact with the volunteers, except for Janet and Miguel Cuevas, and he was interested. They were a colourful lot. A young Chilean had ridden in from his task of riding herd in the higher reaches of the settlement's land, where alpacas were grazed. He wore a broad-brimmed black hat and the riding kit of a *huaso* — extravagantly decorated shirt, skin-tight black trousers and sheepskin chaps

— and his feet were resting in heavy bronze stirrup buckets. There was a German agronomist in *lederhosen* and Bavarian hat, and two girls in Austrian *dirndls*, but most of the youngsters of both sexes wore jeans and coloured shirts, topped by the inevitable ponchos. Men and girls, they all had long hair, and several of the men had wispy beards. They were shouting and laughing as they broke away towards their rooms to prepare for the evening meal.

Castillo's voice over the loudspeaker system stopped them in their tracks. 'I want all volunteers to go *at once* to the assembly hall,' he said. 'This is an order. I shan't keep you long from your dinner. Assemble there at once, please — all of you. Give your names to Ingeniero Lopez as you enter.' There was an astonished hush, then a hubbub of talk.

Craig caught up Rodriguez as he was entering the long building, and spoke urgently. The Peruvian nodded, smiling, and went into a whispered conference with Castillo. The three men made their way to a raised platform at the end of the room, where there was a screen for use on film evenings. Lopez remained at the door, and checked the names of the volunteers against a list.

When they had all arrived, with the exception of Janet Horgan and Miguel Cuevas, Castillo addressed them. He spoke in a hard, cold voice, obviously much upset.

He said he had no complaint to make about the work of the volunteers. They were making an important contribution to the progress of the Centre and the cooperatives. 'You know very well,' he added, 'that this experiment is very close to my heart, and that I am more than grateful to you for your help. But I have just learned — and I cannot tell you how distressed it has made me — that a small group among you have been involved in what I can only call a plot, which if successful would have set back our programme for many months and quite possibly wrecked it altogether.'

There was an incredulous murmur from the crowd below him. He raised his hand for silence, and went on, 'Your political views are your own concern, and you know that we on the Staff have made no attempt to force on you the theories of the Peruvian national revolution. But sabotage is another matter and when — as happened yesterday — one of our foreign helpers was shot and another is missing, and possibly dead, I have no alternative but to take action. The persons responsible must be identified and sent back to Lima immediately, where their own diplomatic missions and the Peruvian authorities will decide what to do with them. If this is not done, I shall at once ask my Government — with very great regret, because of what I owe to you — to withdraw all volunteers from this project.'

There was an astounded silence then a rising chatter of protest. Rodriguez spoke. 'I believe six of you are the persons concerned, and I ask them to stay behind when the rest of you leave, and report to me. The other two members of the group are under arrest. Those who come forward will be held under guard until tomorrow, when I will arrange for their transport to Lima. I am convinced that some of those concerned are not aware of the seriousness of the activity in which they have become involved. It is in their interests to declare themselves now.'

A big Australian stood forward and said in halting Spanish, 'We all know who they are, Major. It's the bunch of reds who've been meeting secretly, or so they thought, in Cuevas' hut. You can't expect any of us to tell tales, but if they don't own up here and now I propose we beat the tripe out of them. The bleeding Commies!' he added in English. 'Sneaking around and playing spies. It isn't what we came here for, too right it isn't.'

A Frenchman shouted, 'Let's all go out of the door, but if they try to come too, we push them back.'

Craig smiled. He had guessed that in a society as tightly-knit as this the 'secret' of the cell was no secret at all.

Castillo shouted above the noise, '*Gracias, amigos*, that is all.'

There was a rush for the door, and several scuffles. When it was over, five young men and a girl remained inside the hall, trying vainly to get out in the face of a menacing barrier of their colleagues.

A tall, fair German turned and walked with an attempt at dignity to the platform. 'Helmut Springer,' he introduced himself to Rodriguez. 'This is an outrage, Senor. It's true that a few of us meet for political discussions with Miguel Cuevas. But the rest of what you said is nonsense.'

'Go and sit down, Herr Springer,' said Rodriguez. He turned to the Manager. 'They should be kept separate from each other, but not in their rooms until those have been searched. If you agree, they can sit here, dotted around the room.'

Castillo nodded, and the other five volunteers were marshalled to their seats. The M.P. sergeant took charge, with three of his men to prevent any attempt at conversation.

Craig and Rodriguez went with Castillo to his office. 'I think one or two of them will make statements,' said Rodriguez. 'The Italian girl looks shattered. And if we have one we have the lot. Except for Cuevas. He's a hard nut to crack.'

'There's the young German,' said Craig. 'He was the one who fetched the nurse to Cuevas. She half spoke his name, before she remembered, and said 'someone'. You could start with him. But what about Cuevas?'

'I think I'll have to leave him until tomorrow. If I start a full interrogation while he's still sick — and the doctor says he hasn't got over the *soroche* yet — his Embassy would make a fearful row. But I'm going to have a go at him tomorrow, if the doctor agrees.'

'Have you arranged transport?' asked Castillo wearily.

'An Airforce plane will arrive here about ten o'clock tomorrow. I shall be very glad when I know they've finally gone.'

'I'd be even happier,' said Craig, 'if I knew what they'd left behind.'

* * *

Craig found Janet staring at what she had written. 'I'm not putting in the names,' she said. 'That's going too far.'

'It's all right, you don't have to. They're all under arrest. You'll go with them tomorrow morning to Lima, by plane. Your room's been searched. You can go there now, and supper will be brought to you. But don't try to leave your room, or speak to any of the others.'

'You don't suppose I want to, do you?' she said bitterly. 'They must all know by now that I was the one that blabbed.'

'No, they don't. They were simply told you were under arrest.'

'Mr. Craig, I don't want to go in that plane. I really do want to find Jack. Can't I go with you tomorrow morning? You see, I think I know where he might be hiding.'

'Where?'

'There's a lake. He took his spinning rod with him and told me he'd bring me back a trout.' She looked up at him. 'That was before I heard he was a police spy.'

Craig swore. 'Why the hell didn't you tell the search-party?'

'They'd left before I woke up this morning. Can I go with you?'

'It's for Rodriguez to decide. I'll tell

him you might be useful.' He frowned. 'It's maddening, having to wait here because of the dark.'

'You don't think he's dead?'

'He must have gone equipped to spend one or two nights on the snow slopes, so he presumably won't die of cold. But Rodriguez knows he's got that blasted machine-gun, and won't hear of trying to find him at night. He thinks he may be trigger-happy.'

* * *

An hour later, they were sitting in the living room of the Manager's house, opposite the administrative buildings, reading the statements which Rodriguez had collected. A *cholo* servant brought in a tray of drinks — Peruvian lager and pisco sours. Lopez was discussing changes in work-schedules with Castillo, who still looked very unhappy. He turned to Rodriguez.

'What do they all say?' he asked abruptly.

'It's the same story — just what Miss

Horgan said. With the exception of a few who won't say anything yet.'

'When will they leave?'

'After re-fuelling, the plane will be ready to leave from Tambo at about eleven tomorrow morning, I should think. You can arrange transport to the airfield?'

Lopez said, 'I've reserved a truck for them. That's the best we can do — and no better than they deserve, anyway. You'll send an escort with them to Lima?'

'Of course. We don't want them to toy with the idea of hijacking the aircraft.' Rodriguez smiled. 'But I think they'll have learned their lesson.'

Castillo sighed. 'I hope so. Madre de Dios! Why couldn't they leave their crazy political ideas at home? I shall miss some of them, you know. Where am I going to get another electrician like young Springer? He did wonders, that boy, and I must say I was really fond of him. And as for Cuevas — those vermifuges and foot-rot injections he used to buy for us have made our sheep and llamas fitter than they've ever been. I suppose it *is* necessary, Rodriguez? Surely if, as you say, they've learned their lesson, can't at least some of them stay?'

'I'm afraid not. My orders are quite explicit. They have to go. What worries me is that they may not be the only ones.'

Castillo stared at him over his glasses. 'Surely you've arrested enough for one day,' he remarked caustically.

'I hope so, but I'm not sure.' He turned to Craig. 'Tell them your theory, Peter.' The Manager and Lopez dropped the papers on a desk, and joined the other two men.

'It's just this, Major Castillo. I can't believe that these rather naive young people were the mainspring of a serious attempt to harbour political criminals and defy the Peruvian authorities by holding some of the volunteers as hostages. Where would they take them? How could they be supplied with food? What about communications with the outside?'

'With your permission, Senor Director?' said Lopez. The Manager nodded, and the young Peruvian went on, 'The whole thing may be a piece of wishful thinking on the part of Miguel Cuevas.

You see, gentlemen, I know Miguel very well. He is exceptionally bright and an excellent veterinary officer, but I also know that he has an urge to dominate other people. He's shown this clearly enough in the way he orders the cattlemen around. I suggest he made up this group of — as Mr. Craig said — rather naive youngsters and fed them ideas of revolutionary activity, which they were very willing to entertain. You shake your heads, because you are thinking of his gunshot wound. But surely, all that is speculative. All we know is that he was shot at, but not how or why. This young girl, Janet Horgan — who outside her nursing duties is quite the most irresponsible of all the volunteers — *says* that Miguel had a gun and that Warne shot at him with — of all things — a machine-gun. I'm afraid I think she made up the whole of this dramatic story. How on earth could Warne get hold of a machine-gun?'

'I don't accept your explanation,' said Rodriguez, 'for one simple reason, which you are not aware of. You have heard that

Cuevas suspected Warne of listening in to his meetings and wanted to lay hands on the taped record which he believed Warne had made. Miss Horgan and several of the volunteers have confirmed this story.'

'But,' protested Castillo, 'we don't even know that there was a tape. As Lopez says, the whole case is pure speculation.'

'Except for one thing,' said Craig, 'Warne's luggage, left with friends of his in Lima, was searched last week and all his tapes were stolen. Nothing else was removed.'

There was a long silence. Then Lopez said, 'I agree. I didn't know that and it makes all the difference. There must be some more serious purpose behind this absurd conspiracy. But what is it?'

Craig said, 'It could be that this one cell that we know of was intended to serve a special purpose. Let's suppose for a moment that there really is some plan to receive a gang of Tupamaros on the run and give them shelter while blackmailing the Peruvian Government with threats to the safety of a number of hostages. The Tupamaros are professionals — young, educated, dedicated people who have achieved remarkable successes. They have forced governments to release hundreds of political prisoners in Brazil, Uruguay and Argentina and they've temporarily occupied whole towns. And how? By holding hostages to ransom.

'The advantage of using the volunteers at this Centre is obvious. They come from many different countries, and that means pressure on the Peruvian Government from several different sides. There *is* a group of Tupamaros on the run in Brazil, and they are believed to have air transport. It's well nigh impossible to guarantee that if they crossed the border into Peru they would be detected in flight. My point is that the possibility of such a plan cannot be discounted completely.'

'But, my dear Craig,' said Castillo, smiling, 'you've seen the Centre. It's full of people, and there's a military base just down the valley. Before anyone could round up some of the volunteers they'd have to deal with me and my staff and several hundred employees at the Centre and in the co-operatives. Within half an hour we'd have troops from Tambo to deal with any refugee Tupamaros.'

'But suppose the volunteers were taken away first, before you even knew anything was happening?'

'That's impossible,' exclaimed Lopez.

'Not,' said Craig, 'if the group of young people we have just arrested were themselves the hostages.'

Lopez slapped his thigh, laughing. 'Very Machiavellian, Mr. Craig! I see what you're getting at. These cell-members are expecting to be told one bright day, 'The time has come, boys and girls. The Tupamaros will be arriving tonight. We must get the refuge ready for them.' They all troop off, leaving their jobs, and are taken secretly to the place they always heard of — but never where it is. Once there, they are held under guard and the mysterious chief of the conspiracy gives his ultimatum to Major Castillo, the base at Tambo, the Peruvian Government and the world. 'Do as we say — or else!' You've worked it out brilliantly, if I may say so — except for one thing.' His pale face was flushed, and he looked at Craig challengingly.

'What's that?'

'Where, in this well-populated valley, could you hide a group of vociferous young people without anyone knowing?'

'That,' said Craig calmly, 'is for you to tell me.'

'And where are the hidden master-minds? On our staff?'

'Perhaps,' said Rodriguez.

'It's quite impossible,' said Castillo indignantly. I'm afraid you're indulging your imagination, Mr. Craig.'

'No, Senor Director,' said Rodriguez. 'He is right to think the thing out, and what he's said makes more sense than the ideas we had already. However, if he's right, at least we've spoiled their game for the moment. There'll be guards around tonight, just in case, and tomorrow I'll get more troops in from the coast. Meanwhile, all the volunteers must stay here at the Centre. I'm sorry, but I'm afraid we shall have to go through the whole Centre with a fine-tooth comb. I agree with you that your own staff are probably above suspicion, but there are the other volunteers and don't let's forget Don Jorge's men.'

'It is extremely upsetting,' said Castillo tightly, 'but I suppose I must leave you to decide. I think I can reassure you on one score. Don Jorge is a wily old man, with his ear very close to the ground. If anyone tried to spread disaffection among his own people, most of whom are still very faithful to him, he'd be the first to know. And incidentally,' he added, rising, as he heard footsteps approaching outside, 'that sounds like him now. He said he'd like to meet Mr. Craig, so I asked him to join us for dinner.'

It was the first time Craig had seen Santa Cruz, and he was impressed by the older man's face and bearing. The clear grey eyes assessed him briefly while courtesies were exchanged.

Santa Cruz sat down with a glass of pisco in his hand. 'I'm delighted to hear, Mr. Craig,' he said in excellent English, 'that you and Major Rodriguez have succeeded in corralling so quickly this bunch of young mavericks. But what about Warne? I hope he's come to no harm.'

'It's very frustrating,' admitted Craig. 'We have reason to think he may be hiding at the lake. It's no use — I can see that — going out to look for him in the dark, but Rodriguez and I will be on our way at six o'clock tomorrow.'

Don Jorge looked thoughtful. 'I wonder why you think he should be there — but I mustn't ask questions. He could certainly have descended by that route. I know Llangacocha well — *cocha* is the Quechua word for lake, by the way — and will tell you something about it, if you're interested.' He looked up as Senor Castillo and his pretty daughter of seventeen entered the room. 'But later, later. Here are the ladies.' He got to his feet with the other men and went forward to kiss hands. 'Dona Lucinda! And Rosita, my child — it's easy to see from where you inherited your beauty.'

A neat left and right, thought Craig, as he in turn bent over Senora Castillo's hand. Lopez made his excuses and left the room.

* * *

After dinner, when the men were sitting at one end of the living room, drinking coffee and brandy, with the two women, segregated by custom, chatting at the other end, Santa Cruz put down his cigar.

'We were talking about Llangacocha,' he said. 'When I was a youngster the glaciers came right down to the head of this valley, just as they did in the Callejon de Huaylas, on the other side of the Cordillera. But they've been retreating steadily — no one seems to know why — and the lower limits of the snows are a thousand metres higher than they were at the turn of the century.'

'Isn't that one of the reasons why you have such terrible natural catastrophes in these mountains?' asked Craig.

'It is. Dozens of new lakes have been forming during recent decades, and indeed they used to grow quite unknown to the people in the valleys below. Now at last air reconnaissance has shown the extent of the menace. As for Llangacocha, I can remember when there was no lake at all. It was a glacier six miles long and a hundred feet deep. Now it's a lake.'

'But why doesn't it empty?'

'The pattern is always the same. The glacier gradually melts, and the meltwater is held back by a terminal moraine, like a cork in a bottle. But some of these natural dams are insecure, being formed of loose rock, and an earthquake or a sudden thaw above the snow line may cause them to burst.'

'As in 1962,' put in Castillo. 'That was in the Callejon. The glacier of Huascaran overhangs a lake. All the lower part has melted away, leaving this gigantic ice cornice. Well, a strip fell off into the lake — millions of tons of it. The tidal wave swept the dam away and within minutes — literally — had obliterated the town of Ranvahirca in the valley below.'

Santa Cruz took up the story. 'In 1970 it was the earthquake that started everything, but another slice of the Huascaran cornice broke off and fell three thousand feet in a straight fall, not into the lake, but on to the mountainside below. What happened then — ' he took a pull at his cigar — 'was remarkable. The avalanche created such heat, by friction, that it travelled down the gorge on a cushion of steam and air.' He saw the look on Craig's face. 'Yes, my dear sir, air. Forty million cubic metres of pulverized ice and mud and water struck the Santa valley, sixteen kilometres below, within two minutes of the moment when the seismographic needles jumped out of their bearings. It was moving at — what would it be? — over three hundred miles an hour, and there were places in which bushes in its direct path were left standing.'

Rodriguez nodded. 'The most extraordinary thing I ever saw. I was working with the rescue teams, and it's not a thing I'll ever forget.'

'Was that how Yungay was buried?' asked Craig.

'Yes. It wasn't in the gorge down which the avalanche came, but the mass was bouncing from side to side, and jumped over a great spur of rock that had always protected the town in the past — and buried it under several metres of debris. Luckily,' continued Santa Cruz, 'we were spared on this side of the range, and in any case Llangacocha is safe enough for the time being. There's no overhang in the Chopicalqui glacier, which formed our lake. And the dam is fairly strong. My father reinforced the earth moraine with a facing of heavy stones, and as the level of the lake rises, year by year, I've added to it and made a concrete sluice. As soon as there's any sign of a thaw a man is sent to raise the gate so that the excess water can flow through without washing over the top of the dam. Otherwise the floods would bring about a rapid erosion, and then,' he added, smiling at Rodriguez, 'I'm afraid the town of Tambo, your excellent military base and three thousand hectares of the best coffee in Peru would be — ' He made a sideways cutting motion with his hand.

'It was a patriotic act by your father, God rest his soul!' said Rodriguez. 'We have military engineers working on a project to reinforce the dam in depth, but it's still only in the planning stage. Your father and indeed you, sir, were ahead of your time.'

Santa Cruz rose and extinguished his cigar. 'Why not?' he said. 'After all, it was his land. As it was mine, until two years ago.' He smiled grimly, and made his way across the room to thank the ladies and say good-bye.

When he had gone Craig said, 'He sounds bitter, and I don't blame him.' He smiled at Castillo. 'Don't get me wrong, Senor Director. But I believe his family were always good landlords.'

'So they were, at least to the extent of developing their land and spending most of their time here. But nevertheless, when my task is finished — and God knows when that will be! — the valley will be producing twice as much food as ever before, except under the Incas. We can't compete with them. And remember it's food we need — Peruvian grain, not imported wheat that drains away our dollars.' He smiled. 'Anyway, Mr. Craig, don't worry about Don Jorge. He's still very rich.'

Senora Castillo came and sat on the arm of her husband's chair. 'It's Don Jorge's pride,' she said. 'All his money can't save the hurt to his pride.'

'You mean,' suggested Craig, 'that he can't bear the thought that someone else should try to develop his valley better than he and his family have done?'

'Yes, that's part of it. But there is more.' She smiled down at her husband and laid her hand on his arm. 'I was born on the *altiplano*, not like my husband, who's a Limeño, and only came to love these valleys after he was sent here on duty. My family owned land in the Callejon de Huaylas, and I can tell you — we didn't like the people of the coast.'

'She still throws that word at me when she's angry,' said Castillo, laughing. ' 'You coastal playboys,' she says — '

'Don't listen to him, senores! I only ever called him that once, and it was on our honeymoon.'

'And I said if you can't be a playboy on your honeymoon — ' began Castillo, but she put her hand over his mouth.

'It's true,' said Rodriguez, 'that the people of the *altiplano* are supposed to be very proud and independent. Didn't the landowners in the Callejon defy the Government once, about a hundred years ago?'

'In eighteen eighty-five,' said Dona Lucinda, proudly, 'and the troops couldn't get into the valley, because we blocked the passes. That's why I can't understand that Don Jorge should take it lying down, after all he's done.'

'His family didn't create the valley,' said Castillo, drily. 'The Recuay civilization was here long before the Incas, and it was highly developed. We still dig up pottery with the sign of the jaguar on it.'

'The jaguar?' said Craig. 'I've seen some of the Recuay pots in Lima, but I didn't realize that extraordinarily angular animal was a jaguar.'

'It was a version of the Cat-God worship that you find all through the early religions of the Andes. The biggest cat of all is an outcrop of dark green granite high up on the slopes of the eastern range, overlooking the valley. The Recuay people sculpted it in the form of a crouching jaguar, and you can still see the resemblance when the sun's in the right direction, although it's been eroded by a thousand years of wind and frost. The Indians are still afraid of it. The Santa Cruz family, incidentally, took it as their crest.'

'Don Jorge's rather like a jaguar himself,' murmured Dona Lucinda, with a surreptitious shiver. 'The Indians call him by that name.'

As they walked back towards the guest-house, where they were to sleep, Rodriguez said, 'I told them we should be leaving at six, Peter, but I think we could get away earlier. There'll be light enough. I'll wake you at half-past four. O.K.?'

'The earlier the better. I'll be ready.'

Afterwards, he was to remember that small change of plan, and all that resulted from it.

# 9

## Thursday Morning

Rodriguez came into Craig's room when the first eerie light, reflected by the high snows of the Cordillera Blanca, was filtering through the window. Craig was already dressed, wearing the extra cardigan which the thoughtful Mrs. Harris had packed in his case. The Peruvian was in battledress, with two ponchos over his arm. He threw one of them on Craig's bed.

'You'll need that. What about boots?' He looked at Craig's feet and said tactfully, 'I'm afraid there's nothing suitable here.' He himself was wearing half-length military boots.

Craig looked down at his size ten brogues. 'I didn't think there would be. These will have to do. Thanks for the poncho. You've got food?'

'And drink. Plenty of both. We'll

probably be glad of it. Also a boat.'

'A boat?'

'It's just possible Warne fell in the lake. The sides are very precipitous in places. And by today,' he added grimly, 'his body may be rising to the surface. Why on earth couldn't that girl have told us about his going to the lake earlier?'

'She thought Warne was a copper's nark.' He used the English words.

'What in heaven's name is that?'

Craig told him. 'And apparently she was asleep when you left to look for him yesterday morning.'

When they went outside Craig found a Land-Rover with a bright yellow inflatable boat strapped on the roof-rack. It was only half-inflated, drooping over the sides. 'We're not going to get very far in that,' he objected, laughing.

'By the time we're at the level of the lake it'll be hard enough. You forget the difference in atmospheric pressure. We'll pick up the nurse at her room. I knocked her up ten minutes ago.'

'You're sure you've no objection?'

'None at all. Neither you nor I know

Warne, and she does. What's more, if he's been running loose with a submachine-gun it may not be a bad thing to have a nurse handy.'

The guard saluted as they came up and knocked on Janet's door. She came out at once, dressed in thick woollen slacks and heavy shoes, with a poncho over her arm. She had a first-aid box in her hand. A handkerchief was tied over her auburn hair and she wore sun-glasses. She looked sensible enough, thought Craig, grudgingly.

Rodriguez ran an expert eye over her revealing roll-neck sweater. 'No room for a weapon there,' he remarked, adding gallantly, 'other than what nature endowed you with, senorita. But for safety's sake, would you open your little box?'

She looked at him coldly, but opened the medical case without a word. Rodriguez examined it quickly and was satisfied. The Land-Rover had followed them and the girl got quickly into the back seat with Craig, while Rodriguez sat by the driver. He handed a heavy-calibre automatic to Craig, who checked the magazine, felt for the safety-catch and put it into his pocket on the side away from the girl. 'Fuzz!' she remarked quietly.

The car swung out of the compound and on to the road that led downhill beside the river and its long row of eucalyptus trees. The whole glory of the Cordillera, brilliantly lit by the rising sun, burst into view. The air was bitingly cold in the shadowed valley. They ran through the sleeping adobe cottages of a small hamlet, through fields of wheat and maize, and so down to a place where a road of loose stones turned off to the left, bridging the river.

The Land-Rover crossed the bridge and began to head straight for the wall of mountains. There were plantations of eucalyptus and spruce on both sides of the road, with the white houses of the foresters gleaming in the semi-darkness. The long jagged shadow cast by the eastern range had already sunk lower on the snows of the Cordillera in front of them, and was approaching the wide strip of glistening whitish-green granite, completely bare except for the thin scatter of shrubs above the tree-line. When the road began to climb, twisting back and forth, one hairpin bend after another, Craig could only occasionally catch a glimpse of the snow peaks that towered above them, dazzlingly beautiful against the deep blue of the sky.

'That's Chopicalqui,' said Rodriguez, pointing. Craig saw an impressive mass of blue ice and golden-white snow appearing above the smooth snow slopes. 'It hides Huascaran, which is higher still.'

A condor planed gently downwards, looking for kids among the scattered herds of llamas on the lower slopes.

* * *

Far below, in the Chasco valley, and on the other side of the Centre, another form of predator was homing in on its prey. The truck descending the road from the head of the valley — the same road that came from the coast, a hundred and fifty miles away — had stopped. A man seated beside the driver was speaking into a radio transmitter. He finished and held the receiver to his ear. Then he put the set back into his breast pocket, unbuttoned the holster of his revolver and spoke to the driver. '*Esta bien*,' he said '*Vamonos*.'

The truck moved off quietly and continued its descent. Near the entrance to the Centre the driver coasted down the remaining few hundred yards, swung in between the buildings and came to a silent stop in the main compound.

Twenty-three men dropped to the ground over the tailgate and ran noiselessly to their destinations. They wore Indian knitted caps with ear-flaps, and their Schmeisser machine-pistols were hidden, for the moment, under their drab ponchos.

It was still only half-past five, and no one in the Centre was stirring, except for the guards. The man at the door of the hut in which the military police had been quartered had his automatic rifle slung over his shoulder, and was taken unawares. He fell to the ground with a knife between his ribs, and the man who had killed him jumped over his body and ran into the hut. Inside, the *agente* who had been guarding Janet Horgan was busy making coffee. He heard a noise outside and grabbed his rifle. The intruder fired three shots, which rang deafeningly through the ears of the sleeping men. The guard died where he stood, and the others were still scrambling to their feet when they saw the ring of grimly pointed weapons and slowly raised their hands. They were herded together and bound hand and foot.

The muzzle of a Schmeisser was thrust through the window of Castillo's bedroom. His wife heard the sound of breaking glass and screamed. Then she saw, across Castillo's head, the face of the man behind the gun. He told her coldly to open the front door, if she wanted her husband to stay alive. Castillo scrambled to his feet, searching the top of the night table for his glasses. She pulled him back on to the bed and ran to open the door.

In the volunteers' quarters four men, two of them Argentines and the others from Chile and Brazil, were already dressed and acting out their parts. Two of them strolled up to the man guarding Miguel Cuevas, and asked him what the shooting was about. As he was peering out into the compound they seized his rifle and threw him to the ground. Plans had been laid very carefully.

In a quarter of an hour it was all over. Miguel had limped out into the patio with a gun in his hand and organized the rounding up of the volunteers, who were pushed into the assembly hut, with guards standing inside the doors. The 'conspirators', who had known nothing of what was to happen, were herded together with the rest.

Helmut Springer broke away and ran to Miguel. 'Give me a gun,' he cried. 'I'll organize this, just as we planned.'

Cuevas pushed him back. 'Go with the others,' he ordered grimly. 'If not, you'll regret it.'

Springer stared at him. 'But what was the use of organizing our group,' he sputtered, 'if you won't let us help now?'

Cuevas smiled. 'You've served your purpose, Helmut. Don't worry, we shan't hurt you. The plans have had to be changed. Nobody's going to be foolish enough to give you a gun, so just go along with the others. You'll get food later.'

Helmut pointed to a man who was speaking to a group of *cholos* who had run up in alarm when they heard the shooting, mostly clerks who worked in the offices and warehouses. They were listening bewildered to what the man said. 'But why don't you arrest *him*?' asked Helmut.

Miguel smiled. 'Lopez? He's a Tupamaro, like me.'

* * *

Half an hour afterwards Don Jorge Santa Cruz and Lopez were listening to reports from a group of men who had assembled in the Manager's office. 'The volunteers?'

Miguel spoke. 'Except for the members of Cell Two they are being collected now, and will be taken to the dining hall. The cooks are preparing their food now. They'll be all right. The lavatories have barred windows and there's a guard inside the door.'

'You've called the roll?'

'Yes.' Miguel hesitated. 'They're all here except one — the Irish nurse. Her guard must have left his post to get himself some coffee in the M.P. hut. He resisted and was shot. I went to the girl's hut but she wasn't there. I suppose she heard him go and ran off to hide. She's taken her poncho.'

Santa Cruz looked at him coldly. 'Go at once and search until you find her. She can't have gone far. The military police?'

'All immobilized and under guard.' He smiled. 'I've locked Castillo in his office. The two women are in the house, too, but they won't stir for fear of what might happen to him, after what I told them.'

'Rodriguez and the Englishman? I want to speak to them.'

'They're not there, Don Jorge. They must have left earlier than they told us.'

Santa Cruz swore. 'You sent men to arrest them?'

'Of course. It was the first thing Carlos did.'

The leader of the Tupamaros who had arrived in the truck nodded. He was a thickset, taciturn Peruvian, with the haunted eyes of a man who had been on the wanted list of every police headquarters in Peru. 'You seem to have slipped up there, Santa Cruz,' he said coldly. 'As arranged, I sent three men to the guest-house as soon as we arrived. They'd gone.' He took off his Indian cap and pushed it into his pocket. 'And so has the Land-Rover.'

Don Jorge chewed his grey moustache, irritably. 'That's the last thing we wanted; it throws the whole plan out of line.' He paced up and down the room. 'If only I knew what our friend Cuevas let Warne overhear.'

Lopez intervened. 'I don't think Warne will be found easily.'

'What d'you mean?'

'They told us last night they had reason to think Warne had gone into hiding. The only reason for that would be if he thought he had killed Cuevas. If so, the moment he sees the Land-Rover he'll go to ground.'

Santa Cruz looked at him reflectively. 'It's possible. But I still don't like it. If they find the boy and he has anything to tell that Rodriguez doesn't know already he'll be on to the Base by radio before we can stop him.'

'But we've got the volunteers. They're being taken to the refuge in an hour's time. We can go ahead with the ultimatum.'

'It's too soon. We want five hours, at least. The Base will try to contact the military police section here, and get no answer, but they'll merely conclude that something's gone wrong with the telephone line. Then all they'll do is send a jeep up the road with a couple of *agentes*. What will you do about that, Paco?'

Lopez smiled. 'Let them come into the Centre, and take them. I've got a guard down the road, with a radio. What about the Indians and the *cholos*? I've calmed them down for the time being.'

'As we planned. I'll summon the foreman and *alcaldes* and tell them there's been a revolution in Lima, and I'm taking back my land. If anyone attempts to go down the road to Tambo he'll be shot. I shall make that clear, and they know I'm a man of my word. They can have a fiesta tomorrow and we'll provide the aguardiente and coca. That'll keep them sweet,' he added contemptuously. 'You do the same with the *cholos* in the village. Once they're back at work we'll have no troube.'

'And the two police officers?' asked Lopez.

'I'll go to the dam myself, and you follow a quarter of an hour afterwards with some of your Tupamaro friends.'

'Rodriguez will be armed,' said Lopez shortly. Santa Cruz seemed to think he was running the show.

The older man smiled. 'If I can't bluff a pair of policemen, Paco, I'm losing my touch. I've bluffed the whole of the military government for the past two years, and they're none the wiser.'

* * *

The Land-Rover crawled round a giddy bend, with a sheer drop to the right, and began to climb a straight stretch across the mountainside. Half-way along there was a place where the rock had been blasted away to allow space for two vehicles to pass, and here the driver stopped.

'We're half-way up,' said Rodriguez. 'Three thousand feet to go before we get to the fork.'

Craig climbed out, rather slowly, because his heart was labouring in the thin air. The driver brought a hamper and produced from it a Thermos of coffee. They all sat at the side of the road, eating sandwiches and drinking the hot, sweet liquid. The Chasco valley, now in full sunlight, lay far below their feet. It was a patchwork of fields and plantations, with small hamlets and isolated farmhouses and co-operative buildings scattered across the broad plain. To the left, in the direction of Tambo, the Chasco disappeared between foothills that crowded in on it. The lower end of the valley was out of sight. On the other side the eastern mountains rose steeply, not as high as the Cordillera Blanca which they were climbing, but with jagged peaks and long white snow slopes. Opposite the Centre, away to the right, a great outcrop of green granite, blown clear of snow, stuck out from the mountain wall. Rodriguez pointed to it. 'The Jaguar,' he said.

'Jack's climbed it,' said the girl, suddenly. 'Look! You can see how he's crouching, with his paws out towards us, and the head above, d'you see? As if he's looking down at the Casa Grande and the Centre.'

The *cholo* driver turned his head. 'I've climbed it, too, *mi Mayor*,' he said proudly. He pointed with the end of a garlic sausage at the slope below the outcrop. 'That's where we camped when I was on the assault course. The morning after, we climbed round the Jaguar's flank and went up from there with crampons.'

'You were trying for the Mountain Battalion, then,' said Rodriguez.

'Si, Senor. I was a good climber, but my map-reading let me down.'

'Bad luck.'

It was curious, in view of what

happened later, how Craig could remember every word of that casual bit of conversation.

* * *

Half an hour afterwards they came to the parting of the ways. For some time they had been travelling up the gorge of the stream that came down from Chopicalqui to join the Chasco. It widened out, and from the left a smaller ravine joined it. The road to the silver mine turned into the ravine, high above a plunging stream that could be heard but not seen through the screen of trees clinging to the precipitous sides. Where the road turned off, the ravine was bridged to carry a narrow dirt road along the side of the main gorge. In the fork of the Y, between the two roads, was a steep bluff of rock, capped with pines.

'That's where we had to go up yesterday,' explained Rodriguez. 'You can see the path. It's not difficult, once you get up into the trees. But several thousand feet further up there's only snow and ice — ' He shivered. 'It forms the base of the Chopicalqui shoulder.'

The Land-Rover took the dirt road, with the high bluff on its left and a sheer drop of two hundred feet or more on the right. On the other side of the gorge the ground rose steeply towards a line of cliffs.

For three miles the road swung upwards, one dizzy turn after another, following the winding course of the gorge. Its surface was scoured by stormwater, and the Land-Rover was permanently in four-wheel drive to keep a grip on the treacherous stones and dried mud.

'What happens when the rains come?' asked Craig.

'This road is protected to some extent by the steepness of the cliffs. The water from the heaviest rain on the slopes above just cascades over it and into the gorge. But the mine road on the other side of the shoulder gets the full force of the storms and is washed away each year. That'll start to happen next month, and I heard Santa Cruz say last night that he was closing the mine early, and had already sent the final batch of miners down to their homes for the winter. He lost two trucks over the edge last year, when the rain came early and he was trying to get the men out before the road closed for the winter. Ten men killed.'

Janet shuddered. 'We had some of the wounded in our hospital,' she said, 'because the other, at the base, was overflowing. I've never seen such injuries. Men impaled on the trees below, after falling hundreds of feet, and others with every bone broken.'

'They're well paid,' said Rodriguez, 'and under our new workers' law the families get heavy compensation. No wonder Don Jorge didn't want to risk it happening again this year.'

During all this last part of the climb it had been like driving up through a narrow, twisting alleyway, but now the Land-Rover laboured its way round the final corner. Ahead, the road ran up to the end of a barrier of earth and stones that blocked the gorge from side to side. Beyond, there was nothing to see but the blue sky and far in the distance the tips of icy mountains.

They heard the sound of falling water above the roar of the low gear and saw a spout of water issuing from the flume in the centre of the dam. It disappeared into a mist of spray far below. The Land-Rover turned into a rough parking place at the side of the dam. Ahead, the view opened out. The sombre green waters of the lake stretched away towards the ice wall of the glacier at the far end, and the full grandeur of Chopicalqui, twenty-one thousand feet high, appeared above it, with a long snow plume blowing off the peak like a banner.

Craig stood beside the car, feeling his heart pound, and a band of pain around his forehead. The last few thousand feet of rapid, twisting climb had taken their toll. He found the girl looking at him with a sort of mocking solicitude. 'It's always worse for the middle-aged,' she said, with an impish grin. 'Would you like some heart pills?'

'No thank you,' he replied, with some asperity. Damn it, he was only thirty-five.

'I am quite used to heights.'

'All the same — ' she began, and broke off. 'Jack!' she screamed, and ran across to the trees at the side, where there was a stone hut, and a young man standing beside a fire, staring at the newcomers uncertainly. He was dressed in jeans and anorak, and his face bore several days' growth of stubble. The girl ran up to him, threw her arms round his neck and burst into tears.

'Jack,' she sobbed, 'you bloody eejit!'

* * *

Warne disengaged himself gently, but kept his arm round her shoulders while he looked at Craig and Rodriguez as they came up. 'She's one of these emotional Irish types,' he explained, in Spanish. 'Why on earth didn't you come yesterday?' Then he started, and asked hurriedly. 'What — what happened to Miguel? Did I kill him?'

'No,' came Janet's voice, muffled by his shoulder. She shook him, delighted to put his mind at rest. 'You only took a slice off his backside.'

'She's right,' said Craig. 'He's not badly hurt, and under a police guard.' The young man stared at him.

'Who are you?' he asked.

'Craig. I'm a British police officer. Now you've got a lot of explaining to do, my lad.' He suddenly felt giddy, and sat down in the doorway of the hut. 'This is Major Rodriguez, Military Security.'

'First,' said Rodriguez, looking at Craig's face, 'we'll have coffee. Alfredo, get the hamper out.'

While they drank, Warne, who had apparently just finished a breakfast of fried trout, told his story. He finished, 'You see, I could hear the jeep going down all right, and I thought they'd be rushing up here to arrest me. So I decided to wait for the police, rather than risk running into some of Cuevas' gang, out for my blood. And yesterday, when nobody came, I felt sure the police hadn't been told and — well, I was pretty worried and holed up. It was only just now, as I was having breakfast, that I made up my mind to face it out. Thank

God Miguel isn't damaged.'

'He's got a very sore behind,' said Janet, 'and serve him right.'

Warne turned to Rodriguez. 'So what am I accused of, exactly? Don't worry, I'll go quietly. That blasted gun's in the hut.'

'Nobody's accusing you of anything yet. Incidentally, you've said nothing about the tape.'

'How d'you know about the tape?'

'Just tell us, please.'

'Well, I wanted to know what was going on so secretly in Miguel's hut.'

'Why?' put in Rodriguez.

'Well — it was partly because I didn't want Janet to get too involved in — '

She pushed him away. 'I'm quite capable of thinking for myself.'

'No, you're not. So I fixed up a microphone and attached it to my tape-recorder, and triggered it off with a thing that — '

'A thing called a Viva Voce,' said Craig. 'We found it.'

Warne stared at him. 'You couldn't have. It was — '

'In the cistern in the men's loo, that's

where you put it, surely?'

'Yes.' He continued, in a slightly deflated tone, 'I got a tape, but I couldn't make head or tail of most of it.'

Craig and Rodriguez exchanged puzzled glances. 'You couldn't understand what was being said. Why?' asked Rodriguez.

'Some of it was clear. It was obvious that they were hatching some sort of plot. But the rest was in Quechua, which was very odd, because Miguel never let on that he knew more than a few words. But of course he's been here over two years.'

'Where is the tape?'

'In my pack, over there.' He pointed to his rucksack. 'I didn't want it to be found, you see, if they happened to discover the mike.'

'Which they did,' said Craig, drily.

'Oh my God, that must have put the fat in the fire. So that's why Miguel came to look for me?'

'Exactly. That and the fact that he thought you were eavesdropping on our behalf,' said Rodriguez, smiling. 'Now, get your things together. It's time we went back.'

Warne hesitated. 'There's one thing I didn't tell you, but I suppose I ought to put that aquasuit back.'

'What are you talking about?'

'You see, on Tuesday, before all this happened with Miguel, I thought I'd swim to the island, that one over there.' He pointed.

'You must have been mad,' said Rodriguez angrily. 'It's glacier water. You're lucky to be alive.'

'Well, it *was* tough, but there's a hut on the island and I saw this aquasuit inside, so I found the key and borrowed it. To swim back with. It's cached under some rocks along the shore, where I landed, and I'd better get it. I don't want to be accused of pinching, on top of everything else. Not that the owner deserves to have it back,' he added angrily.

'Why not?'

'Because he keeps stores of explosives in that hut, too. For fishing, I suppose. All marked with the skull and crossbones.'

Rodriguez exclaimed. 'Dynamite?'

'I suppose so. Several boxes of it. He probably thinks it's quite safe, because it's well hidden and there isn't a boat on the lake.'

Rodriguez stood up. 'That's one thing I'll take care of,' he said grimly. 'No one's got a right to keep explosives lying around. It must be someone from Don Jorge's mine. Were there detonators as well?'

'I don't know. The boxes were all sealed with metal tape.'

'So you don't know for certain that they contain explosives?'

'They're marked '*Explosivos Peruanos*'.'

'I see. But we've got to find out. It could be that someone is using the stuff for something else. Alfredo!'

'*Mi Mayor.*'

'Get the boat ready.' The driver began to untie the ropes that held the boat, now fully inflated in the lower atmospheric pressure of the mountains, on the roof-rack. Rodriguez opened the tool-box and took out a claw hammer, a tyre-lever and a screw-driver. He glanced at Craig, still sitting on the door-step of the hut, and went over to him. 'How are you feeling now?'

'O.K. I'd like to go with you. There'll be room for three, I should think.'

'Let's see you walk about a bit first.' The two men strolled across the dam and looked down into the stonelined flume. It was about eight feet deep, but the water in the lake was well below the level of the dam and only the lower section of the gate was in position, holding back some four feet of water. Above it, the water spilled over smoothly and fell splashing into the flume. Between the concrete uprights that held the two gates a plank bridge crossed the falling water. The gears for raising and lowering the gates were operated by a windlass on the nearer side.

Beyond the sluice, the dam stretched on for another hundred yards and ended in a mass of rocks and stones that had fallen from the steep slope on the northern side. Among them a vicuna balanced delicately on its slender legs, foraging for food, and turned its long neck to gaze at the intruders with a cold disdainful stare. Unhurriedly, it pranced away, and began to scale the hill-side.

Alfredo called. He was putting the boat

into the water. Rodriguez told him to stay at the dam to guard the Land-Rover and collect the sub-machine-gun from the hut where Warne had left it.

Janet was taking her place in the boat when Rodriguez stopped her. 'I'd rather you remained here, Miss Horgan. If there are explosives in those boxes the fewer who go the better. Would you please find out from Mr. Warne where the aquasuit is hidden, and go and collect it. We'll pick you up on the shore on our way back.'

She looked rebellious, but agreed. The three men pushed off and Warne took up the oars. Ten minutes passed before they were tied up at the island. Warne led the way to the hut, pushed the door open and let Rodriguez go ahead. Then, with a certain sense of drama, he hauled the table to one side, picked up the llama skin and pointed to the trap beneath. Rodriguez pulled it up and stared at the array of boxes. He pulled one out on to the floor and examined the markings. There was a stencilled sign that Warne had not noticed.

Rodriguez got up quickly, brushing the

dust from his knees. 'It's gelignite,' he said briefly. 'From the silver mine, as I thought. The fools! If they leave it long enough it'll go off by itself.' He picked up the claw-hammer.

Craig took the tyre-lever and between them they broke the metal ribbon and unscrewed the top of the box. Inside were waxed parcels, like overgrown sausages, lying in rows, three deep. The Peruvian gingerly stripped back one of the coverings.

'It's not sweating,' he said with a sigh of relief. 'They had the sense to leave it underground. The inside of this hut must vary between boiling hot by day and below freezing at night, and that's more than gelignite can stand. We won't touch it now. I'll get the engineers to fetch it.'

Craig was standing near the wall of the hut, looking at a rough sketch made in chalk on the boards. 'How d'you explain this, Bernardo?'

Rodriguez joined him. There were two horizontal lines, joined by a vertical stroke — like an H lying on its side. Left of the vertical was a curving line of dots leading from a point on the upper horizontal to join the lower line where the vertical crossed it.

'I'm not sure,' said Rodriguez, 'but I don't think it's got anything to do with fishing. Nor have those.' He pointed to the row of drainage pipes lying across the roof beams.

Warne was watching the grave faces of the two older men. 'What's it all about?' he asked curiously.

'I don't know,' said Craig, 'but I agree with the Major. The sooner we get this investigated the better.' He started. 'Oh my God! The aquasuit.'

'Exactly,' said Rodriguez. 'For fixing charges underwater to destroy the facing. Let's get back to the boat.'

'Wait,' said Craig. 'Jack, can you see if there's anything else down in that hole?'

The young man lay on the floor and moved the boxes around. 'There is something behind them, but I can't reach it. Hang on to my legs.' They held his feet while he wriggled his body through the aperture in the floor and groped with his hands. He gave a cry of triumph, and a moment later handed back a long bar with a square socket in the end, containing a spring catch. 'Hold on,' he called in a muffled voice. 'There's something else, but it's big and awkward. Here it comes.'

When he had scrambled to his feet he found the others staring down at a thing like a giant corkscrew, three feet long, with a four-inch bore. The central shaft was square ended, and fitted into the socket in the long bar, being held in place by the catch.

'There's a tommy-bar down there, too,' said Warne. 'Look! There are holes for it in the end of the two shafts. But what's it *for*?' He saw Craig looking up at the stack of pipes.

'Yes,' said Rodriguez, 'that's it. Insert the augur into a pipe and start boring, pulling up the earth as you go. Then fit on the extension, add another length of pipe, and down another three feet, and so on. Do it carefully, and you've got a hole nine feet deep, neatly lined with pipe. You lower the gelignite down on the end of the detonator wires and stuff the pipes with packed earth. It's clever. *Por Dios*! Very clever and efficient.'

'And the sketch,' said Craig quietly, 'shows where they'd plant the pipes. Look! The central line is the flume, and the line of dots are the charges. Nine feet deep! What lunatic would plan a thing like that?'

'You mean the sketch is of the dam?' asked Warne, bewildered. 'But no one could deliberately want to *blow it up*!'

'I don't see any other explanation,' said Rodriguez shortly. 'I must go straight back and report. I ought to have spoken to H.Q. before, when we found Warne, but this is even more important. The sooner I can get troops here the better. No one's going to blow that dam while I'm around.'

'What about Janet?' asked Warne.

'We'll signal to her from the boat. I'm afraid she'll have to walk. This news can't wait.'

As they stepped out of the rubber boat on to the shingle, near the stone hut, they heard the roar of a car engine approaching fast, and a moment later a gleaming Buick station-wagon came into view and halted alongside the Land-Rover. Don Jorge Santa Cruz emerged from it, wearing an embroidered poncho over a suit of old tweeds.

'Splendid!' he said in English, as he came towards them. 'You have found the errant sheep. I was going to help you search for him.' Then he saw the boat, and his eyes narrowed. 'Looking for him in the lake?' he enquired sarcastically.

'You'll forgive me, Don Jorge,' said Rodriguez, 'if I leave Mr. Craig to explain what's happened. It's very important. I must use my radio.' He began to walk towards the Land-Rover. The driver got out and opened the off-side door.

'Wait a moment, Major.' Rodriguez turned round. 'You're going to telephone your base?'

'Yes,' said Rodriguez shortly.

'May I ask why?'

Rodriguez gave him a cold stare, then shrugged, and said, 'There is a stock of explosives on that island, probably stolen from your mine. I'll get the engineers up here, to take charge of it.' He continued to walk to the car.

'Stop!' It was a peremptory command. Santa Cruz was moving slowly towards Rodriguez. There was a look of cold ferocity on his face, and Craig recalled that the Indians called him the Jaguar.

Rodriguez turned. 'Don Jorge, I do not take orders from you.'

Craig sensed danger, but the man said more mildly, 'I'm sorry, but you see I can explain everything, if only you'll be kind enough to listen. There was a theft of gelignite from the mine two weeks ago. I think you've stumbled on the place where the thieves cached it.'

'Did they,' asked Craig slowly, 'also steal an augur for making holes in the dam?'

There was silence for a moment, broken by Don Jorge's voice, lowered to a hissing whisper. 'You'll suffer, my friends, for this inquisitiveness.' He sprang to the side, and a Luger appeared in his hand. He shouted something in a clicking, guttural language. Rodriguez, who understood Quechua, whirled round, snatching out his revolver.

Craig jumped behind Santa Cruz and shoved the muzzle of his automatic into his back. 'Behind you,' he shouted to Rodriguez. He was too late. A burst of automatic fire came from the Buick, and the Major's body was flung into the air, to fall forward on its face. Alfredo had jumped out of the Land-Rover, his automatic pistol in his hands, and was raising it to fire when the second burst from the big station-wagon cut him down.

'Drop your gun, Santa Cruz,' said Craig between his teeth, 'and put your hands on your head.' He kept the man's body between him and the Indian who was emerging from the Buick, a young man holding a Schmeisser. Craig had never seen him before. He heard Warne's voice, 'I'm just behind you.'

'Good. I said, *drop your gun*, Santa Cruz. I liked Rodriguez. He was a friend of mine. Do what I say or I'll blow your spine apart.'

An automatic fell to the ground and Don Jorge put his hands on his head. A bullet from Craig's gun hit the ground at the feet of the young Indian and showered him with dirt. He dropped the Schmeisser and held up his hands.

'Get it, Warne.' The boy ran forward, picked up the gun and held it ready to fire. His face was white, but his hands were steady.

'Keep it pointed at that man,' said Craig in Spanish, so that there should be no misunderstanding, 'and if he moves pull the trigger and keep it pulled. He's a murderer and may have another gun on him.' Warne did as he was told.

Craig spoke to Santa Cruz. 'Put your hands behind your back.' He pulled his handkerchief from his pocket with his left hand.

'You won't get away with this, Craig. Ugh!' He felt a vicious stab from the muzzle of the gun in his back.

'I won't warn you again,' said Craig quietly. The man's hands came down and reached behind his back. Craig pushed the pistol into his pocket and tied the wrists together in a tight figure of eight. 'Now lie down, over there' — he pushed him — 'away from your murderous friend.'

Santa Cruz lay down, and Craig made the Indian do the same, after feeling over his body for a gun. But there was none. 'Stand away from them, and if *either* moves, spray them both. I've got to ring the base.'

He had reached the transmitter in the Land-Rover when he heard the noise of a truck wheezing its way up the road. Craig jumped down quickly, picked up the automatic pistol lying by Alfredo's dead body and covered the truck as it came to a stop on the edge of the hard. He could see two men in front, but the rear was hidden by the cab. With a sigh of relief he recognized Lopez.

The Deputy Manager opened the door and stepped down. He saw the two prostrate forms on the ground, the dead men, and the gun in Craig's hands, and cried angrily 'What the hell's been happening?'

'They've killed Rodriguez and Alfredo.'

'*Don Jorge* did that? He must have gone out of his mind.'

'Perhaps he has, but I'm taking no

chances. You'll have to get the truck off the road; it's blocking the other two cars. Will you do that, please? I've got to telephone to the base.'

He heard Lopez call out a command in Quechua and the truck began to move. Craig's foot was on the step of the Land-Rover when the truck stopped beside him.

Lopez said coldly, 'Turn round, Mr. Craig.'

He turned, and found a man leaning over the side of the truck, pointing a Schmeisser at him.

'Drop your gun,' shouted Lopez. Craig dropped it, cursing himself for having taken something for granted.

Another man leapt over the side of the truck and advanced towards Warne. He had an automatic in his hand.

'Get back,' cried Warne, swinging the gun to cover him.

'Don't be silly, Jack. If you don't drop it we'll have to fill Mr. Craig with lead.' He was a tall, pale-faced Chilean whom Warne knew well. After all, they had shared meals in the volunteers' mess.

'But *you* aren't one of them — ' he began.

'Drop it, Jack.' Warne threw a despairing glance at Craig, who nodded. The gun clattered to the ground.

Santa Cruz got to his feet, laughing. 'Will someone untie me? That was well-done, Paco. Where's Miguel?'

'He was still looking for the Irish girl when we left,' said Lopez.

Craig saw the startled look on Warne's face, and willed him to be silent. The boy said nothing.

'All right,' said Santa Cruz. 'Get a rope and tie them up.' With sudden viciousness he kicked Rodriguez' body, lying face down on the broken surface of the dam, in a pool of blood. 'You can drop them both in the overflow,' he said between his teeth. 'Soldiers don't deserve burial.'

# 10

## Thursday Afternoon

The plan to move the volunteers to the refuge had been postponed, and they were given lunch in the students' dining room. Some of the anger and frustration at being confined had passed, but they were still in no mood to be friendly with the remaining six members of Miguel's cell who, they had decided, were stool-pigeons.

'Why d'you think they've been put together with us?' shouted the Australian. 'I'll tell you why. Their job is to listen to what we say among ourselves and spill it all to Miguel. That's so, Helmut Springer, you rotten Kraut, isn't it?'

Springer said, 'No, it isn't. I don't care whether you believe us or not, but all we were planning to do was give help to some political refugees who are on the run in Brazil.'

'But you agreed to hold us as hostages, didn't you? Marisa blurted that out this morning.'

Helmut cast a withering glance at the weeping Italian girl. 'Yes. We did. But it seems we were only a screen for the real plot. I don't understand what's going on any more than you do. All I know is that Lopez and that capitalist swine Santa Cruz are involved, and I wouldn't work with them even if they asked me.'

There was a growl of disbelief from the others. 'You keep yourself and your Commie friends away from us, that's all I say,' said the Australian.

The door opened and Miguel came in. Half a dozen volunteers jumped from their benches and advanced on him, shouting, but the guards pushed them back with their rifle butts.

Miguel said, 'If you misbehave you won't get food. Now listen, all of you. You will be well cared for, and released as soon as our ultimatum to the Peruvian Government is accepted. And I can assure you it will be.'

Someone shouted 'How d'you know

this? They've probably got troops coming up the valley already.'

Miguel smiled. 'They wouldn't get far, because the road from Tambo has been blocked. In addition, they'll have another reason for doing what we say, and one that'll carry a lot more weight than the fate of a couple of dozen volunteers. In any case, we're going to move you to a place of safety, so that if there is any attempt at armed action you won't be in danger. Two trucks are waiting outside. You will go in one and the military police prisoners in the other. And don't think you'll have any chance of escape. Your baggage has been packed for you and is in the truck. All except shoes, which you'll collect later, together with those you're wearing now. Take them off and leave them here when you go out.'

'You think we can't run without them?' asked one of the volunteers scornfully.

'Not unless you want to get frost-bite,' answered Miguel. 'You're going to the silver mine, where you'll be quite comfortable and well-fed. You'll get your shoes back when you arrive there. If you try to escape from the mine' — he shrugged his shoulders — 'you'll be shot.'

* * *

From the window of the stone hut by the side of the dam Craig had watched, in an agony of frustration, the boats passing between the island and the camp which had been set up between the sluice and the parking place. The inflatable rubber boat had been used, and another that had been brought up on the truck. There seemed to be six men involved, as well as the two Indian drivers, and they had been rapidly set to work boring holes in the earth of the dam to sink the pipes they brought from the island. The boxes of explosives were broken open and charges lowered down the pipes, with detonators and cable attached. The ends of the cables all disappeared into the command tent, in which Santa Cruz had made his headquarters.

Craig had seen the man speaking for a long time into the microphone of the police radio in the Land-Rover. Then he had gone over to the Buick and pulled up a telescopic aerial from the wing of the car. For some time he sat in the station-wagon, talking into a microphone. When all this had been done Don Jorge had strolled away, lighting a cigar, to watch the operations on the dam.

It was two o'clock when the men broke off for lunch round a fire on the hard. Two billicans of hot stew and some bread were handed through the little window of the hut to Craig and Warne, whose hands had been freed. Later, the door opened and they were ordered out, ahead of the guard, and brought over to where Santa Cruz sat comfortably in a collapsible chair near his tent.

'Sit down, both of you,' he said cheerfully. 'Try those gelignite boxes; they're quite empty now.' They sat down. 'I don't bear you any ill-will, Craig. Why should I? Nor, indeed, to this young fool whose interference has forced me to bring forward my — er — operation by some six weeks. But don't count on my good humour, Warne. Answer my questions truthfully and promptly. That's all I ask.'

'You can jump in the bloody lake,' said Warne gruffly.

'Tell him what he wants to know, Jack,' said Craig. 'It'll do no harm now.'

'Thank you, Craig. You see, Mr. Warne, if you don't, there are men among my operatives who will get the truth out of you very painfully, but fast. And I don't include Miguel Cuevas, who has his own particular grudge. Don't worry. I'll see that he doesn't indulge it — provided you behave reasonably. He's organizing the removal of your fellow volunteers to a safe place, where they can't escape and can be easily guarded.'

'You've got control of the Centre then?' asked Craig. It would have given him a lot of pleasure to throw Santa Cruz into the ravine after the bodies of Rodriguez and Alfredo, but the first requirement was to find out exactly what was going on.

'Yes indeed. Some time after you left, so unexpectedly early, one of my mine trucks arrived from a place in the coastal plain, where the men in it had been hiding. They are Peruvian Tupamaros, all badly wanted by the Peruvian Government. The Brazilians arrive later. But tell me, why so early? You told us six o'clock.'

'We decided there would be light enough at five.'

'I see. And where did you find Warne?'

'Here.'

'Why did you go over to the island?'

'Warne had swum over to it two days ago, and had found the explosives.'

'What a very inquisitive young man you are, Warne. Now tell me, did you record certain conversations on this tape-cassette?' He pulled it out of his pocket?

Warne looked at Craig, who nodded. 'Yes, I did.'

'And you played it back, of course?'

'Yes, but most of it was in Quechua, and I didn't understand it.'

Santa Cruz looked startled. 'I know what was on that tape, but didn't you get it translated for you?'

'No. I just kept the tape.'

'You're lying, young man,' said Santa Cruz harshly. 'You understood enough to get a message to Lima and cause Mr.

Craig to be sent here to investigate.'

'I did not,' said Warne sullenly.

'He's not lying, Santa Cruz,' said Craig. 'I only came to the Centre because Warne was missing, and the Ambassador asked me to do so.'

'The excellent Mr. Townsend? He's a great friend of mine.' He changed his tone. 'What about the Spanish part of the tape, Warne? You could understand that.'

'It made no sense. Miguel and the others were talking about some plan to take refugees to a place of safety. That's all.'

Santa Cruz moved his shoulders, irritably. He looked disconcerted. 'Are you asking me to believe, Craig, that you knew nothing about this operation when you left the Centre this morning?'

'Yes. I could see that something funny was going on, but that's all. We decided, after hearing about the tape last night, that the first thing was to find Warne.'

'Something funny? You have a curious sense of humour. But no, I remember now. This is funny, peculiar — not just funny?'

'Yes.'

'And you did not telephone to Lima about it?'

'No. You can check that, of course.'

'Quite right. I did check, and found that neither you nor Warne had made any call. It puzzled me, just as it puzzled me that Warne should have gone off on his climbing expedition without a care on his mind, apparently, at the very time I thought he must have been expecting you, Craig. Did you just happen to be in Lima?'

'No. I was invited to give lectures to the Peruvian security services.'

'On guerrilla warfare,' said Santa Cruz, laughing.

'On counter-subversion generally.'

'My first reaction, when Rodriguez told me that story, was to laugh heartily. He asked me what I found amusing, and I had to invent some excuse. But when I heard that within a few hours of arriving in the Centre you and Rodriguez had arrested Cuevas, I began to think it was altogether too much of a coincidence. Do you tell me, Craig, that you knew nothing about the tape Warne had found until one of the volunteers told you about it last evening?'

'Nothing at all,' said Craig, lying. There was no need to mention Warne's letters to his mother; the boy was in enough trouble already.

'So the only reason to arrest Cuevas was because you found he'd been wounded?'

'And because of his manner when questioned.'

'So you bullied the Irish nurse into telling you the rest?'

Craig made no reply.

'I know police methods, you see,' continued Santa Cruz coldly. 'You seem to have frightened the girl silly. She ran away during the night, when her guard had left his post, and still hasn't been found.'

'The main evidence was the bullet marks in Cuevas' jeep.'

'All the same,' said Santa Cruz, reflectively, 'I'd like to know where she is now.'

Not half as much as I should, thought

Craig. Had she slipped into the lake? Or was she jut keeping her red head down?

'However,' said Santa Cruz, 'returning to your story, I am inclined to believe it. In fact, it seems we could have contained the whole situation if that hot-head Cuevas hadn't rushed off, without awaiting orders, to settle his account with Warne. Once he started showing off his Schmeisser machine-pistol the fat was, as you say, in the fire. Lopez tells me, Craig, that last night you accurately deduced that there was a real plot behind the façade. That was clever, and we did not want a full-scale investigation going on at the Centre, so we had to act . . . ' He extinguished his cigar and rose, stretching himself. 'Well, gentlemen, it's time for my siesta, and you must return to your hut. By all means relieve yourselves first, if you wish. The guard will accompany you to the bushes. Incidentally, I've given Lima twenty-four hours to make up their minds.'

'About what?'

'Ah, I forgot you didn't know,' said Santa Cruz carelessly. 'It's quite simple.

Unless they agree to my demands by noon tomorrow I shall take reprisals, of two kinds. One, the twenty-four volunteers whom I hold in custody will be liquidated one by one.' Warne half rose to his feet, but Craig thrust him down. 'That is the beauty of my plan,' continued Santa Cruz, his eyes glinting. 'No less than eight different countries are represented among those young people, and the fact that I am holding them to ransom will be in all the newspapers by now. I leaked the story to the representatives of Reuters and Agence Havas.'

'And what is your other reprisal?' asked Craig. The man was obviously willing to tell.

'I shall burst this dam, of course. The whole of the lower Chasco valley will be flooded and the town of Tambo, with its damned military base, will be swept away. I have no love for the military, as you may have observed.' He looked at Craig reproachfully. 'But you haven't asked me what I'm demanding.'

'I'm sure you'll tell me.

'Why not? For my Tupamaro friends,

without whose cooperation the whole plan would have been impossible, freedom to use this valley as a refuge and headquarters for their colleagues in all South American countries. For a period of six months. The work of this ridiculous Centre will continue, since it will make the Tupamaros independent of outside food supplies. At least, I shan't be here to see the mess they make of my valley, since I have asked for the funds I hold in Peruvian banks — *my* money, in fact — to be released from embargo and deposited in my Swiss account. Once that is done I'm quite willing to leave my country to go to the devil in its own way.' He yawned. 'The military have been told not to over-fly any part of this area and to let planes use my runway without interference. That will give the Brazilians a chance to land, and as for me, there are half a dozen places I can reach in my Cessna, with no questions asked.' He looked at Craig. 'So those are my terms. Can you blame me?' He sounded as if he really wanted to know Craig's opinion.

'Blame a man who plans to murder half

the population of the Chasco valley? Oh yes. I blame you all right.'

'My dear fellow, you've got it wrong. There has been full warning. And just in case the military haven't told the local inhabitants what is happening, I am about to have the sluicegate opened. That by itself won't cause damage to the dam, of course, owing to my family's foresight, but it'll send a big wave down the valley and warn the people to take refuge on higher ground. The military will be the ones to suffer if I should be forced to blow up the channel we have mined.' He pointed to the tops of the line of pipes which had been sunk vertically in the surface of the dam. Between this line and the flume was a narrow wedge of dam, its point towards the gorge.

'At the bottom of those pipes,' explained Santa Cruz, 'there is a total of three hundred kilos of gelignite, well tamped down. If I explode them — you see where the cables converge on my tent — the facing on the lake side of the dam will be breached and several feet of water will scour out a channel through the holes made by the other charges. Within an hour, I reckon, all the ground between the new channel and the flume will have been washed down into the gorge, the stone lining of the flume will be undermined and the wedge of impatient water remaining will, I calculate, burst the dam completely — in a most spectacular manner. The whole lake will empty into the Chasco valley.'

Warne burst out, 'You must be mad!'

'I am not mad. If the Lima Government will do what I want all will be well. No one will have been hurt. But if not — first the volunteers, one by one. Then the dam.'

'You don't imagine they can agree, do you?' asked Craig, desperately.

'Oh yes, I do. I hold the whip hand. If the Brazilians could release ninety prisoners — enemies of the regime, they were called — to set free one foreign diplomat, d'you suppose this Government is any tougher? They're both military regimes. The Lima gang will capitulate.'

'What happens to us?'

Santa Cruz smiled. 'I wondered when

you were coming to that. I'll release you, but not yet. Oh dear no! Two more hostages, after all, to spin out the agony. What I will do, however, is to put you both out of the way, just in case the Army attempt something foolish. You seem to like that island; well, you can have it. In fact, I'll see you're taken there at once. There are stores and blankets, so you won't freeze during the night. And you'll be well guarded.'

He laughed loudly, and there was a crazy look in his eyes that confirmed the suspicion in Craig's mind. 'If the worst comes, as you say, to the worst, you'll be able to *walk* ashore.' He shook with laughter, and took out his handkerchief to wipe his eyes. 'But if you do, be careful, I beg of you. There's fifty feet of water round the island, but even when that's gone — there's ten feet of mud underneath.'

* * *

It was late in the afternoon. 'He *must* be mad,' said Warne. They were sitting in the wooden hut on the island, with their backs to the wall. Their hands and feet were tied. The Indian driver who was acting as guard was outside, peering through the window every now and then to make sure they were not moving.

'Yes, I think he is, to some extent. But I think the device to burst the dam is feasible — and diabolical. If he'd wanted the lake to drain slowly, all he needed to do was blow up the flume and the facing, but this plan means he's determined to make the dam actually burst, for maximum effect. The Chasco bed simply couldn't take a flood of that size, and it'd spread up the valley and drown half your fields and plantations before it drained off. That's why he's used the aquasuit to place charges deep in the facing on the lake side of the dam.'

'But if he lets water through the sluice, won't that drain off a lot of lake water before mid-day tomorrow?'

'I'd guess he'll let it out for half an hour, say, and then lower the gate. Then repeat the operation from time to time to keep the people down below nervous, always expecting it's the real thing.'

'But it may not happen, may it? The Government will give in.'

'I don't see the Peruvians doing that,' said Craig thoughtfully. 'I agree we've heard no planes, so they're making it appear that they're willing to do part of what Santa Cruz asks. But I'd expect them to have a bash. But how? The terrain's so impossible for *coup de main* attacks.'

'What's that?'

'A small, very skilled party infiltrating into enemy H.Q. and knocking it out or capturing hostages. Like the attempt in Africa to kidnap Rommel.'

'There'd still be the volunteers.'

'Yes. He's divided his two forms of reprisal very neatly — one here and one at the 'safe place', where-ever that is.'

'I think I know where,' said Warne thoughtfully. 'The silver mine. You see, there's nowhere in the valley where you could hide a group of people, all probably shouting their heads off, if I know my friends, without someone finding out at once. But at the mine — '

'I think you've got it,' said Craig, breaking in, 'because Rodriguez said Santa Cruz had withdrawn the miners early. He said it was because of the rain last year that washed away part of the road before they could get the men down to the valley for the winter. But if you're right it was to clear the place so that they could house the volunteers there — and I suppose those M.P.s who were at the Centre when the putsch took place, if there're any left alive.'

'If we could get away from here,' said Warne, 'we might be able to warn the military.'

'We might. I'm going to try to unbind your wrists. Keep watching the window, and if you see any sign of the guard pull your hands away. Press your wrists together.'

It was no use. His fingers were numb from the tightness of his own bonds, and his teeth could get no grip.

Warne said, 'When he gives us food he'll have to untie us.'

'No, he won't. But it's worth trying.'

He called out, '*Amigo*, what about some food?'

The Indian's head appeared in the window. 'Wait,' he said tersely, and disappeared.

'He's chewing coca all the time,' said Warne. 'I hope it slows up his reflexes.'

'If he gets near enough I'm going to have a go. You agree we try?'

'Of course.'

'Good man. I think I'd better do it, because I've probably had more experience at this sort of thing. I shall want your help.'

'O.K.'

'If he comes in I'll try either to kick him in the crotch or butt him in the guts. Either way, if I connect, he won't be able to use his gun for a few seconds. That's where you jump on him — lie on top of him if you can, so that he can't roll out sideways. I'll only need a moment to grab his gun and hit him with it.'

Warne took a deep breath. 'Fine.'

When the Indian came in with two plates of tinned meat, however, he took no chances. He threw the door open, with the muzzle of his automatic pistol in front of him. He saw the two men sitting quietly against the wall on the rear side of the hut and relaxed. He put the plates on the floor near the door. Craig held out his hands, but the guard shook his head.

'You give him, he give you,' he said in broken Spanish.

'Wait,' said Craig. 'I've got to relieve myself.'

The Indian hesitated for a moment, then nodded. 'You outside, he stay.' He stood well back while Craig went out of the door, moving in little jumps, like a rabbit, and turned towards the nearest bush. The guard followed, grinning as he saw Craig's difficulties in getting his flies open. When the operation was finished Craig turned round and began to jump his way back. Then he stumbled.

It was a forlorn hope. He pitched forward and fell, near where the guard was standing. His arms went out and he caught the man's feet with his tied hands and pulled. But the Indian fell over backwards and rolled away, still holding his gun. When he scrambled to his feet he was hissing with rage. He rushed at Craig and kicked him on to his back. Then he reversed the gun and lifted it to bring the butt down on Craig's head.

There was an unearthly scream behind him. He swung round, and cowered at the sight of a weird shape against the silvery leaves of the buddleia bushes, a figure of shining black, with great black webbed feet and webbed hands outstretched towards him. He uttered a moan of terror and threw up his arms to cover his eyes, dropping the gun.

Warne acted fast. He had jumped his way through the door when he heard the scuffle and with one final awkward leap got his linked hands over the Indian's head and fell backwards, pulling the man on top of him. Craig was picking up the gun when he heard a sharp crack. One of the webbed hands had hit the guard's head with a stone the size of a large brick. He groaned and rolled over on to the sand.

'My God,' said Warne, still lying on his back. 'It's you, Irish.'

'It is that,' said Janet.

'Untie my hands,' cried Craig, throwing the gun out of reach and sitting down on the back of the prostrate Indian.

'Wait a moment.' She raised the stone again.

'Hold it!' shouted Warne. 'You don't want to kill him, do you?'

'Why not? It's what he was trying to do to the fuzz. But don't worry. They've got skulls of iron, these boys.'

'No, give me the stone. And for God's sake untie our hands.'

She had strong, capable fingers and the two men were freed before the Indian came to his senses. He opened his eyes, but one glance at the black figure bending over him, with red hair streaming in the evening breeze, was enough, and he closed them again, moaning.

They tied him up and carried him into the hut, propping him against a wall. 'Did anyone see you, Janet?' asked Craig.

'No. I didn't dare risk the swim until it was nearly dark.' She had stripped off the flippers and the webbed gloves, and unzipped the aquasuit, appearing in her sweater and slacks. 'I'm going to be bloody cold; I had to leave the poncho in the bushes on the other side. And I'm starved.' She saw the plates on the floor and picked one up.

Warne said he would look for more food, and ran out into the growing dusk.

'You're a brave girl, Irish,' said Craig. 'You kept your head down all day?'

'Holy Mother! I did so. I was watching you rowing that boat back, and wondering why Jack signalled to me to walk. Pretty inconsiderate I thought, seeing how awkward that damned suit was to carry through the bushes. It's not as if there was a bloody path along the shore. But I was on my way, when I heard the shouts.' She stopped to pick up the wooden spoon and attack the meat with it. 'I dropped the suit and crept nearer, and saw them collar you and tie you up. I knew they'd do the same to me if I uttered a squeak, so I went back and hid. Then I saw that when they brought you to the island they only left one guard with you, so I thought I'd try and do him.'

'Bless you!' Craig brought one of the blankets and draped it around her shoulders, while she continued to eat, ravenously. Warne came back with a pan of highly scented stew. 'He had a fire out there, and I've put on a can of water. We'll have coffee.' He took down a tin from the shelf where there was a stock of packaged food. 'Are you O.K., Janet?'

'Yes, love. Feeling a lot better. Can I eat the other plateful?'

'It's all yours. We'll have the stew.' He looked at Craig. 'What do we do now?'

'Will one of you tell me what it's all about?' asked the girl.

'Jack'll tell you. I'm going to have a recce.' Craig went out and walked past the smouldering fire and up on to the ridge that ran along the back of the island. As he came towards the dam end he was aware of a glow ahead, and when he peered through the bushes on the bluff above the shore he could see the headlights of a car trained on the island, no doubt so that if the Indian had wanted to signal for any reason he would be seen from the dam. The glare prevented Craig from seeing other lights, but he felt sure that there would be sentries taking duty in shifts. He returned to the hut, picking up the billy-can of water and some tin mugs and spoons as he went. He thought it best to make plenty of noise as he approached the door, but it made not the slightest difference. Warne and the girl were sitting on the floor, wrapped in each other's arms, and oblivious of all else.

'Coffee,' he called, and they disengaged, blinking at him happily. The girl got up to make coffee, while Craig opened tins of meat, biscuits and butter. 'You and I had better eat something, as well as that stew,' said Craig to Warne.

'What about me?' said Janet indignantly. 'I'm still hungry.'

'You'd better not have any more, after fasting all day.'

'She's got a digestion like a horse,' said Warne affectionately. 'It's well known, isn't it, Irish?' She aimed a playful blow at him.

'All right, then. And we'll talk while we eat. That may slow her down a bit. Did you have time to tell her about the gelignite, Jack?'

'Roughly. What I forgot is something

that's been on my mind. D'you remember Santa Cruz saying he had twenty-four volunteers to hold as hostages?'

'So he did. What's odd about that?'

'Well, we were thirty, all told. Take away me and Irish, and Miguel, and the rest of his group — that's nine. And there was the Chilean who came to the dam in Lopez' truck, and probably other volunteers who were in the know, or they'd never have been able to take the Centre by surprise. So how does he make twenty-four?'

'You're right. It's just what I thought.' Craig turned to the girl. 'Your cell was just a front, except for Miguel. Santa Cruz was counting you and the other members of your group among the hostages.'

'So Miguel played us all for suckers, did he? I know you said so, but I didn't believe you. Wait till I get my hands on that bastard!'

Warne was counting on his fingers. 'Thirty, less Miguel, less me, less twenty-four. It makes four volunteers who formed a sort of separate cell. Then he's got some of the Indians, we know that, and the Tups who arrived in the truck, and of course Lopez, blast him!'

'And a bunch of Brazilians due to arrive by plane,' said Craig. 'It adds up to a lot of chaps. But remember they'll have to divide their forces — quite a number to keep order at the Centre and watch the Tambo road, then others at the mine — if your idea is right — and at the dam. How many did you see at the dam?'

'About six, and two drivers — including this one. We can't take on that lot, can we?'

'No, we can't, unless we can catch them completely by surprise. We've only got one weapon, this man's machine pistol. And in any case there's no boat.'

'We've got the aquasuit,' said Warne thoughtfully.

Janet had been listening to them with rising apprehension. 'Listen, both of you. Why can't we just stay here? We've got food and warmth, and a gun to scare people off with — we could remain here for days, and they couldn't touch us. If they sent a boat to fetch us we could sink it before it got anywhere near.'

'We can't let Santa Cruz get away with it,' said Warne firmly.

'Oh *men*!' she cried impatiently. 'Why the hell can't you let Santa Cruz carry out his plan? The Government will give in. He's got all the cards. Now if we could get ashore — somehow — couldn't we make it over the mountains and down into the Callejon de Huaylas?'

'I could,' said Warne, 'but it'd be too tough for you two, without climbing boots or anything. Anyway, you're talking nonsense, love. We can't let him open the valley for all the Tupamaros to use as a rest camp.'

'Why not? They're fighting for freedom.'

'Balls! Miguel's a Tupamaro, and you've seen how twisty he is. They're out for themselves. Half of them are just gangsters, raiding banks — '

'They only do that when they need the money,' she retorted, pushing out her lower lip.

'Oh my God, won't you ever learn? That's what all criminals say — 'Sorry, I had to knock the old lady down. I needed the money.' '

They were looking at each other, hackles raised and Craig intervened. 'Let's keep politics out of this. What seems more serious about Santa Cruz's plan is that it may backfire.'

'What d'you mean?' said Janet, still staring angrily at Warne.

'I think he's slightly round the bend. There was a wild gleam in his eyes when he was talking about flooding the valley. He's not doing all this just to help the Tupamaros.'

'I know,' said Warne. 'That's what he said. He wants to get his money back.'

'But even more, he wants to get his revenge on the military.' Craig paused. 'I wouldn't put it past him to try to blow the dam in any case.'

Warne thought for a moment. 'You may be right. All those elaborate preparations, so carefully worked out. He sounded — you're right, there was a sort of loving relish in his voice when he was talking about them. But — well, it's difficult to think someone could really intend, whatever happened, to ruin all the work that's gone into making the Chasco valley what it is.'

'But damn it!' cried the girl, exasperated. 'He'd have no excuse. As I said, the Government's bound to give in.'

'Are they? I'm not so sure. They're a very tough and capable body of men, and I don't see them giving in easily. Then Santa Cruz might try something, and I'm scared of what he might do.'

Warne turned to the girl. 'He said he'd liquidate the hostages one by one, if the Peruvians didn't surrender.'

'Mary Mother of God, you didn't tell me that! I suppose you must be right. No true freedom-fighter would kill people of our age, we're the ones who support them.'

Wisely, Warne held his tongue. Craig said, 'I'm afraid that's just what has been planned, to bring maximum foreign pressure on the Government. In theory, the blowing of the dam is the last resort.'

'Well, then,' said Janet. 'We've got to stop them.' The Indian groaned, and she sprang to her feet. 'Oh God, I forgot the crack I gave him. I'd better have a look.' She fetched water and sponged the swelling on his forehead. 'It's O.K.'

'Coca,' said the man beseechingly. '*En la borsa*.'

'He just wants a chew,' she said, and began searching his pockets. She brought out a small gourd of white powder and a leather pouch of coca leaves.

'You're not going to let him have it?' asked Craig, horrified.

'Of course I am. He's been used to it all his life and it'll ease the pain. Without it he'd get desperate. They have a tremendous capacity for this stuff.' She dipped several leaves in the powder, and put them into the Indian's mouth. He began to chew slowly, and a bittersweet smell spread through the room. 'He'll be happy now for hours,' she said, re-joining the two men. She yawned. 'I'm sleepy.'

The air was now bitingly cold, and they lay close to each other, hugging their blankets. 'We'd better get some sleep, I agree,' said Craig, 'because I don't see we can do anything until morning. But first, let's work out a plan. Our object is to remove the danger of exploding the dam. So, either we have to take the men down there by surprise, or at least remove the charges from the pipes.'

'Oh, fine,' said Warne, 'but how?'

'The first thing is to get ashore without being seen. Someone will have to come here with the boat tomorrow morning to relieve the guard.' He looked at the Indian, beatifically chewing his cud. 'He probably won't tell us when it'll be.'

'That's easy,' said the girl. She went across to the guard, who was stretching out his bound hands towards the pouch of coca leaves, and took it away from him. 'When do they come for you?' she asked him.

He said nothing, but his eyes strayed to the coca pouch. She put it into her pocket. '*Pues?*'

'*A los cinco y meia,*' he muttered. She gave him one leaf from the pouch.

'Our sadistic friend,' said Craig, 'has the answer. Half past five. We'll take turns, Jack and I, to keep watch. He may be double-crossing. When they come for him we'll jump them, but where we can't be seen from the shore. I'll leave you two to get some sleep — and I mean sleep,' he added, grinning. 'I'll take the first three hours and will try to work out something. At least we'll get the boat and another gun, I hope. Sleep well.'

* * *

The pilot of the old Dakota was a young Brazilian from Porto Alegre, who had done his military service in the Airforce. Behind him sat eighteen men in their early twenties, bound together — like him — by the Tupamaro oath and the shared experience of many bank raids, a successful attack on a prison in Goias, the blowing up of an army depot in the Mato Grosso and — most satisfying of all — the swopping of a Paraguayan consul for eleven of their friends in a Rio gaol. But the heat had been on for the past three months and their nerves were on edge; some had died or been captured by the Brazilian special security forces, others had been too sick to move and many of the men who had boarded the plane on the jungle airstrip near the Purus river were disillusioned and quarrelsome. The Cause was no longer what it had been.

The co-pilot who acted as navigator appeared through the cockpit door. 'We're over Peru, boys,' he cried, and they cheered and shouted their Portuguese slogans. Anything was better than that long head-hunt through jungle and savannah which some had suffered in the Mato Grosso before they could make the rendezvous.

The plane had been hidden for two weeks by the side of the airstrip, covered over with branches and bamboo fronds, while they had planned and carried out the raid on the small airport of Boca do Acre for the fuel they needed and brought it back through the jungle trails in a stolen truck. The Brazilian troops had missed them by only an hour, and they'd had to hide the truck and sweat out days of damp heat and plagues of insects. One man had died of snake-bite and three of the others were still recovering from malaria.

They looked out of the windows eagerly at the dark green floor of trees a few hundred feet below. Six hundred miles to go, with just enough fuel to do it. The plane flew on through the short twilight, then the dark, until the moon rose and the pilot could see the great rivers flowing north to join up and form the Amazon. The Ucayali, then the steep climb over the Cordillera Azul, the white water of the Huallaga and finally the Maranon. The plane still held the heavy, sweet air of the jungle, but the heat had dissipated and it needed all the warmth the engines could supply to keep out the bitter cold. The men, accustomed to night temperatures of ninety degrees, huddled in their blankets.

The navigator saw the moon glinting again on a high ridge of snow peaks, and at last made contact with the transmitter in the Casa Grande. The pilot flew slowly over the last range and began to circle, straining his eyes to distinguish between the twinkling lights far below. Suddenly, there was a rectangle of illumination, and as he came lower he could see the headlights shining across the airstrip. He glanced at his fuel indicator, made a dummy run over the Casa Grande and its little hangar, and up again to turn before landing.

It was a bumpy strip for a plane the size of the Dakota, and it bounced badly before the brakes took hold and brought it to a shuddering stop at the extreme end of the field, just before the trees. The pilot sat still for a minute, his hands trembling.

The navigator glanced at him. He could hear the other Tupamaros shouting excitedly behind the half-closed door. He put his hand on the pilot's shoulder, and squeezed gently. '*E terminado*, Joaquim. *Agora vamos*.'

But Joaquim Freitas didn't move. He was thinking, 'It *isn't* over. This is just the beginning of exile. We'll never go back.' He thought longingly of lush green fields, his favourite horse, the full life he had left at his father's ranch in Rio Grande do Sul to join the Airforce. Afterwards he had lingered in Rio, learning how not to be spotted as a provincial, meeting girls who gave themselves laughing, unlike the buxom, well-protected young women of the South. And the talk in the students' cafes — grand, effervescent stuff, dreams of an ideal world once youth had taken over.

The first year of his life as a Tupamaro had been satisfying enough, and exciting — the training, the clandestine meetings, the first dangerous clashes with the police, successful attacks and mounting publicity — but afterwards the spark had gone out, and it became the life of outlaws. The members of the movement who were hidden in ministries, the professions and local government did their best to help their friends on the run, but they couldn't prevent the police net tightening or facilitate escape to another region. The attacks went on, but the ideological motive was missing; they robbed a bank to get money to live on, to survive, not to help the poor or plan a bold piece of political blackmail. The quarrels had grown more bitter.

'Joaquim! *Che cousa ha? Vamos!*'

And now it had come to this. Strangers in a very strange, cold land, unable to speak the language except haltingly. With the prospect of leaving again for some other refuge as soon as this became too hot to hold them.

Wearily, he took off the brakes and revved his port engine to make the turn.

A crowd of men ran towards the Dakota as it taxied to a stop by the hangar. The Brazilians opened the door and jumped down one by one into the frigid air. There was a buzz of voices in Spanish and Portuguese.

In the background a silent line of dark, expressionless Indian faces stared at the newcomers.

# 11

## Friday Morning

Between two and five in the morning Craig again stood on guard. A brilliant moon had risen during his first watch, and he'd spent some time exploring the island. But there was nothing which could conceivably form the basis of a raft except the hut itself, which was strongly bolted together at the corners and strengthened with angle irons. Without spanners there was no hope of unscrewing the bolts.

So it would have to be the boat. But if one, or at most two men rowed out to relieve the guard, how would it look when *three* people were aboard when it returned to the dam? The girl had made it clear that she wasn't going to be left on her own again. And even if he got over that difficulty, surely someone would see and recognize them before they landed, and raise the alarm? He evolved a plan.

Then, feeling fresher after three hours' sleep, he turned his thoughts to what was happening elsewhere, trying to put himself in the place of the military strategists in Lima. They had until mid-day to fulfil their side of the bargain, if it was to be accepted. That meant continuing to ban flights over the Chasco valley, allowing free movement for planes arriving and leaving the little airstrip, and transferring the contents of Santa Cruz' Peruvian bank accounts to the Swiss bank he had nominated. As for aerial reconnaissance there had been no sound of planes overhead all the previous day, so the Government was giving the impression of playing ball. But would they not try something? He thought they would.

During meetings with the groups of officers to whom he had given his lectures he had met several impressive young men from the Ranger units, trained to track down guerrilleros in the jungle, where some scattered relicts of the extremist M.I.R. and F.L.P. were still holding out.

But this terrain, sixteen thousand feet up, was another matter. He recalled a remark by Rodriguez to Alfredo, when they were talking about the rock called the Jaguar: 'So you were trying for the Mountain Battalion?' It sounded as if the Peruvian Army had made provision for mountain operations.

* * *

They had. It was three o'clock in the morning at the temporary headquarters of the Mountain Battalion in the Callejon de Huaylas, near where the town of Yungay had been entombed by the avalanche in 1970. In one of the re-built houses the Adjutant was talking to an officer in the white and grey battle-dress of the Battalion. He had his finger on a large scale map of the area surrounding the Chasco valley on the other side of the Cordillera.

'Your men left at eighteen hundred hours, and you reckon they should be on the Chopicalqui shoulder by dawn?'

'Yes, sir. I shall be dropped by

helicopter to join them as soon as they signal their arrival. They will camp in the tents I shall bring with me, eat, and sleep for two hours. We should have reached our position above the dam by nine o'clock'

'Tell me again what you will aim to do then.'

'Rest the men for half an hour and feed them, without showing smoke. A patrol of picked men will then approach the southern end of the Llanga dam and observe what is happening. They will be dressed as mountain *cholos*, with Indian balaclavas, ponchos and woollen trousers. If challenged' — he swallowed — 'they will run away.'

'Correct.' The Adjutant lit a cigarette. 'What then?'

'Return to the Company H.Q., which by then will be located half-way down from the col, and report. A message will be sent to you, *mi Mayor*, and we'll await orders.' He hesitated. 'I shall lead the patrol.'

The Adjutant smiled. 'Who says so?'

'I should like to do that, sir. I know

the area well and am an experienced mountain-climber. My second-in-command, Lieutenant Passos, is a responsible officer, as you know, and quite capable of taking over if necessary.'

'All right, Captain Mendieta. I agree. You understand that if the alarm were raised it would be disastrous. Your patrol's first task is reconnaissance — no more. What d'you think of these?' He picked up a series of aerial photographs. 'Taken yesterday afternoon at twenty thousand feet through a gap in the clouds. The pilot couldn't risk getting nearer, for fear of being spotted, but he had the sun behind him, which helped. Santa Cruz made no mention of it when he spoke to the Tambo base later. The noise of the water escaping over the sluice probably drowned that of the plane.'

The first photograph showed drifting clouds, through which there were glimpses of the white shoulder of a mountain sloping down to a lake on one side and a narrow ravine on the other, with a road. The next print was a blow-up of the end of the lake, showing the dam and the white line of the flume crossing it to disappear in a patch of mist at the head of the gorge. On the dam were several vehicles close together at the southern side, and two tents. The Adjutant picked up a magnifying glass.

'If you look here' — he pointed with a pencil — 'you'll see some round dots, between the truck and the tents, and there are lines — here — connecting the dots with the smaller tent. We assume those are cables joining the buried charges with the command tent. Inside that tent, which of course is your main objective, Santa Cruz will have an exploder. It could be the old-fashioned kind with a handle which you depress, or one using a battery with a transformer and a switch. Those are the things to go for, if you get a chance. Santa Cruz can come afterwards. Throw those in the lake and half his ultimatum falls to the ground.'

'But what about the other half, sir? The volunteers?'

'Yes. The volunteers. There's been a lot

of pressure on the Government from abroad but we've made no promises. Nevertheless, the President himself has said that no action must be taken by your Company unless you can be sure of doing two things at once — liquidate the explosive mechanism *and* capture Tupamaros. We want as many as possible, and alive. Santa Cruz, if possible. Then we can bargain for the lives of the volunteers. I wish to God I knew where they were.' He looked up at the tense face of Captain Mendieta. 'Is all this clear?'

'Yes, sir. One point.'

'What is it?'

'The narrow ravine on the other side of the shoulder, with a road running up it. Where does it go?'

'To a silver mine at the head of the ravine. You can't see the buildings because the cloud's in the way.' He looked up. 'Why d'you ask?'

'I wondered whether that's where the volunteers have been taken.'

'It could be. But you see, there's no sign of movement on the stretch of road we can see in the print. Jesus Maria! The hostages could be anywhere. That's why we've got to gamble on getting Tupamaro prisoners and using them as bargaining counters. All right. You know the orders, but I'll repeat the gist of them. You will not engage the enemy without first reporting to me and getting my agreement. If you form a plan of attack it must include the capture of Tupamaros as well as the destruction of the exploder. You can be sure that according to what proposals you make I will give you as much freedom of action as possible. That will do, Mendieta. *Vai con Dios*!'

Mendieta grinned. 'It looks as if I'll need Him, *mi Mayor*.' He saluted and went out into the freezing cold of the night.

* * *

There were streaks of orange light on the clouds and the shapes of the mountains were edged with gold. Warne was with Craig when they saw, from the cover of the shrubs among which they were lying, the bright yellow blotch of the inflatable boat moving towards them across the calm water of the lake. There was only one man in it, as they could see when he came closer. He was still a hundred yards away when the two wormed their way backwards until they were out of sight. They heard him hauling the boat up the beach and the crunch of his shoes on the shingle. Warne remained concealed behind a quenuala bush and Craig stood inside the hut, behind the open door. The coca-chewing Indian had been gagged and covered with a blanket. The girl lay by him, also swathed in blankets, with her auburn hair covered.

It was all over very quickly. Seeing, as he expected, two figures on the floor of the hut, the guard stepped inside to look for his friend. Craig's right hand, with the thumb stuck out at right-angles to tighten the karate edge, struck him at the side of the neck, hard.

Five minutes later Warne, dressed in black rubber, was ready. Craig looked at their young, cheerful faces, and wondered whether he had the right to risk their lives. 'I've told you,' he said, 'that it's a pretty forlorn hope, taking possession of that camp against a bunch of armed men, and in daylight. The only thing we've got working for us are surprise, the fact that they're apparently still sleeping and the fire-power of two machine-pistols, which is considerable. All the same, you don't have to go along with me — '

'Listen to the heroic fuzz,' said the girl, affectionately. 'Don't be silly. I've told you, you're not going to leave me alone again, and it's no use trying to persuade Jack to be sensible. I've tried.'

'I'll get going,' said Warne, drawing a deep breath. He picked up his gun, walked down to the shore and let himself in without a splash, swimming away under water and coming up from time to time to breathe. The girl stood watching anxiously until he landed, and when she turned to Craig there were tears in her eyes.

'You've got a nerve,' she said bitterly, 'risking his life for a crazy plan like this.' She rubbed her eyes with her sleeve. 'But don't worry. I shan't let you down. I hope.' She smiled at Craig, uncertainly.

He took her arm and led her back to the hut.

They left the coca leaves and lime-gourd for the two Indians, both tightly bound, and went out, locking the door. 'They'll release each other in time, if they want to,' said Craig, as they made their way to the boat, 'but the window's too small to get through, so they'll be stuck there for quite a while. It was a good idea of yours to leave the coca handy.'

'I'm scared,' she said. 'You know that?'

'So am I. Anyone who goes into action without being scared is a fool. And this bit of action is damned tricky. Now listen again. This is what we've got to do.'

* * *

When Jack landed, the sun had not yet reached the lake and there was still the thin mist lying just above the water. He felt sure he couldn't have been seen from the dam. He stripped off the aquasuit and put on his shoes, which he had kept dry inside it. Then he pulled the plug of torn handkerchief out of the muzzle of the

Schmeisser and held the gun upside-down. No drops came out. He worked the lever, and the first of twenty-eight rounds slid into the breach.

His face was stiff with cold, but he rubbed it warm and tested his leg muscles. He took up the automatic pistol, pushed back the safety-catch and began to walk towards the dam, pushing his way through the thin screen of trees. Across four hundred yards of water he could see from time to time the yellow blur of the boat in the mist. It was zig-zagging about from side to side and aiming generally at the far side of the dam, near where the great landslide swept down from the high crags to water level.

It had been Janet's idea that Craig should steer a wavy course, to give the impression that he was high on coca. He was wearing the Indian guard's woollen cap, with its earflaps, and his poncho. The girl was out of sight, lying in the bottom of the boat under a blanket.

Jack came to the last turn of the lake shore and peered round a low bluff. Thirty yards away was the hard turning area at the near end of the dam, with the stone hut, then the Land-Rover and the Buick and finally the truck. Beyond were two tents, a long one for the Tupamaros and a small one for Santa Cruz, which lay only about thirty yards from the sinister line of pipe tops appearing out of the surface of the dam. Further away still he could see the flume, with its plank bridge, and in the distance the stony debris at the foot of the slide, to which Craig was heading.

He listened, and realized that the sluice gate had been lowered for the night, partly to conserve water and partly to stop the noise. He drew back and climbed through the trees until he came out on top of the little cliff, where he lay down and poked the muzzle of the gun forward through the branches of a juniper bush. It was sparse cover, but he would only need it for a very short time.

Craig had said there would probably be two guards, one patrolling the dam and the other watching the end of the road as it came up the gorge. Warne could only see one, who was now walking across the bridge towards the slide. The man was shouting something, probably asking the drunken boatman what he meant by landing so far from the camp. Craig waved his arms excitedly, and let the boat hit the dam with a bump. The guard continued to walk towards him, and was just behind Craig as he turned back to pull the boat up on the beach.

The man was taken completely by surprise. Craig had whirled round and caught him with his fist on the side of the jaw before he could move his gun. It was a clean knockout, and before the guard came to he had Janet sitting on his back, tying his arms together with a rope brought from the hut.

Craig was already running across the bridge towards the command tent. On the other side, a hundred yards away, he saw a man emerging from among the parked cars, and prayed that Warne could see him, too. He did. There was a crisp, short rattle of automatic fire, and the man fell.

Craig knew that all hell would break loose in a moment, but he ran to the smaller tent, jerked the flies open — and stopped short. The tent was quite empty. No Santa Cruz, and worse still, no exploder. The wires from the charges ended in neatly labelled terminals on a wooden board which lay on top of a packing case. There was a sudden loud racket of fire outside, and Craig dropped to the ground and peered through the tent door.

The Tupamaros were used to early morning alarms. Within five seconds of wakening to the crack of Warne's gun each man had seized the knife that lay by his side and slashed a rent in the tent's wall. Jack had turned his Schmeisser on the larger tent, but he couldn't bring himself to fire at sleeping men. As he watched, hesitating, they burst out in all directions, and at that long range it was impossible to pick them off. He fired a long burst, fanning the gun, and saw one man fall. Another, unaware of Craig's presence, ran towards the command tent. A bullet took him in the chest, and he fell at Craig's feet.

The other two Tupamaros seemed to

have vanished, and what had happened to Santa Cruz?

The soft rock of the cliff on which Warne was lying suddenly seemed to explode under his body, as two bursts of automatic fire found their mark. A flying stone hit him on the head, and he felt himself slipping. There came again the thud of heavy-calibre bullets smashing into the little cliff, and it collapsed like a house of cards. He pitched forward and slid down to hit the beach below with his head. He was unconscious when the two Tupamaros ran, crouching, to snatch the gun from his outstretched hand and twist his arms behind his back.

Craig saw it happen, but dared not fire for fear of hitting Warne. He groaned in desperation, and stooping down seized a handful of the cables where they entered the tent, trying with all his strength to pull them out of the pipes. But they wouldn't give. The earth rammed down hard on top of the charges took care of that. He heard Santa Cruz' voice.

'Drop your weapon and put up your hands, Craig. If not they'll kill you.'

Craig took a quick look round the corner of the tent. There was a single crack, and a bullet buzzed past him. The shot had come from the Buick, he thought, but his line of fire was being blocked by the truck, which had moved out and was coming towards him. He fired two bursts, one through the windscreen and the other straight into the radiator. There was another rattle of fire from behind the Buick, and as he threw himself to the ground he heard again that vicious buzz. But the truck had stopped.

A frenzied shriek broke out behind him, recognizably Janet's. 'Not that, too,' he groaned, and turned his head. The guard whom he had knocked out was carrying the girl in his arms across the bridge. He looked at Craig, grinning, and made as if to throw her into the flume, and Craig knew he was beaten. He dropped the automatic pistol and got to his feet, raising his hands. Someone was coming up behind him — and he knew nothing more. This time, they were taking no chances.

* * *

It was eight o'clock, and the sun burned down fiercely on the sweating faces of the men descending in file the steep slope of the col, between the steel-blue ice buttresses. Suddenly, the leading man dropped sideways on to the snow, unslinging his gun. Ahead, he saw a figure appearing from behind an overhanging serac, someone who was crawling up the slope on hands and knees, and who seemed not to hear the scrunch and squeak of boots on the hard-packed snow until he was surrounded. Then he lifted a ravaged face, screwing up his unprotected eyes. It was a young man in jeans and a striped poncho, and his feet seemed to be clothed in frozen snow.

'Who are you, *hijo*?' asked Mendieta gently. He used his hand to shade the man's eyes. They stared at him sightlessly.

'Helmut Springer. German volunteer. The others are in the silver mine. I escaped. I can't see you, only snow.'

A vacuum flask of hot soup was held to his lips and he drank eagerly. Then he lay back and began to mutter sleepily in German. Mendieta shook him. 'Don't go to sleep,' he ordered sharply, and turned to one of the men. 'Get his shoes off and massage his feet. They'll be frost-bitten. And put a bandage over his eyes.' He held the flask again to the blistered lips. 'Listen, *hijo*. We are going to release the hostages. Where are they?'

'In the mine dormitory, back at the ravine. All the windows are barred except in the lavatory, because there's a deep drop there.' His face contorted as the blood began to flow again in his feet and legs. For a time he could only groan. Then he said, 'I'm a climber. I got down the soil pipe and into the ravine. Then up the other side. I was trying to get across into the Callejon.'

Madre de Dios, thought Mendieta, the boy must have been desperate. He knew nothing of the build-up in Springer's mind during the long cold night, when the thought of having to see again the contempt in his friends' eyes and the triumph in those of Miguel had left him with only one wish, to get away at any cost.

'We'll take you to the Callejon,' said Mendieta quietly, 'but on a stretcher. Signaller!'

'*Mi Capitan*?' The man had already taken his transmitter from his pack.

'Use the emergency signal to get Base.' He turned to Lieutenant Passos, who had brought blankets. 'That's it, hombre. Get him comfortable, but don't let him sleep. There's a lot more I want him to tell me.' He pulled a map out of the pocket of his anorak and began to study it

* * *

The Adjutant sat in his Callejon headquarters listening to Mendieta's report. He tapped the map in front of him with his pencil.

'Hang on, Mendieta. I must speak to Lima first.'

Crouched in the snow, with the receiver clamped to his ear, Mendieta heard the Adjutant's voice speaking on the other radio. He grinned ruefully, imagining the

Chief of Staff in his great panelled office in Lima, directing other people's fates. The Adjutant came on the line again.

'Mendieta? Can you hear me strongly? Good. I have G.H.Q.'s agreement for my plan, which is this. You will split our two sections. You will lead one to the mine valley, choosing the best route you can devise. Get as much information as you can from Springer and send him back here for treatment with two bearers. Take the mining camp by surprise. There will probably be only a few guards there. Signal your success and we'll send an aircraft to pass over the lake at two thousand feet. The other section, under Lieutenant Passos, will take no action until they see the plane. They will then attack the men holding the dam with massive fire, using a diversion tactic if possible, to catch the enemy by surprise. They will neutralize the explosive devices, take prisoners for use as hostages and report success by radio.'

'It *sounds* easy, *mi Mayor*,' said Mendieta.

'There is no need to be sarcastic,

Captain. Listen, Mendieta. I know, and so does the Chief of Staff, that we are setting you an extremely difficult task. But there's no time for you to reconnoitre, report back, receive further orders and so on. The ultimatum expires at noon, and this man Santa Cruz seems crazy enough to do anything. So you'll have to carry out this plan to the best of your ability, of which I think highly. You have freedom to interpret the plan in any way you like, as long as the result is the same. Is that clear?'

'Yes, *mi Mayor*, and — er — thank you. There's only one thing.'

'Tell me.'

'I doubt whether we shall be able to make radio contact with you either at the dam or in the mine valley. The mountains will be in the way.'

'I agree. That is the point in sending up the aircraft, so that Passos can be in no doubt of the timing for his attack. When you capture the mine, if you cannot signal to me show a V sign in the centre of the compound — big, so that the plane can spot it from high altitude. I don't like showing our hand before it's time, but we'll have to risk the plane being seen by the enemy. O.K.?'

'Yes, sir.'

'Good luck.'

'Just a moment, sir. You said Passos could use massive fire at the dam. That will mean casualties.'

'Right. As long as you get some Tupamaros alive. We still have to liberate the Centre. But you can take it that everyone there is an enemy. We assume Craig and Rodriguez must have been taken prisoner when they took over the Centre.'

* * *

At eight o'clock Lieutenant Passos and his section were hidden in the scrub a thousand feet above the dam, resting after the long scramble down the snow and shale slopes. He called his sergeant and made him squat down beside him.

Sergeant Huaman was a short, broad-shouldered man with the dark skin and deep chest he had inherited from his

Indian father and the cheerful optimistic grin of his mother, a *chola* from Cajamarca.

'I want you to listen carefully, Huaman, because the job I'm going to give you is vital to the success of the operation.'

'Senor.'

'In a few minutes I shall move down with the rest of the Section until we are hiding just above the dam I showed you on the map. Our aim is to attack as soon as we see a plane above the lake, and take possession of the dam. But it has to be done very quickly, using the element of surprise, because there is a man down there who is planning to blow up the dam and flood the whole of the lower part of the Chasco valley, including Tambo. It would be a great disaster.'

'*Claro, mi Tenente*.'

'Right. Now what I want you to do is create a diversion. You've heard me speak about this tactic in my lectures. If *you* can attract the rebels who are on guard away from where the rest of us are waiting *we* shall have a better chance of seizing the tent from which we believe the explosive charges are fired.' He looked anxiously at Huaman's impassive face. 'That means I want you to pretend to attack from the other side.'

'There is a gorge between, senor. And the only bridge is at the dam itself, according to the map.'

'Precisely. You'll have to get across the gorge lower down and work your way up the opposite bank without being seen.'

Huaman pushed back his Indian cap and scratched his head. 'It shouldn't be difficult. There won't be much water at this time of year.'

'I'm afraid you're wrong. There may be a sizeable torrent in the stream bed. The flood-gate was opened yesterday, and it may still be letting through a lot of water.'

The Sergeant's dark face was split in an enormous grin. 'Two ice-axes, senor, and a lot of rope.'

'Good man! You'll need your axes anyway. The gorge looks to be very narrow and deep. Pick two men to go with you. Now remember, Sergeant. You must on no account be seen, or take any action against the enemy until you spot that aircraft. By then, with any luck, you'll be in position on the other side of the dam, but we shan't move until you start firing. Try to lure them across the dam, thinking there's only one of you.'

'How many of them are there, senor?'

'We just don't know. That's a risk we've got to take.'

An hour afterwards the little patrol reached the road half a mile below the dam, and five minutes later they stood twenty feet above the boiling torrent, penned in by steep banks. On the other side, eight feet away, small trees grew thickly, protected from the wind.

Huaman tied together the two axes so as to form a grapnel, attached the end of his climbing rope and made a cast. At the third attempt the grapnel hooked itself firmly into the roots of a tree. He tested it with all his strength, but it stayed firm. Bracing himself, he took the strain while his two men swarmed across, hand over hand. He waited while they climbed up the cliff, pulling the rope behind them, while he paid it out and attached another to give greater length.

When they had reached a spot high up, from which the rope hung down almost vertically, they passed it twice round the bole of a tree and anchored themselves. Huaman pulled the rope taut and jumped to grasp it two feet above his head. He swung across the torrent and caught hold of a bush with his axe. It held, and he pulled himself ashore. Winding the rope round his waist he climbed up to where his men were waiting. They clambered to the top of the cliff and looked back at the other side of the gorge, scarred by the ledge carved out of it to take the road to the dam.

They heard the drone of an engine, and froze, hoping that their drab ponchos would not be seen against the shale and scrub of the hillside.

It was a jeep, driven furiously up the road towards the dam. Miguel Cuevas was at the wheel. His pale face was set, and he kept his foot on the accelerator as the jeep swung round one dizzy corner after another. He had no eyes for the men cowering in the trees atop the opposite cliff.

* * *

When Craig opened his eyes the sun was high, slanting steeply through the little window of the stone hut on to the earth floor, on which — as it seemed to Craig — far too much of his life-blood was lying around, already half-congealed.

The pain in his head was intense, and he felt sick. He closed his eyes again.

Some time later he heard the key turn in the lock and two people came in. He looked up, and struggled into a sitting position. Santa Cruz had an automatic in one hand and was grasping Janet's arm with the other. There was a purple bruise on her cheek, but she was dry-eyed and defiant. She had her medical box and a bottle of water.

'All right, he's yours — for five minutes. Have you got what you want?' Santa Cruz stood back against the wall.

The girl ignored him. 'When did you get your last tetanus jab?' she asked, lifting the hair on the back of Craig's head gently and looking at the swelling and the deep cut the butt of the gun had made in his scalp.

'Two weeks ago,' he muttered.

'Good. This'll hurt a bit, but I'll give you an analgesic afterwards.' She cleaned the wound and put on a dressing. 'Is that comfortable?'

'You're an angel, Janet. Is Jack all right?'

She smiled. 'Yes, he's O.K. now, bless him.' She picked up a hypodermic syringe and broke open a little plastic tube.

'What are you doing?' asked Santa Cruz. 'I agreed we didn't want him to die of tetanus, but that's all.' He looked at his watch. 'It's ten o'clock. I may want him to be fit to talk at mid-day.' He took the syringe away from her. 'I don't want him unconscious. Give him some aspirin.'

The girl scowled at him, but he took no notice. She shook some tablets into her hand and gave them to Craig with a drink from the bottle. 'I'm sorry I let you down, Peter,' she said miserably.

'My fault. I suppose he worked his hands free?'

She nodded.

'Who did that to your face?'

'Miguel. He says Helmut's escaped.'

'Be quiet,' said Santa Cruz quickly. He took the girl by the arm. 'Out you go. Get into Cuevas' jeep.'

'What are you going to do with her?' asked Craig.

He thought for a moment that the man would go without replying, but Santa Cruz turned at the door and said, smiling, 'She and Warne are going to join the other hostages in their secret prison.'

'It won't be a secret long,' shouted the girl from outside, 'with Helmut on the loose.'

'Unless he can fly,' remarked Santa Cruz caustically, 'there's nowhere he can get to before my ultimatum expires at noon.' He locked the door behind him, and Craig heard him call, 'Cuevas.'

Craig heard Miguel's voice answering. 'Tie up the girl and Warne,' said Santa Cruz, 'and attach them to the jeep. I don't want to hear about any more persons escaping from your custody.' There was a thinly veiled threat in his voice and the Argentine's sullen reply showed what he was thinking.

# 12

## Friday Noon

The silver mine lay at the head of the ravine, where the stream issued from a hole in the sheer face of the mountain. Generations of Indian slaves, and during the past seventy years the miners of the Santa Cruz family, had formed from the mine waste and the rocks that fell from the mountain side a broad platform for the buildings and plant. Outside the gate in the wall of the compound were the remains of the Inca village, heavily overgrown with scrub and fire trees, and it was here, behind a wall of clean-cut Inca stone, that a man lay hidden, peering through the bushes at the gate. He wore an Indian knitted cap and his battle-dress was covered by a striped poncho.

There were two Tupamaros on guard behind the closed gates, and as the man watched another joined them. 'In ten minutes you can open up,' he said. 'Cuevas will be arriving in the jeep with two prisoners.' He strolled back to the administrative buildings, and the two men resumed their watch on the road.

The man from the Mountain Battalion crawled back until he was out of sight and ran along the road to where Captain Mendieta and his platoon lay in the bushes, a quarter of a mile from the mine compound.

Mendieta listened to his report, and considered. He had to get into the compound very quickly and release the hostages before they could be used as bargaining counters. The scout had seen none of them in the compound, so it could be assumed that they were still penned up in the dormitory Helmut Springer had described, with guards both inside and in the guard room next door, which gave access to the compound. It all depended, thought Mendieta, on whether the jeep had a good tow-rope. Surely one would be standard equipment in this sort of territory? He gave rapid orders.

* * *

Miguel Cuevas was in a very bad temper. This man Santa Cruz had bawled him out in front of his fellow Tupamaros, first for having gone after Warne without orders, then for letting him escape and finally for allowing Springer, too, to get away. What was he expected to do? Stay in the dormitory all night and accompany every hostage to the latrine? The aristocratic Don Jorge was getting too big for his shining riding boots.

His eyes were on the road, because the jeep was slithering wildly on the loose stones. He saw what he thought was a snake on the road, and accelerated to crush it. No snakes at this altitude, a warning bell rang in his mind, but too late. The 'snake' leapt high in the air and became a rigid line of rope across his path, windscreen-level, unspeakably threatening. Instinctively, he jammed on his brakes and skidded to a halt just short of it.

He saw the man coming at him with a knife and desperately reached for his Schmeisser. As his hands closed over the stock he heard a shout from behind and turned round. He had time only to catch a glimpse of the top of Warne's head before it crashed into his face. The man with the knife had vaulted over the side of the jeep and had the point at Miguel's throat before he could get his wits back. Mendieta ran up, an automatic in his hand.

'*Amigos*!' screamed the girl. He leaned over the side, and saw that the two pairs of wrists had been securely tied to the handrail behind the driver's seat.

'So you're the prisoners,' said Mendieta, laughing. 'Untie them, quickly. Where have you come from?'

'The dam,' said Warne, rubbing his head. 'He was taking us to join the others. The policeman, Craig, is still there, locked up in a stone hut near the parking space.'

'*Madre de Dios!*' Mendieta remembered the orders given to Passos, to take anyone he found at the dam for an enemy. 'What happened to Major Rodriguez?'

'The bastards killed him,' muttered Janet.

'Oh did they? That's another score to

settle. All right, explanations later. Get out, please. I'm taking this jeep.'

'What are you going to do?' asked Warne. 'Seize the mine?'

'Yes,' he replied impatiently. 'Get out, please.'

'If we stay in the jeep it'll be good cover for you,' said Warne eagerly. 'Look at the colour of her hair. We'd be inside the compound before they knew what was happening.' The girl nodded, and clung to her seat.

Mendieta smiled. 'You've got guts, *amigos*, but no. There'll be shooting. Out you get.' He turned to the man with the knife. 'Tie up the Tupamaro and leave him here.' He spoke to Warne. 'I need all the men I've got. You can stay here and guard him. Take his gun. Was it you who did that to this man's face?'

'Yes.'

'What with? I couldn't see.'

'My head.' Warne rubbed it again, and looked at the blood on his hand. 'That was his teeth, I suppose. I hope I've bust them. He hit the girl while she was tied up.'

'Well, thanks. And don't kill him, will you? Just see he doesn't get away. I take it you haven't been to the mine?'

'No. At the dam the whole time, or on that island.'

'Island?' The Captain looked puzzled. 'Tell me later. If I haven't sent a car for you in half an hour, escape as best you can.' He turned his attention to the jeep.

Sure enough, neatly coiled and strapped to the front bumper, was a thick cable, with hooks at each end. And in the tool-box was a heavy pair of pliers. He gave them to his sergeant, and told him what he wanted done. The man nodded, and marched off his men in single file along the side of the road. Two others remained with Mendieta, who made them crouch in the back of the jeep, huddled in their ponchos. Then he attached the hook of the tow-rope to the shackle on the chassis and gave the slack of the rope to the men in the back. He drove off slowly, leaving the rest of the platoon time to approach the Inca village without being seen, and waving an approving hand to one of his men who was perched on top of a telephone pole.

Three minutes later he passed his men, who had taken up their positions, and saw the guard opening the gates as he caught sight of the jeep. Beyond, he caught glimpses of the broad compound, with ore-heaps, railway lines, offices and workshops on the left and on the right the long dormitory building. He roared through the gate, waving his hand. Before the guards realized that something was wrong there was a rattle of automatic fire and one of them fell. The other, trying desperately to close the iron gates, was hit by a burst of fire from the sergeant's gun. He spun round and his body was thrown backwards a couple of yards, to lie on the dusty earth of the compound, and the troops of the Mountain Battalion jumped over it as they ran to attack their targets.

Fifty yards ahead of them the jeep had made a tight right-hand turn and was facing the grilled windows of the dormitory, behind which Mendieta could see the crowded faces of the volunteers. One of the men in the back of the jeep kept up short bursts of fire on the guard-room door, while the other vaulted to the ground and ran forward to hook the towing cable to the iron grill of the nearest window. Mendieta reversed and slowly took up the strain.

The bars were set firmly in the oak frame, but the strength of the cable was decisive. With a great wrenching and splintering noise the frame and part of the wooden wall burst outwards, and the volunteers poured out through the gap. '*Lie down!*' shouted Mendieta, as he jumped out and forced his way through the crush.

The two guards inside the room, unable to see what was happening because the volunteers were in the way, were taken by surprise when they heard the crash, and now lay on the floor, buried under a group of infuriated volunteers. The Tupamaros in the guard-room were caught between the fire of Mendieta from the dormitory and the troops, who smashed down the door from outside and came in firing. The noise of the automatics stopped suddenly.

Mendieta did not pause. He stumbled

over the bodies in the guard-room and ran out into the compound. On the opposite side some of his men were attacking the door of the administrative building.

There had been only one Tupamaro in the mine office when the attack took place. He was the signals officer of the group, and as soon as he heard the firing he locked the door, ran to the telephone and pressed the call button which rang a bell in the Casa Grande, fifteen miles away in the Chasco valley. A man answered — but as he spoke the line went dead. The signaller guessed that the man at the other end would try the radio, and hastily picked up the receiver. He heard the voice of Lopez.

'The military are here,' said the Tupamaro quickly. 'They're releasing the volunteers.' He could hear the polylingual shouting in the square outside. There was a bang on the door, and it shook violently.

'It's not possible,' began Lopez angrily —

'Good-bye, comrade,' said the man in the mine office. The door burst open. He swung round with the microphone in one hand and his automatic in the other. As he raised it they shot him.

Beyond the office were the sleeping quarters of the clerical staff, and here Mendieta found the captured military policemen, bound and tied to their beds. The man guarding them already had his hands in the air.

Five minutes later the roll-call was taken. Two of the volunteers were suffering from gunshot wounds in the legs and four were slightly injured, one Mountain Battalion man was dead and five wounded. Six Tupamaros, including three wounded, were prisoners, and four were dead. The M.P.s were all unhurt, and took over the guarding of the prisoners with relish.

Mendieta ran to the mine office, stepped over the dead body of the signals officer and began to tune the transmitter to the frequency of his Base in the Callejon de Huaylas. He heard a well-known call-sign and replied. The Adjutant came on the air.

Mendieta made his report, adding that

he had been unable to prevent the signals officer from warning the Centre.

The Adjutant swore. 'I was afraid of that. Listen. They've got reinforcements at the Centre. The aircraft that was looking for your V signal, if you couldn't get through to me, has just reported seeing a Dakota on the airstrip, which must mean that the Brazilians have landed. They must have kept below our radar level. Now those men won't be fit as yet to fight at the altitude of the mine or the dam, but Lopez may send some of his own men to try and reach you. Get Warne and the girl back to the mine with their prisoner and hold your position. Wait. Take any men you can spare and set up a block at the fork in the roads, so that they can't send any men up to the dam. Don't try to link up with Passos. The plane is just about to overfly the lake, and as soon as he sees it he'll attack — I hope. Your first responsibility is to guard the volunteers and the prisoners. Understood?'

'*Perfectamente, mi Mayor*. Can you contact Passos?'

'No. His set's too weak, with that blasted mountain in the way. We'll get the aircraft to keep an eye on what's happening. Stay in touch.'

'Yes, sir.'

'You've done well, my lad. *Caray*! You've done very well. Now let's see if your young man Passos can finish the exercise.'

* * *

There was still a band of pain around Craig's head when he awoke, but the throbbing had passed. He looked around. The stone hut was entirely bare. He wondered what had happened to Warne and Janet, and remembered, with a chill of apprehension, that they were both held at the mine as hostages. This was his fault, he knew; he should never have let them help him in that crazy, abortive attack. He sat up, and remained for a time with his head between his hands, then got slowly to his feet. The door was locked, of course. He went over to the little window that gave on to the parking space.

Something was happening. Through the clear air of the mountains he could hear Santa Cruz talking rapidly into the transmitter in the Buick, which was parked a dozen yards from the hut. The truck Craig had earlier disabled was still where it had been, with two men working under the raised bonnet.

'Listen, Lopez,' Santa Cruz was saying. 'Where is the truck with the reinforcements now?' There was a pause. 'Good. Tell them by radio to stop at the fork and block it. If they've got time they should use their grenades to cut the bridge on the mine road. They must stop the military from getting through to the Centre . . . Yes, I know, but remember we've still got the dam, and we still hold Craig and the hostages you have at the Centre. So we still have the whip hand. I'll clear the dam now, so that they can see we mean business. Adios!'

So the Peruvian Army *was* in on the act, thought Craig, his heart lifting. And if they were sending men down the road from the mine it could only mean that the mine was the 'secret prison' Santa Cruz had spoken about, and that the troops had taken it. So with any luck Jack and the girl would be free. That was what Santa Cruz had meant by saying 'we still have Craig'.

He heard further orders, and a few minutes later the Land-Rover and the Buick were parked one behind the other at the entrance to the road. The drivers were the Indians whom Craig had left on the island, one of them with a bandage round his head. Santa Cruz emerged from the Buick with a cylinder in his arms. There was no mistaking the shape of the exploder, with its handle extending at one end. He took it into the smaller of the two tents.

Ten minutes passed. Craig heard the sound of a jet aircraft and saw the Peruvian run out of his tent and stare upwards. The plane seemed to be circling overhead, out of Craig's sight. Then the sound died away.

There was a single, sharp *crack*. Far

away at the other end of the dam, where the landslide came down to the shore, the head of a man could be seen above one of the fallen rocks. He fired again, and a bullet hit the steel side of the disabled truck with a loud *ping*. The effect was electric.

Santa Cruz stared across the broad sweep of the dam incredulously, then rapped out an order. The men who had been busy with the truck already had their Schmeissers in their hands, and raced across the bridge to face the challenge, firing as they ran. Spurts of dust and stones flew up from the rocks under the slide. There was no reply, and the Tupamaros edged forward on their stomachs to close the range. The Indian drivers had also snatched up their guns and were standing by the cars, uncertain what to do. They were still gazing across the dam when they felt strong arms around their necks and were pulled to the ground with knives pricking at their throats. They made no sound.

Craig had a seat in the stalls for this sudden and skilled attack, and heard footsteps passing the hut. Then he saw them, men in drab ponchos moving out towards Santa Cruz, who still had his back turned.

Craig could well imagine what he was thinking. How was it possible that a man with a gun had reached the other side of the dam? Where there wasn't even a llama track. Almost visibly, Santa Cruz concluded that it must be a diversion to distract his attention, and whirled round. The men in ponchos were still thirty yards away as he dived into his tent.

Shots rang out. Heavy slugs from the platoon's machine-pistols smashed the tentpole and the canvas fell in enveloping swathes on the man inside. He lay still, and Passos approached cautiously. 'Get out of it quickly,' he shouted, 'or I fire.'

'*Esta bien*.' Santa Cruz appeared to be extricating himself, groping under the canvas as if to raise himself to his feet. Then he flung himself downwards.

Craig ducked, instinctively, as the whole hut rocked. A great wall of earth and loose stones and pieces of pipe rose into the air on the far side of the fallen tent, and a fountain of spray shot up from the lake edge. The muffled roar of the explosion followed. Passos and his men, thrown to the ground by the shock-wave, lay with their hands protecting their heads from the rain of debris. The whole dam was trembling under their bodies. Craig heard the first deadly rush of water into the trench excavated by the charges.

Passos ran forward and jerked away the canvas, half burried in earth and stones, that covered Santa Cruz' body. Craig could scarcely see what happened next for the cloud of red dust that hung over the dam, but he saw a scuffle, an automatic, kicked from the older man's hand, describing a gleaming arc through the air to land ten yards away, and finally Santa Cruz' figure being dragged to its feet and pushed forward by the muzzle of a gun until he was standing on the edge of the trench. For a moment Craig thought that Passos was going to throw the man into the swirling torrent of mud and water. He dropped his gun and held him on the brink, shouting at him. Santa Cruz struggled frantically, but was powerless to free himself.

Suddenly the lieutenant dropped his hands, picked up his weapon and turned round. Without looking back he rejoined his men, his face white with anger. Above the roar of the water he shouted, 'Tie him hand and foot and throw him in the Land-Rover. We'll save him for the firing-squad. Fermin, do the same for the two Indians, and stay with them on guard.'

Beyond, on the far side of the dam, Craig saw the two Tupamaros lying on the ground their hands in the air, and three men with automatic pistols in their hands advancing from the foot of the slide. He recalled having heard shots just after the explosion. The men had turned to look, and Huaman was not one to miss an opportunity.

Craig shouted. Passos stared at the window of the hut, astonished, and ran to release him. 'You're the Englishman?'

'Yes. Listen, Lieutenant. There were six Tupamaros here, and the two Indians. We killed three. One's missing. He might be on guard down the road.'

Passos swore, and issued quick orders. Two of his men ran beyond the cars to where the road began. He called to Craig, 'We've got to save the dam, hombre. Come and look.'

They ran past the fallen tent. At the lake end of the trench the water was pouring smoothly through the breach in the stone facing and finding its way amid the tumbled debris towards the gorge. The side fell in, a few yards from the gap, but the pressure built up and the obstruction was swept away. As the two men ran down the bank they saw the mass of mud and stone and shale burst out and join the water from the flume in a great gush that flew over the edge of the drop. Within seconds the channel was flushed out and the water poured into the gorge in a steady stream, eroding the sides and bed of the trench as it went. Passos shouted an order; he wanted bushes from the hillside. Craig seized his arm.

'It's useless,' he shouted. 'I saw a spout at the water's edge when the charges went off. The stone facing there has been breached low down.'

'Let's waste no time talking,' said Passos roughly.

Craig held on to his arm. 'Listen. *Santa Cruz told me how it would work*. The water will dig its way downwards and eat away the ground between this ditch and the flume if we let it. Then the whole dam will burst.'

'The whole dam? It's impossible.'

'No, it's what he planned. We've got to block the ditch at the lake end, where there's still facing. Come and see.'

The gap in the stone slabs was four feet wide. 'We've got to block it here,' Craig repeated, shouting above the roar of the water, 'before the slabs on either side are pushed in. Have you any grenades?'

'Yes,' said Passos shortly. '*Madre de Dios*, what use are bombs now?' He broke away and began to run towards the hillside.

Craig shouted after him at the top of his voice, 'Blow up the hut and use the roof.' Passos stopped dead, and turned back. 'It's strong enough. Under that corrugated iron there's a thick layer of planks held together by battens.' He had inspected the inside of the roof when he was a prisoner in the hut. It had been built to withstand winter storms and he had seen the rows of heavy bolts that held the iron sheeting to the battens beneath.

A strained smile came over Passos' face. 'Thanks, *amigo*,' he said, and called to his men. They scattered hurriedly and took cover. So did Craig.

The lieutenant ran to the hut and closed the door securely. Then he took two grenades from his pockets, pulled out the pins and dropped the bombs through the little window. He trotted back unhurriedly and lay down behind a tree. Craig smiled. It was a textbook case of an officer showing a good example of coolness to his men.

There was a sharp double crack and the door fell flat. The walls shuddered and cracked but remained in position. The roof sailed into the air and fell back, half lying on the walls and half overlapping them. The men cheered and ran to work it off the walls and on to the ground, but it was a great weight, and Passos called to the pair who had been searching unsuccessfully for the missing Tupamaro. Between them they dragged the roof to the gap in the dam and strung climbing ropes across it from side to side, attaching more ropes fetched from the broken tents. Two of the battens had split and the roof had buckled, but not badly.

The slabs at the side of the gap had already given way and were being trundled down the ditch by the current. On the other side Huaman appeared with his two men. His dark face was grinning broadly as he looked at the trussed roof, and he took his rope and threw across the end, signalling to his men to do the same. This was an operation after his own heart, and Passos let him organize it.

Six men took the strain on the ropes as the roof was tilted over the edge of the steep stone facing and allowed to slide down until the top edge was below the bottom of the gap. The weight of the corrugated iron countered the buoyancy of the woodwork.

Then, from the other side of the gap

Huaman and his men hauled on their ropes until the roof was below the gap and both teams strained to raise it slowly, pressed tight against the sides of the breach by the pressure of water. Up it came, until the men, their faces pouring with sweat, saw the top edge break surface. The roar of water ceased. The roof was pinned against the dam and Passos, who could see the lower boards bending inwards under the pressure of six feet of water, left a man at each side to hold the ropes and urged the others to push in the sides of the ditch.

The men dug at the loose earth and debris with their ice-axes and threw stones, brushwood and anything they could lay hands on. The trench was filling when Craig shouted, 'Not near the gap, *hombre. Deje-lo.*' But he was too late. One of the soldiers had enthusiastically demolished part of the wall of the trench that lay behind the stone facing which was all that held the blockage in position. Craig could see the heavy facing slabs begin to move, and grabbed the man back just in time to save him. The facing on the near side burst inwards, and a rush of water swirled round the edge of the roof and fell into the ditch.

The man holding the end of the rope felt the earth slipping under his feet and let go. The corner of the roof fell out of sight and the tug of the rope at the other corner was too great for the man on Huaman's side. The roof slid downwards into the depths of the lake. Within seconds the water, crashing through the breach, had swept away everything they had thrown into the trench. Craig looked at Passos. They were back where they had started, with a dangerously widened channel.

Passos swore fluently. Craig sat on the ground, the wound in his head throbbing with pain. He gasped for breath. He turned to cast his eye around the dam, searching for anything which could be used to stop the flood before it was too late.

Passos said, 'We've tried, but we can't work miracles. Look at it! Washing away the sides and going deeper all the time. My job is to get my men away before the whole dam goes.'

'The truck!' cried Craig hoarsely. He staggered to his feet and ran unsteadily to the disabled truck. Passos went past him and climbed into the cab. He tried the ignition, but there was no result. He jumped down and peered under the open bonnet. '*Jesus Maria*! Did we do that?'

'No, I did,' said Craig. 'They were working on it when — look,' he pointed. 'They've got the cables from the distributor stripped where they were cut. Tie the ends together. She might still fire.'

Passos worked quickly, twisting together the stripped ends of wire. He jumped into the cab again. The engine fired, jerkily, 'Only a few cylinders,' he shouted, 'but it may pull her. Stand back, man.'

'No, you don't.' Craig hauled himself painfully into the cab. 'Let me do it. If anything happened to you where would I be with twelve Peruvians to command?'

Passos glanced at the look on Craig's grimy features and gave in. 'O.K.,' he said, 'but tie this round your waist.' He held the other end of the rope while Craig did so. 'How are you going to do it?'

'Steer with one hand and hold the door open with the other. Get the men out of the way.'

He selected four-wheel drive and let the clutch in gently. The truck began to move, slowly climbing over the rock-strewn surface. Passos walked alongside, keeping the rope taut.

Craig made a turn and approached the lake end of the ditch at right angles. He slid away from the steering wheel to the right-hand side of the seat and pushed the door open with his free hand.

His whole body was trembling. If he got too close to the gap the truck might tip over into the lake; if too far away it would barely close the ditch, which had widened alarmingly on the near side of the breach. If he went too slowly the front wheels would sink into the loose earth of the bank and nothing would shift it then. He revved the engine to a spluttering roar and let in the clutch until it was fully engaged The truck charged across the last few yards.

He peered through the sweat running

into his eyes and judged the distance, keeping his foot down. There was an urgent pull on the rope from Passos, running whitefaced by his side.

'Not yet . . . *Now!*' As Craig felt the front wheels dip he pulled the wheel over to the right, hard, and threw himself to the right. Passos jerked him out of the cab like a landed fish, and he lay on the edge of the channel, winded, as the truck plunged head-first into it.

There was a colossal splash, and he felt water cascading over him. Then Passos' arms were pulling him to his feet. Together, they looked down at the truck. '*Hombre*,' said Passos in an awestruck voice, throwing his arm round Craig's shoulders, 'you might have been practising for weeks.'

That last tug on the wheel had flung the tail of the truck forwards as it fell. It lay on its side, diagonally across the ditch, with the tailgate just inside the gap in the facing. The water was boiling angrily over the tail and racing past the wheels but its deadly force was broken — for the moment.

'Get stones,' muttered Craig, shakily.

'Use the truck to give them hold. But where — ?'

'That's my job, *amigo*. Get your strength.' Passos ran to the Land-Rover, brought it round and rammed the side of the hut, gently at first, using the heavy bumper as a battering ram, backwards and forwards. The wall, already badly shaken by the explosion, began to rock, and more cracks appeared between the foot-square blocks. Like most Andean buildings, it had been built in the traditional way, without much mortar. In an earthquake-prone country, a wall that disintegrates under vibration is better than one that falls flat and buries people.

Men brought up a small tree and with two of them on each side swung it against the end walls, where the Land-Rover could not be used. The heavy stones loosened, and as they became free the soldiers staggered off to dump them in the ditch — down by the sides of the truck, between the tailgate and the facing slabs, any place where the water could erode. Others brought more brushwood, the canvas from the tents, blankets and sleeping bags, and jammed them into crevices.

There was a cry from the lake, and Craig raised his eyes to see Huaman and his two men in the rubber boat. For a moment he thought they would be carried over the tailgate, for there was still a deep rush of water pouring over the end of the truck, but Huaman had worked it out. He paddled hard to force the bow against the stone facing on the near side and let the current slam the boat across the gap. It buckled and squeezed through, but men were lying on their stomachs, holding it in place while others manoeuvred it on top of the side of the truck and loaded it with stones, which they jammed under the thwarts. When the rubber boat was well weighted down the men, under Huaman's directions, spiced with obscene Quechuan oaths, lowered it over the side so that it was held in place by the wheels of the truck, and stopped the gap.

More brushwood and more building blocks were brought, and suddenly the last major leaks were filled and strengthened, and the roar of the torrent ceased once more. There was still a rush of water across the top of the obstacle, but there was no vice in it, and it ran down into the trench and flowed away peacefully.

The filling in went on for a time. Passos inspected the trench from end to end, and was satisfied. The dam had been saved.

Craig sat on the ground wiping his sweating, filthy face with his hand. Then he stumbled, inexpressibly weary, to the shore at the end of the dam and lay down, bathing his aching head and arms in the icy water. The dressing Janet had put on had been lost somewhere along the line, but the wound was bleeding no longer. He felt Passos' hand on his shoulder. They shook hands, unsmiling. Neither had much breath for speaking. The sun still blazed down, but the anabatic wind had begun its daily task, sweeping up the gorge and over the lake towards the mountains. Cat's-paws chased each other across the calm waters of Llangacocha.

Craig said, 'It wouldn't be possible to have better people with me in a jam, Lieutenant. You've trained them well. They don't wait to be told.'

'Like Chapas, for instance,' said Passos, laughing. 'The cretin who brought your first plan to nothing. I'm going to make him dive down and attach ropes to that roof, if it hasn't slipped too far. That'll teach him.' He sat thinking for a moment. 'I mustn't underestimate the force of the water-pressure, low down. It can't burrow under the truck — it's too heavy. But it can still push round the sides, eating its way as it goes. If we can strap that roof over the gap, with the truck and boat behind to support it, and get a lot of sandbags from the Base to fill in the whole trench, I reckon it'll hold till the engineers can get to work.'

'I think you're right.' Craig shivered suddenly. 'I'll never forget the way the water began to swallow up the banks like a ravenous beast; it was as if nothing would stop it. And I'll never forgive the man who started it. I suppose he's safe?'

Passos started. 'Dios! I'd forgotten him. And those two Indians. I'd better check everything's O.K. before I try to get through to Base. I wonder — ' He stopped, frozen into immobility.

From the direction of the Buick there was a long-drawn-out scream, the cry of a man in mortal agony.

# 13

## Friday Afternoon

As they ran towards the car they heard the engine start, and the Buick took off down the road. There were two men in the front seat and two behind. At the side of the road the guard, Fermin, lay on his face, writhing in pain. Passos snatched his automatic from his holster and fired, but the car vanished round the corner of the cliff. Fermin gave a convulsive shudder and lay still, the handle of a knife sticking out from between his shoulder blades.

Passos cursed. 'The man we couldn't find,' he said bitterly. 'I called off my two men, thinking he'd run for it, but he must have hidden in the rocks down the road.' Huaman had brought up the Land-Rover. Passos gave him instructions as he scrambled into the driver's seat. 'Take over, Sergeant. Everyone on guard in shifts of three. Give them food. Call Base if you can tell them what's happened.'

Craig picked up the dead guard's automatic pistol and climbed in. 'Can you catch up with him?'

'We have a chance,' shouted Passos above the roar of the engine in four-wheel drive, as he skidded round the first bend. 'This vehicle's a lot better than the Buick on a track like this.' Craig clung to the bracing bar. The Land-Rover slithered round two more turns and they could see, for a fleeting instant, the other car a quarter of a mile ahead, where a lower stretch of the gorge came into view. The dust of its passage still lingered in the air and as the gap between them diminished the air got thicker and more impenetrable, but Passos seemed to steer by instinct.

Five minutes later they were racing down the last section before the junction of the two valleys, the great spur of mountain hiding the mine road on their right. The Buick, bucking wildly on its soft springs, was only two hundred yards ahead and Passos kept his foot on the accelerator. They were still closing the other car when they swept round the last bend and saw the open space and the bridge where their track joined the mine road. The Buick came to a skidding halt in a cloud of dust near a group of men with automatic weapons in their hands. Passos jammed on his brakes, stopped dead and reversed expertly, retiring into the dust caused by his own sliding stop. Craig heard the snarl of heavy-calibre bullets passing near, and the slap of one hitting the Land-Rover.

'We can't take them on here,' gasped Passos. 'They'd massacre us with those Schmeissers if they got nearer.' He had his left hand on top of the wheel and was looking back over his right shoulder, still reversing fast. 'I'll try the other side of that bend, where we'll have cover. They know we can't turn on this road, so they'll follow.'

The vehicle whirled backwards round the bend and stopped. Before the wheels had stopped moving Craig had jumped out and was running back to the corner of the cliff. He saw two men approaching, one running forward, the other ready to fire. A stream of bullets hit the crumbling red rock near his head and showered him with dirt. One hit a stone and ricocheted away across the gorge, buzzing like an angry hornet.

Craig waited until the first man was within range, stepped round the corner and fired a short burst. The man stopped as if he had hit a brick wall, and crumpled into a heap on the road. As Craig ducked hastily back the second man fired, and more chips flew from the rock. He could hear the man coming, his boots stumbling in the stony litter under the overhanging cliff. The footsteps ceased, then came on again, and as they did so Craig took a leap sideways into the middle of the track and fired.

The man under the cliff was only twenty yards away, with a grenade in his hand, pulling out the pin with his teeth. He was raising his right hand to throw when a bullet from Craig's gun took him in the left shoulder. He spun round and fell against the cliff, with his hand holding the grenade between his body and the rock wall.

Craig made a convulsive jump backwards and threw himself on the ground. 'Really,' he said to himself irritably, 'we've had enough bangs for one day.'

What came was more than he had expected. There was the sharp report of the grenade, and then a growing roar that made the whole gorge reverberate, and a sudden wind whistled round his ears.

The roar increased to a deafening pitch, and round the corner of the cliff came a billowing cloud of grey and red dust. Craig and Passos lay still until the noise died to the rattle of rocks bounding into the gorge. They got to their feet shakily, and peered round the corner of the cliff.

For some time they had to close their eyes against the dust that the anabatic wind was steadily blowing up-valley. Then they could see dimly that the road had been submerged by a great spread of fallen earth, rocks and tangled, uprooted trees, which stretched in an unbroken slope from a scar a hundred feet up the mountain side, across the road, and over the edge of the gorge.

Craig rubbed his eyes, trying to get rid of the gritty dirt. 'It's going to take a bit of clearing away,' he said.

Passos laughed shortly. 'So that's what they call British understatement, is it? We're stuck, my friend. If I attempted to cut into that slope to make a track for the Land-Rover I'd lose men, and not by Tupamaro bullets. It'll take the engineers a week, with bulldozers. I know these landslides. Touch them, and it's like making a pass at the colonel's wife. Too tricky for comfort, believe me.'

Craig laughed. 'What now, then?'

Passos got into the car. They had heard no sound from the other side of the blockage in the road. Somewhere, below hundreds of tons of debris, were the remains of the Tupamaro whose grenade had started the slide. 'Back to the dam,' said Passos, 'and report. I'll have to reverse back to the next bend, where I think I can turn.'

'Go slowly, for God's sake,' Craig urged.

Passos turned and looked at him in surprise as he put his foot down on the accelerator. 'I'm a careful driver,' he said. The car rocketed backwards up the twisty track.

* * *

When they arrived at the dam Sergeant Huaman ran up and saluted. 'I can't get contact with Base, *mi Tenente*.'

'All right, Sergeant. Listen. The Tupamaros have blocked the road this side of the junction with the mine road. They caused a landslide accidentally.' (It was nice of him to put it that way, thought Craig. After all, it was he, Craig, who had started it.) 'Now, they may try to attack us — they've got reinforcements — and retake the dam, but if so they'll have to make their way around the landslide and along the road, or up the other side of the gorge, as you did. Place guards on both approaches. Is the dam holding?'

Huaman's sweating dark face grinned happily. 'Si, senor. We used the other rubber boat — the one they brought up on the truck, I suppose.' He added anxiously, 'It's not Government issue.'

Passos laughed and clapped him on the back. 'Well done, *hijo*. So the ditch is getting dry?'

'Si, senor.'

'Good. We'll use it as a trench if we're attacked. Make some firing stands, with stone loop-holes. We don't want to be taken by surprise. And first, get me some bandages. I want to look at Mr. Craig's head-wound. And tell them to bring food and water.'

'My head's all right.'

'No, it isn't. Lie down for a bit and I'll see to it.'

Craig was glad to, and later, when his head had been washed and a new bandage applied, and he was eating canned beans with relish, he felt a lot better. They were sitting in the shade of the trees when he remembered something.

'Just before your appearance on the dam I heard Santa Cruz talking on his radio to Lopez, the official at the Centre who's sided with the Tupamaros. He must have heard that the hostages at the mine had been released, because he spoke about stopping the military from going *down* the mine road. He said the reinforcements in the truck should destroy a bridge. Have you got the map?'

Passos produced it and they looked at it together. 'There it is, half a mile up the mine road from the junction. My Company Commander, Captain Mendieta, went with the other platoon to attack the mine and it's true he succeeded, because otherwise we shouldn't have seen the plane.'

'I see. That was the signal for you to attack?'

'Yes, sir. I wonder where the reinforcements came from; they explain, of course, the men we saw down at the join of the roads. I'm going to have another shot at getting the Base on the air, but I'm afraid it's this mountain in the way. Get some sleep. You may need it.'

Half an hour afterwards Craig awoke. Passos was shaking his arm. 'There's a message from Base. They sent up a scout plane and we heard the pilot's signal quite strongly. There's a job for me to do.'

‘For us.’

‘At your own risk, sir.’

‘O.K. What is it?’

‘Base say the truck with the Tupamaros who were at the junction has started down the road to the Chasco valley. Captain Mendieta is in control at the mine and will stay there, but he’s sending eight men to meet us at the junction. They’ll have to descend the ravine, because the Tupamaros have blown the bridge on the road.’

‘What’s the job?’

Passos drew a deep breath. ‘A Dakota has been seen on the airstrip at the Centre. They think it brought Tupamaros from Brazil. So that explains the reinforcements we were talking about. I’m to take the section to the airstrip after nightfall, without being seen, and prevent the aircraft from leaving.’

‘Why don’t they just move up the road from the Base at Tambo?’

‘They couldn’t do it without warning, because the Tupamaros have a road block not far from the Base, and the Adjutant is flying to the Base to co-ordinate an attack at dawn. In the meantime he wants me to prevent the Tups from escaping in the Dakota, taking the hostages they hold at the Centre with them.' He paused. 'You see, they've still got the Manager and his family in their power.'

'I see. How do we get round the landslide? Over the top?'

'Yes. You don't have to come with us, Mr. Craig.' He smiled. 'You've done enough, you know. I'd rather you stayed here.'

'Have you or any of your men visited the Centre?'

'No.'

'Well, I have. I may be able to help you. And I'm feeling fine, so let's get moving. It's going to take several hours on foot.'

# 14

## Friday Evening

There was tension between Lopez and Don Jorge Santa Cruz. The quarrel had exploded half an hour before, Lopez blaming the older man for everything that had gone wrong. Santa Cruz had replied coldly that at the worst they still had the means to escape. The Dakota was re-fuelled and ready to leave; so was his Cessna. But with luck, he had added in a friendlier tone, the Government would give in to the threat of reprisals against Castillo, his family and twelve other officials working at the Centre, who were also held in custody. Lopez had agreed, but reluctantly, mistrusting Santa Cruz.

The lights came on in the compound outside. Lopez glanced out of the window and swore furiously. He seized the other man by the arm. 'Is this your doing?'

Under the bright lights a massed crowd

of men was gradually filling the open space, *cholos* and Indians — the latter grouped in their traditional *ayllus*, with the headmen in front, holding their silver-decorated staves of office. More men came pouring into the compound as they watched, until it was almost filled. 'They want a *cabildo*,' said Santa Cruz calmly. 'I'd better speak to them.' He added scornfully, 'Don't worry, Lopez. They're children; they'll do as I tell them.'

He walked out of the door and stood at the top of the steps. There was a moment of silence, then the crowd began to murmur angrily. An old man with white hair showing under his balaclava stepped forward. He raised his *vara* in salutation and stamped the butt on the ground. There was complete silence. 'We are asking for an open *cabildo*, Don Jorge,' he said in Quechua.

'What are you doing, Don Jesus?' asked Santa Cruz sternly. 'Asking for a meeting this day, when I gave you leave to hold a fiesta with your *ayllus* and provided pisco and coca, just as my father and grandfather always did, in better times?'

'Your father — may he rest in peace! — would not have tried to flood our valley. There are many of us who have our farms in the lower lands, where the flood would have blotted them out. It is not only the coffee of the co-operative you would have destroyed. You are no longer our master, Don Jorge. It is Major Castillo, whom you hold prisoner. Set him free, and all the others who are prisoners, and we will go away. He is a good man, and we need his guidance if all is to be done as it should be done, before the rains.'

Santa Cruz whispered to Lopez, who stood behind him. The man disappeared into the house.

'Who says I did such a disgraceful thing?' asked Santa Cruz contemptuously. 'It is untrue.'

'Bring Simon,' said the old man, turning to those about him. Two men dragged forward one of the Indians who had been on guard at the dam. He stared at the ground. The *alcalde* said, 'He got drunk at the fiesta, and told his *chola* that you were only able to escape from the dam, after you had blown it up, because he helped you.'

'It is a lie,' said Santa Cruz. 'The man is dreaming. I was not even at the dam, was I, Simon?' His menacing stare was fixed on the cowering Indian.

The man said nothing. The old man struck him with his *vara*. 'Answer him, Simon. You saw what the men did to Yana.'

'You blew a hole in the dam, senor.' The words came out slowly. 'The soldiers filled it. It would have flooded our fields.'

'Bring that man here,' cried Santa Cruz in a fury. Men with Schmeissers in their hands were filling the doorway behind him.

The *alcalde* stood his ground. He rapped out a command, and the Indian was pulled back into the crowd. Two of the Tupamaros ran forward, pointing their guns at the old man, but there was a sudden, menacing roar from the *ayllus* — more impressive because until then they had been silent. Santa Cruz called the Tupamaros back. He went forward himself, and faced the *alcalde*.

'Simon is a liar,' he said, staring into the wrinkled old face, 'and you are a fool to believe him.'

The old man held his ground. 'Why are you holding the Major prisoner? You told us there had been a revolution; but the Major has done no harm to anyone. Why will you not let him get on with his work?'

'You forget yourself, Don Jesus. That is not a matter for you.'

'You are not our master any longer. Set the Manager free, and we'll go away.'

'And if I do not?' asked Santa Cruz, scornfully.

'Then we will destroy the aircraft that are on your runway.'

'If you touch them you will die. Go to your homes. I will send more coca. You are an old man who likes to make mischief, but I will forgive you because you have always been my friend.'

The *alcalde* turned to his fellow headmen, 'Who is our friend, Don Jorge or *Senor Director Mayor Castillo*?'

There was a roar of 'Castillo' from the whole crowd.

Santa Cruz said slowly, 'This saddens

me. But I will do what you ask.' He turned to Lopez. 'Set the Manager free.'

'You're mad. They can't do anything. If we fire over their heads — '

'Try that, and we shall all be lynched. They are too many for us,' said Santa Cruz in a low voice. 'Let him go. We can get him back easily enough. Set his wife and daughter free as well.'

Lopez ran into the house and returned a moment later with Castillo, who ignored Santa Cruz and stood staring out across the brightly-lit square at the massed ranks of the Indians.

'You are free to join your Indian friends,' said Santa Cruz, bitingly.

Castillo, without replying, walked briskly down the steps and across to where the old *alcalde* stood. He embraced him formally and said, 'You did well to come here, Don Jesus, and I am grateful. There is much to be done.' He turned to address the Indians. 'Thank you, my friends. Some of you may return home now, but I would like others to remain, in case these evil men go back on their word. I will hold a meeting tomorrow morning at eight o'clock to discuss any complaints of damage to property or theft of stores by these foreigners. I shall also want to see foremen and co-operative managers to hear about the work-schedules. That is all.'

He went back into the house, walking past Santa Cruz and Lopez as if they did not exist. Lopez stared after him. 'He thinks he's in charge again,' he said, sneering.

'Let him think what he likes. He's still where we can lay hands on him.'

The Indians drifted away, talking volubly now. Lopez spoke to one of the Tupamaros, a small Brazilian with dark-rimmed eyes.

'Alcyr,' he said, speaking in slow Spanish so that the man could understand. 'You and Manoel had better guard the Dakota. And see that no one goes near the hangar. Take a radio with you, and if there's a movement of Indians on the runway shoot over their heads and call me at once. I don't like the look of this.'

Santa Cruz said, 'I've known Jesus since I was born. He's always been a loyal servant.' His hands clenched. 'I'd like to flay that drunken fool Simon.'

They went into the Manager's office and sat down. Half a dozen Tupamaros crowded in after them, demanding to know what had happened. The whole exchange in the compound had been in Quechua, which only Santa Cruz and Lopez could understand.

Lopez explained. Then he turned coldly to Santa Cruz. 'What you forget is that these people are no longer your servants. You told us that if we didn't interfere with them and gave them extra pisco and coca they would be content. Thanks to your loyal servant, Simon, they all know that you tried to submerge their land under miles of mud.' He rose and looked out of the window. Small groups of men in ponchos were still standing in doorways, silent and watchful.

One of the Tupamaros spoke. 'We can take in Castillo again and drive those Indians off the Centre. Then we can still bargain with the Government.'

Santa Cruz shook his head. 'You couldn't do it without a riot, in the mood they're in now. Our bargaining position is at an end. We shall have to escape before the Government finds that out. I have friends in the Apurimac valley with an airstrip. We could leave in the two aircraft at dawn, while the military are still expecting us to come to terms. They'll have no air patrols up, least of all to the east, where we shall be flying.'

There was a murmur of dissent from the Tupamaros. One said bluntly to Lopez, 'We don't wish to put our trust in Santa Cruz, Paco. If we can leave by air we fly to Ecuador. We have contacts there and could take possession of a small airport and hold hostages.'

'What airfield?'

'Zamora, just over the border.' It was Joaquim, the pilot of the Dakota, speaking. 'There's jungle country there, and we're more used to that than these repulsive mountains.'

'It's true,' said Lopez thoughtfully. 'We've thirty-three men, counting those on guard on the road, all trained guerrilla fighters with automatic weapons and plenty of ammunition. We could take the airfield, make a sortie into the town and rob a bank, get stores — All we'd need to stop the Ecuadorians interfering is a few hostages taken at the airport. It's what our Argentine friends did near Cordoba. The Ecuadorian students would flock to join us. What do the rest of you say?'

'We'd be better off back in Brazil,' said Joaquim, sourly.

'We couldn't get over the Cordillera Azul without being spotted. But we can cross these mountains, to the east, into the Maranon valley and follow it down, below radar sighting, and be over the Ecuadorian frontier before they can put up fighter planes from Cajamarca.'

The Tupamaros agreed, and Lopez was turning to Santa Cruz when there was a bleeping noise from his breast pocket. He pulled out the small radio set and answered. One of the Brazilians guarding the Dakota was speaking, loudly and hurriedly, in atrocious Spanish.

Lopez listened, and swore. 'How many

are there, Alcyr? . . . Turn the lights on. If they get nearer, fire over their heads. No, hombre, not to kill — frighten them. Make them go away . . . What's that? What is *gado*?'

'*Gado*,' said Santa Cruz dully, 'is Portuguese for cattle.'

But the Brazilian had already made his meaning clear. Lopez pushed the radio back into his pocket and turned to the men around him. His face was white. 'The Indians are all over the airstrip, but keeping well away from the Dakota.' He laughed shortly. 'After all, there's no need for them to go any nearer.'

'What's that?' shouted Santa Cruz. 'They haven't — ?'

'Oh yes, they have. They've driven your precious herd of Herefords on to the strip.' He strode up and down, thinking furiously. Then he turned to the Tupamaros. 'There's only one thing to be done, and if Santa Cruz doesn't like it he can stay here and fight his own battle.'

* * *

Jack Warne had persuaded Mendieta that he could help Passos to approach the airstrip unseen, since he knew the tracks through the plantations and corn fields in the valley. Now he stood with seven other men at the join of the roads from the mine and dam, and watched curiously the ragged group of men who were being lowered, one at a time, on a rope which dangled down the side of the bluff between the two roads. The long scramble around the top of the landslide through the thick bushes and over treacherous slopes of shale had taken its toll of clothes and tempers. He scarcely recognized Craig, whose face, under the dirty bandage, was as dark as an Indian's from the effects of sun and grime.

The two groups joined up and Passos ordered a rest of ten minutes, while coffee was drunk and the men from the dam stretched themselves out on the warm earth. Then the real descent began.

It was like a gigantic staircase, for they used the shortcuts Warne showed them, which led straight downwards across the zig-zags of the mine road, and by the time they reached the place where Rodriguez had stopped the Land-Rover on the way up — it was only thirty-six hours before, but it seemed eternity — Craig's head was bursting with pain and his calves felt as if made of red-hot iron. Passos called a halt, and they ate and drank, drenched with sweat, staring across the valley of the Chasco at the snowy tops of the eastern range. There was the Jaguar, thought Craig, now lit up redly by the setting sun. He found Warne beside him, and pointed. 'Janet said you'd climbed that rock. It really looked like a Jaguar yesterday. Not so much now.'

'Did she? Yes, I did. There's a pass just near it — can you see? — and one of these glacial lakes full of good trout.' He paused. 'She's a funny girl, Janet.' He glanced at Craig. 'But gutty, you must admit. I don't think those revolutionary ideas of hers go more than skin deep.'

'I doubt if she'll have any left, after this lark. They conned her into it, Jack. Because they wanted a nurse. Played on her feelings about poor hunted men. There's nothing wrong with Janet, and she's got character, all right.'

'Too much bloody character,' said Warne. He heard Passos shout '*Vamos!*', and jumped from the road into a scarcely visible track between the bushes, moving with the sure-footedness of a llama.

Later on the light went, and Passos fell at one point and broke his pocket radio. He swore fluently. 'I wanted to make contact with Base when we get down to the Chasco,' he explained bitterly, stumbling on after Warne.

It was like a bad dream, always downwards, stamping their heels into the shifting ground, with the pressure building up on their eardrums. When they came out on to the flat stretch of road through the eucalyptus plantations they had descended six thousand feet. Craig was walking like an automaton. They rested for a quarter of an hour, and he stretched out his legs painfully and lay flat, breathing in the denser air of the valley, scented with pine and eucalyptus.

On again. As they approached the valley road Passos called out sharply, 'Take cover. Quick.' The men jumped into the ditch at the side of the road and watched with puzzled eyes as two trucks came past, slowly, blacked out and steering by the dim light of the rising moon. They rumbled quietly past and disappeared in the direction of Tambo, down the valley. Passos called to Craig, 'How many men do you reckon?'

'Thirty or forty, judging from the number of heads I could see. The trucks were full of them.'

'*Jesus Maria!* How I need that transmitter.' He looked at Craig uncertainly. 'I think they're going to try to raid the Base at Tambo, or take hostages from the village. I must warn the Commandant. Would you — ?'

'Try to find a telephone? It'd be too late, man. Those trucks will be in Tambo in a quarter of an hour.'

'No, Mr. Craig. I didn't mean that. If they're trying to make a raid and return to the Centre with their hostages I've got to get there first. Even if they've left a guard it can't be a very strong one, and I can take them by surprise. But I've still got orders to prevent that Dakota from taking off.' He hesitated. 'I'm sorry to ask you to do this, but whoever is in charge may have to take decisions fast, and frankly, I'd rather it was you, if you feel fit for it.'

Craig nodded, and got to his feet. 'How many men can you spare?'

'Four, and Warne, of course. He can show you the way. I'll give you grenades! Blow one of its wheels off.'

'Oh God! More bangs. O.K. We'll stay on the airstrip until you make contact. Have you any idea where the plane is?'

'Yes, they told me that. When last seen she was near the trees on the west side. Thanks a lot, Mr. Craig. And *vaya con Dios*!'

Four miles more, thought Craig. But flat. He led the way across the bridge, and called on Warne to show him the best route. The rest of Passos' platoon went off up the road in single file, while Warne took a track through a coffee plantation and later branched off towards the South. There was no sign of life anywhere, except for an occasional lit-up window in one of the whitewashed cottages. Warne was puzzled.

'The men ought to be sitting outside their front doors, smoking or chewing coca, at this time in the evening. What's happened to them?'

'Don't ask me. How far are we from the airfield?'

'A few more fields.'

They were big fields. An hour later Warne spoke quietly, signalling to the men behind to stop. 'The airstrip is just beyond those trees. Look! The moon's shining on something over there.' He ran forward towards the left and peered through the screen of trees, then signalled to Craig to join him. Craig spread his men out, and they approached in line abreast, with their guns ready to fire.

But there was no need for caution. When they came through the last trees they could see a crowd of Indians around the plane, smoking and laughing. Among them were two of Passos' men.

It was something of an anti-climax.

* * *

The Tupamaro driver of the leading truck saw the road in front of him narrow, as it came to a stretch between a line of low cliffs and the river. He flicked on his headlights briefly and slowed down. A man with a gun in his hands ran out from the shelter of the cliff. Lopez leaned out of the cab and spoke to him. '*Que tal*, Garcia. How far ahead are the troops?'

'They left half an hour ago,' said the Tupamaro. Six other men joined him. 'They must have packed it in for the night.'

'O.K. Get in, all of you.' Lopez called through the little window behind him. 'Help them to climb in.'

'Are you taking us back?'

'No, *amigo*. We're going forward. The others will tell you the plan. *Venceremos!*' The truck began to gather speed.

Three miles further on they came to the outskirts of Tambo. The road ran along the edge of the deep river bed and was bordered on the right by the first houses of the little town. There were no lights to be seen, and the truck ran down silently between the houses and the river.

Ahead, the driver could see a solitary lamp-post. He switched on his headlights and accelerated.

Where the road entered the riverside square a lane ran in from the right. Something huge, and coloured a bright yellow, came lumbering out of the lane into the glare of the headlights, swivelled round the corner and stopped, facing the first truck.

The burst of fire from Lopez' Schmeisser rattled harmlessly off the broad raised shovel of the bulldozer. The driver of the truck slammed on his brakes.

'Go ahead!' screamed Lopez. 'There's room to pass.'

The man let in his clutch. There seemed to be enough space to get by — just enough. He was approaching fast when he saw two objects thrown from the windows of one of the unlit houses on his right. They rolled on the road. Wildly, he accelerated, but just as he tried to pass the bulldozer one of the grenades exploded between his rear wheels. The truck was blown off course, and as the driver wrenched at the wheel he felt the bank crumble, and the heavily-laden truck skidded over the edge into the swollen stream beneath. The second truck swerved away from the broken edge of the road and hit the yellow shield head-on.

Men in battledress poured out of the silent houses.

# 15

## Friday Night

There was a brightly-striped woollen hammock slung across the end of Castillo's office, and Craig sat down on its edge and leaned back against the cloth. His second mug of cold beer was in his hand; with the other he rubbed his stubbly chin and looked up at the Manager. 'How did you manage to warn Tambo?'

'They'd smashed my transmitter and cut the telephone wire. What they didn't know was that there was a direct line from the generating station, so I took my Vespa and was speaking to the Commandant a few minutes after they'd left. By the time I'd got back here and the line was repaired he rang through and told me what had happened.' His face was still blotchy from the copious tears he had shed, his arms round the necks of Craig and Passos, when he had made them tell the whole story of how they had saved the dam, and his precious valley.

'You ran a risk,' said Craig. 'They might have left a guard at the generator-house. Did they *all* go?'

'They must have thought they could hi-jack one of the transport planes at the Base,' said Passos. 'We've searched the whole Centre and there's no trace of a Tupamaro.'

'And Santa Cruz?'

'He must have gone with them. They haven't found all the bodies that fell into the river at Tambo, but he must be among them. He hadn't a hope of getting away, even in his Cessna, with all those cows browsing on the strip. And he knew that if the Indians caught him he wouldn't live long.'

Craig nodded. He put his empty glass on the floor and swung his legs up, one after the other, stiffly, and lay back. He looked up at Castillo apologetically. 'Sorry,' he muttered. 'I feel a bit tired.' He fell asleep.

Passos bent over the hammock and

shook him gently by the arm, but it was no use. 'He won't wake up,' he said with a tired laugh. 'I was going to lead him to that bath you promised.'

'Let him sleep it out.' The Manager brought blankets and tucked them round Craig's body. 'There's blood on his shirt collar.'

Passos stood up, stretching. 'He had a nasty crack from one of the Tupamaros, but I put a dressing on it and it seems all right. It didn't stop him from working like a madman to plug that damned trench. He was everywhere. Without him we couldn't have done it.' He paused, looking down at Craig's grimy, lined face. 'It's curious, you know, but although he's so much senior to me he took my orders and acted on them just like a well-trained subaltern. Never questioned anything, but a lot of the ideas came from him. Like using the truck, for example. He's been a good comrade,' he ended, awkwardly.

Someone knocked at the door and an old man came in. It was Fidel, the butler from the Casa Grande, holding a long key in his hand. Passos' sergeant, with a gun slung over his shoulder, followed.

He said, 'The old man didn't want to hand over the key to anyone but you, sir. But the Cessna's safe inside the hangar and I locked the door myself. The Dakota's under guard.'

'Thank you.' Castillo took the key, looking down at the bent head of the Indian servant. 'You will not see Don Jorge again, Fidel,' he said gently. 'I know how much you loved him, but he has acted like a very wicked man. I shall see that you and your family are looked after. In the meantime you can go on living in your rooms in the Casa Grande, and be responsible for keeping everything safe.' He threw the key into the drawer of his desk and locked it.

The dark, wrinkled face stared up at him for a moment, expressionless. The old man muttered, 'Si, senor,' bent down to kiss Castillo's hand and shuffled out of the room.

Passos was leaving when Castillo called him. He turned, and found the Manager looking at him hesitantly over his half-spectacles. 'That truck, Lieutenant

— the one you used to block the trench up there.'

'Sir?'

'Can we save it? We've few enough as it is.'

Passos gazed at him for a moment, speechless, then laughed shortly. 'No, *mi Mayor*. Not unless you want to burst the dam. The truck'll be buried under a metre of stones and earth, if the guards I left there have done what I ordered.' He turned to the door. 'I'll sign an indent for it. Good-night, *mi Mayor*.'

# 16

## Saturday Morning

The lamps in the Manager's office had been extinguished, but the moon was high and some light came in through the windows giving on to the compound — enough for the man who entered quietly through the door at the rear. He had a long knife in his hand, and coming to the desk thrust it carefully between the top and the edge of the drawer. There was a sharp splintering sound, and Craig stirred in his sleep.

The man whirled round and caught sight of the hammock under the side window. It was swinging slightly. He went across, making no sound, and peered down at the sleeping man. Craig was lying straight, not diagonally as a Peruvian would. One arm was under his body, and the other by his side. The man bent down and shone a torch for a fraction of a second, not at the face but near it. Then he straightened up, smiling to himself, and moved away to the desk. He took a key from the drawer, picked up a heavy wooden ruler and returned to the hammock. 'Craig,' he called softly, and switched the full light of the torch on the sleeper's eyes. They opened, blinking, and Craig raised his head. Santa Cruz hit it hard, across the forehead.

He went quickly to the door at the back of the room and hissed. The old man Fidel appeared and Santa Cruz led him to the hammock. A shadow passed the window and both men froze. But the guard merely tried the handle of the door at the top of the steps and went on his way, satisfied.

Santa Cruz whispered some words in Quechua, and the butler nodded. Between them they lifted the hammock off its hooks and carried it, one at each end, into a passage that led to an open door at the side of the building. Outside was a space between the offices and the chapel, brilliantly lit by the light of the moon.

Santa Cruz let down his end of the hammock, took the knife in his hand and crossed quickly to the deep shade by the chapel wall. He crept to the end of the building and looked round the corner. There was no one in sight. Running back, he picked up the ropes of the hammock and they moved forward.

They had to pause three times to allow the old man to get his breath back, before they reached, on the other side of the chapel, the little door in the high wall of the Casa Grande. Beyond, for the moment, they were safe from observation. They were in the formal garden, with its carefully tended lawns and flower beds, and on the close grass their footsteps made no noise. The smell of tobacco flowers and magnolias was thick in the still night air.

They passed the big swimming pool, the garages facing the closed main entrance, and the rose garden, and leaving the great house on their right came to a small gate. Again, Santa Cruz put down his burden, satisfied himself that Craig's face, under the swelling bruise, was vacant of all expression, and went out through the gate.

The eucalyptus trees grew closely on the other side, but a path led through them towards the dark side-wall of the hangar. How many times, thought Santa Cruz, had he come home this way, after a visit to an outlying farm, leaving the mechanics to return the plane to its hangar, walking quickly in his dusty clothes through the cool scented garden to the luxury of a hot bath, a change to his velvet smoking jacket and silk shirt, and then down to drinks with his wife and guests. It had been a civilized life, and it was all over. He would never see the Casa Grande again.

They laboured through the trees, pausing again to make sure that no guard had strayed from the front of the hangar, and entered it through a side door, which Santa Cruz unlocked with the key he had taken from the drawer. Inside, it was pitch dark, for there were no windows and the electrically-operated roll-door at the front was down. Fidel found a switch, and the whole of the hangar was ablaze with light.

There stood the little high-wing monoplane which Santa Cruz had bought five years ago, and which was his pride and joy. The light shone on the sign of the couchant jaguar on its fuselage, and the paintwork was spotless. As always, the little plane was fuelled and ready for flight whenever the whim took its master.

* * *

Craig had come to his senses during the swaying journey from Castillo's office. There was a blinding pain in his forehead, but he found he could think, if not very clearly. Lying deep in the hammock he hadn't the ghost of a chance of catching the two men by surprise, but at least he had kept his face calm and expressionless when he knew he was being inspected.

He felt them lay him down on the cold floor of the hangar, fold the sides of the hammock over his body, and then the ends as well, so that they covered his head and feet. There was a pause, as a rope was brought and tied round his arms below the elbows. They had to raise his body to pass the rope underneath, and beneath the thick folds of cloth he imperceptibly worked his arms to his sides and pushed them outward as the rope was tightened. They tied him again at upper arm and knee levels, and he could imagine Santa Cruz looking down at the bundle of heavy cloth on the ground, trussed like a sausage, and feeling satisfied that should he recover consciousness he would be unable to set himself free. In fact, Craig knew something about escape methods. He had the amount of play in the rope he needed, and could free himself any time he wanted. But not yet; he had no wish to feel a knife between his ribs.

The sill of the rear door of the Cessna was only a foot above the floor. Santa Cruz came up, wearing his flying suit. With Fidel's help he hauled Craig into the plane and settled his body in the seat behind the pilot's. He adjusted the seat belt round the inert bundle and latched it, pulling it tight. Then he slipped into the pilot's seat and checked his gauges.

Everything was in order. He glanced at the place by his side, and laid out the safety straps so that Fidel could put them on easily. The old man was standing by the side of the thirty-foot roller-door, with his hand on the switch that operated it.

Santa Cruz took out a handkerchief, and carefully and slowly wiped his face and hands. He drew a deep breath, put his finger on the starter button and nodded to the old man. The great door began to rumble upwards. Fidel ran to the side door and switched off the lights. Through the widening gap under the roller-door they could see the moonlight on the grass outside. The Herefords were huddled together under the trees at the side of the strip.

'Quick, Fidel,' shouted Santa Cruz. The servant shambled forward and stood by the open door of the cockpit, staring up into his master's face. The engines fired, one after the other, and the roar of the turbo-supercharged exhaust filled the hangar.

'Get in, you fool.' Santa Cruz' voice was cracked with anger.

The old man shook his head. 'No,

senor. I've helped you to escape, but that's enough. Good-bye, *Padron*.' He slammed the door shut. Frantically, Santa Cruz wound down the window.

'Do as you're told, you cretin. I *need* you, for him.' He jerked his thumb over his shoulder at the bundle in the seat behind.

'Adios, Don Jorge.' Fidel had tears in his rheumy old eyes, but he turned his back and walked to the door in the side wail.

Santa Cruz heard faintly, above the roar of the engines, a shout from outside. He took off the brakes and edged open the throttle. The little aircraft, booming throatily as the turbo-jet exhaust began to help the twin props, ran forward on its three wheels. A man who had arrived, breathless, in front of the door was knocked down by the wing. Others, with guns in their hands, were racing across from the side of the runway, where the long shape of the Dakota shimmered under the moon. They fired, but were too distant for accurate aim. A bullet hit one of the struts with a loud *ping*, but that was all. The Cessna gathered speed, jolting over the thin couch grass.

The guards fell behind. Suddenly, the bumping stopped and Santa Cruz opened the throttle wide and flew out over the end of the strip, gaining height. Before making his turn into the east wind he glanced back over his shoulder at the rear seat. The bundle had slumped forward, only held in place by the seat-belt. Satisfied, he banked steeply and headed towards the glittering peaks of the eastern range.

⋆ ⋆ ⋆

Right-hand turn, thought Craig in the stuffy darkness. Now straight. Is he going to turn again? . . . No. Straight towards the mountains on the east of the valley. He must be heading for the gap Warne had pointed out, near the rock they called the Jaguar.

There was something odd about the engine noise — and then he remembered. These planes were often fitted for use at high altitudes with turbo-superchargers, that gave them almost as much thrust as at sea-level. That was why Santa Cruz — it was he, of course; there was no mistaking that high, aristocratic voice, even speaking Quechua — that was why he had no need to circle before climbing over the range. Craig felt his weight swing backwards as the rate of climb increased. Once the man was negotiating his way through that long pass he would have his attention fixed on his instruments and on the mountains looming on either side. Craig controlled his impatience until he felt a slight change of course and the buffeting of the wind, funnelled by the gap. Then he acted, fast.

Feeling through the thick folds of cloth for the belt clasp he triggered it, bracing his legs to avoid being tipped off the seat by the next turn. Then he crossed his arms and worked the slackened rope up, above his elbows. Wriggling his hand into his pocket he brought out his knife, opened it and began to saw through the cloth at the ropes. He bent forward until he judged he must be out of sight of the front seat, emerged from the bundle of folded hammock and let it fall while he freed his legs.

The concentrated effort made his temples throb, but he could afford time to rest. A small object was clipped to the cabin wall near his head. He explored it with his fingers and smiled grimly. That would do for a start. When the next buffet of wind jolted the plane he prised the little aerosol fire-extinguisher away from its clips. He took off the cap and felt for the trigger, glancing upwards at the head of the man in front. But Santa Cruz was intent on his job and could hear nothing above the throaty roar of the engines, sucking in the thin air and ejecting a pressurized stream through the exhaust.

Craig picked up one of the pieces of rope and began to make a running noose.

* * *

The pass through the mountains was over twenty miles long. The narrow valley between the peaks opened out, and Santa Cruz saw a glacier lake shining like silver three hundred feet below. Like Llanga, on the other side of the Chasco, it was stocked with his fish. How many times, he thought nostalgically, had he climbed over the snow slopes as a young man and spent the day hooking the rainbow trout — monsters, some of them, fifteen kilos in weight. He jerked his thoughts away as the pass closed in again. This was the worst part, even by daylight.

The wind was roaring up the further slopes and pouring through the gap in the range, and the plane swayed and side-slipped as he guided it between the high grey walls, with patches of snow filling the crevices where the wind could not sweep it away. Only two more treacherous bends. His eyes were bright with excitement. The Indians had been right to call him The Jaguar, because like the king of the sierra he worked best alone. He was free of Lopez and his gang of quarrelsome bandits. Alone with the man who had wrecked his plan of revenge.

One more bend. The gap was widening out. Suddenly, the mountains on either side fell away and he was flying out above precipices that dropped thousands of feet to the steep slopes of broken schist below. Beyond lay the great valley of the Maranon, and on the lush banks of the broad river was the hacienda of his friend.

He was safe. Suddenly, his thoughts went to his unwilling passenger and he was turning, left hand on the holster strapped to his belt, when there was a loud hiss in his right ear and a choking mist filled the cockpit in front of him and formed a frozen cloud on the windscreen. He dabbed with both hands at the glass, trying to clear it.

Craig's left hand snatched the gun from its place; his right dropped the extinguisher and slipped the noose over Santa Cruz' head. And pulled it tight.

'All right, Santa Cruz. I'll give you some rope so that you can wipe the windscreen.' The Peruvian did as he was told. The main thing was to be able to see. His head was jerked backwards again and held against the support.

'Turn back.'

'No.' The noose tightened, then slackened off.

'Yes, you will.'

The aircraft kept its course. Craig pulled again. When Santa Cruz could speak he said, 'It's not much good trying to throttle me, Craig. That'd be the end of us both.'

'Oh no, it wouldn't. I can easily kill you and take over the controls, I know these planes.' That was a lie. 'Come on. Get into the other seat.' The rope tightened again and Santa Cruz found his head being tugged sideways. He threw up his hand, and Craig let the noose go slack.

'All right,' said Santa Cruz, gasping. 'But listen, Craig. I have friends down in that valley who'll hide me until the search is over and I can get across the Ecuadorian border. I'll give you twenty thousand dollars, in your own secret account in Switzerland, if you'll let me land where I want.'

'Turn round and go back. Back through that pass and land on the runway, at the Centre. *Do as I say*.'

'Fifty thousand dollars.' The noose was tightened savagely. The man threw up his hand again, and when the awful pressure on his throat was released he sat still for a moment, choking for breath, and then slowly pressed on the rudder-bar. The plane came round and began to climb.

'You're taking me to my death, you know that.' There was no answer. 'What does it matter to you? You're not a Peruvian. If we went on, no one would know. You'd be held in comfort until I could get away and the police would find you. You'd have a hundred thousand — ' His voice was choked off.

'Through that pass,' said the cold voice behind him. 'You forget I saw what you tried to do to that valley and the people in it. If you're shot it's what you deserve.' The plane completed the circle, still climbing. 'O.K. I see you've got to gain height. But don't make me angry again.'

'Give me room. I can't see clearly.' He was putting his hand to his pocket as he spoke. The noose tightened.

'Don't take your hands off that wheel until I tell you.' He threw a handkerchief on to the man's lap. 'Now. Use your left hand and wipe the screen.'

The plane turned and began to approach the gap in the mountains. Craig watched the manoeuvre with grudging respect. Santa Cruz was a skilled pilot and he knew his aircraft. He brought it in close over the sill of the pass and swept on between the towering walls, neatly banking at the turns and riding the following wind that beat at the ailerons and tended to push the tail from one side to the other. It was bitterly cold in the cabin. Craig bent down swiftly, keeping the automatic under his eyes on the rear seat, and picked up the woollen hammock. He wrapped it round his shoulders and tied the folds at the waist with a piece of the cut rope. But he never let go of the other rope that led to the noose around Santa Cruz' neck.

The Peruvian was silent, and Craig wondered apprehensively what he was thinking about. The aircraft flew across the glacier lake, through the long gorge between the snow peaks and out at last to where they could see the Chasco gleaming faintly in the distance, and the twinkling lights of the Centre. Santa Cruz eased the wheel forward and opened the throttle.

'Go slower, you fool,' shouted Craig. 'You'll never make the turn at this speed. *Throttle back!*' He tugged at the noose, but Santa Cruz had thrust his hand up between the rope and his throat. In the same moment he stamped on the rudder bar and pulled back the wheel.

The plane zoomed upwards, turning on the tip of its port wing. Craig was flung against the cabin wall and the rope jerked from his hand.

Santa Cruz was secure in his seat-belt. He whipped the noose off his head and slung it over the wheel. Straightening out, he drove straight at the buttress that stood out from the eastern range, its crouching cat lines sharp under the moon. He held the throttle wide.

Craig scrambled to his feet and found the end of the rope. '*Turn*, you madman!' he shouted, tugging violently. But the noose was held by the wheel standard. 'D'you want to be killed?' He beat on the man's shoulders.

Santa Cruz laughed aloud. 'Yes, and

you with me.' He pointed ahead. 'There he is, Craig. That's the Jaguar. I'm bringing him his kill.'

He's off his head, thought Craig. The Jaguar rock seemed to rush towards them, as if the beast itself were making its spring.

And then Santa Cruz screamed.

He pulled the wheel right back and threw up his hands to cover his eyes. The aircraft stood on its tail and the east wind thrust at the underside of the wings with all its force. Forward speed was lost, and the Cessna drifted tail down over the head of the granite jaguar towards the snow slopes beyond.

Craig had been thrown to the rear, beside the sliding door. The end of the hammock, still tied round his waist, fell over his head and he could see nothing.

There was a rending crash as the tail struck the slope and tore off. The door slammed open, pitching Craig out into the freezing wind. The fore part of the plane cart-wheeled away, with Santa Cruz still screaming uncontrollably.

But Craig knew nothing of the crash

that followed, and the pall of black smoke from the burning fuel tanks. Entangled in folds of heavy cloth he was rolling down the snow slope, gathering a white shroud as he went.

# 17

## Monday Morning

Craig had a dream that went on and on, about a black cat with claws outstretched coming at him in mid-spring. And someone screaming. It switched to a glittering whiteness, that tossed him about, bore him down and covered him with a smothering, freezing blanket that grew tighter and tighter, and even colder. He awoke shaking with fear.

There was a starchy rustle, and a remembered Irish voice. 'Poor old fuzz, you are having a go. Go to sleep again, love. I'll hold your hand.' There was extraordinary comfort in the strong warm fingers testing his pulse and stroking his head, where it wasn't covered in bandages. He fell asleep.

This time there was no nightmare, and he slept for several hours, to awaken in a darkened room. He turned his head. He couldn't see very well in the dim light, but someone was coming towards him. The same starchy rustle.

'Is that you, Irish?'

'It is that.' She switched on a small light near his head, and he could see her auburn hair under the nurse's cap.

'I'm hungry.'

'You can have some soup. I'll bring it.'

'Not bloody soup. Something I can bite.'

'Always one for violence, aren't you?' She lifted his head and turned the pillow. It was cool on the back of his neck. 'You'll have the bloody soup, and like it.'

She brought a cup with a spout and held his head, feeding him like a child. It was undignified, but there seemed something wrong with his hands. He turned his face away from the feeding-cup. 'I haven't lost any bits and pieces, have I?' he asked anxiously.

'No, Mr. Craig,' she said, and laughed. It was like music. 'You're all intact, but your hands will take a week or two. Jack says you looked like a big fat snowman when he found you. You'd rolled down three hundred feet, gathering snow all the time. That's what saved your toes, and other bits you were so anxious about. That and the hammock.' She brought the cup again to his lips. 'Is that what the smart fuzz officer wears in mountain country?'

He saw her wide grin and the grey eyes laughing at him, and smiled back. But what was that she had said? 'Jack?'

'You owe your life to him, by all acounts. He saw the fire on the mountain and told them he knew the climb and could lead the rescue team. Passos went with them.'

'They're all right?'

'Yes. Right as rain.'

'Can I see them?'

'You won't see anybody but me and the doctors for a bit longer. Least of all the press. They're swarming all over the place.'

'Santa Cruz?'

'He's dead.'

'That's good. He wouldn't have wanted to live after — ' He lay back on the pillow, remembering the spectacle of a character disintegrating before his eyes, a man one moment and a terrified animal the next.

She watched his face, worried. 'Don't think about it, love.'

'I must.' He closed his eyes. 'Tell Jack his uncle will have the whole story — from me.' He chuckled. 'Doesn't know I've met his uncle. That may sober him up a bit.'

'He may act like an eejit,' she said defensively, 'but all he needs is someone steady to keep an eye on him. Like me, for instance.'

THE END

We do hope that you have enjoyed reading this large print book.

Did you know that all of our titles are available for purchase?

We publish a wide range of high quality large print books including:
**Romances, Mysteries, Classics**
**General Fiction**
**Non Fiction and Westerns**

Special interest titles available in large print are:
**The Little Oxford Dictionary**
**Music Book, Song Book**
**Hymn Book, Service Book**

Also available from us courtesy of Oxford University Press:
**Young Readers' Dictionary**
**(large print edition)**
**Young Readers' Thesaurus**
**(large print edition)**

*Other titles in the*
*Linford Mystery Library:*

## DEATH CALLED AT NIGHT

**R. A. Bennett**

Jimmy Ellis believes his parents have died in a car crash when as a young boy he is taken to live with relatives in Australia. The years pass happily, then the nightmare comes. Terrifying images flit through his mind in the dark — all through the eyes of a child, a witness to grisly events seventeen years before. He begins to delve into the past, and soon he finds himself on the trail of a double murderer — a murderer who is prepared to kill again.